666 Park Avenue

666 Park Avenue

GABRIELLA PIERCE

wm

WILLIAM MORROW

An Imprint of HarperCollins*Publishers*

666 PARK AVENUE. Copyright © 2011 by Alloy Entertainment. All rights reserved. Printed in the United States of America. No part of this book may be used or reproduced in any manner whatsoever without written permission except in the case of brief quotations embodied in critical articles and reviews. For information address HarperCollins Publishers, 10 East 53rd Street, New York, NY 10022.

HarperCollins books may be purchased for educational, business, or sales promotional use. For information please write: Special Markets Department, HarperCollins Publishers, 10 East 53rd Street, New York, NY 10022.

alloy**entertainment**

Produced by Alloy Entertainment
151 West 26th Street, New York, NY 10001

FIRST EDITION

Designed by Diahann Sturge

Library of Congress Cataloging-in-Publication Data is available upon request.

ISBN 978-0-06-143477-8

12 13 14 15   OV/RRD   10 9 8 7 6 5 4 3 2 1

666 Park Avenue

One

"Twirl."

Jane Boyle spun obligingly, her skirt flaring in a satisfying burst of green silk. She craned her neck for a glimpse of the back in the boutique's narrow mirror, but it was hard to tell what she'd look like when she wasn't twisting around like a lime-colored flamingo. This, she reminded herself, was why friends were so essential to the shopping process—especially when shopping to impress a man who was an unrepentant fan of the back view. Jane had spent every lunch hour that week hunting for the perfect dress, but by Thursday it had become clear that she needed an expert's help.

Fortunately, Atelier Antoine, the boutique architectural design firm where Jane had worked for the past two years, was also home to Elodie Dessaix, a fiercely talented shopper. Elodie was nearly as invested in Jane's budding romance as she was in finding the perfect Swarovski-studded slingbacks. Jane cocked an eyebrow at her friend, whose long, brown legs were swinging cheerfully from her perch on a stool in the changing room of the *très chic* and *très cher* Soie et Vin boutique.

After a thoughtful pause, Elodie shook her head. "It's just so *green*," she explained unhelpfully in her charming British-French lilt before shoving a dusty-lavender sheath dress into Jane's hands.

"I'll freeze," Jane muttered grouchily. She started to hand the dress back, but the steely look in Elodie's espresso eyes changed her mind. "Are we down to the dregs?"

Elodie nodded crisply, her curly black bob swinging above her shoulders. Jane headed back into the gold-and-marble dressing room, complete with an ornate gilt-framed mirror. It had been Elodie's idea to target the pricey boutiques just steps off the fabled Champs-Elysées. "Quality shows," she had argued passionately and convincingly. Jane had allowed herself to be persuaded because, in her trim camel-hair coat and suede Lacroix heels, Elodie looked like a million bucks.

The drawback of the plan was soon apparent, though: Jane could only afford to shop the clearance rack, and even that was a stretch at some of the places Elodie had dragged her into. And the drawback of *that* was it was the middle of December and Jane was contemplating putting on a gauzy halter dress that had all the substance of tissue paper.

At least I'll look like I belong with Malcolm, she told herself grimly as she pulled over her head what felt like the hundredth dress. The thought of Malcolm brought a rush of heat to her cheeks and, well, other parts of her, too.

Malcolm Doran had swept her off her feet—literally—a month before, when they'd met over a chipped fifth-century vase at an antiquities auction. She had been there bidding on pieces with Madame Godinaux, her first solo client; Malcolm was expanding his enormous art collection. He was tall, with broad shoulders, dark blond hair, and perfectly kissable lips. The attraction had been immediate and overwhelming, and she'd lingered outside after the auction to light a cigarette in the bitter winter chill, hoping for another glimpse of him. Two puffs in, she had begun to try to talk her naïve and giddy self down. Malcolm's accent and business card agreed: he was American. Whether he was in France for business or pleasure, he wouldn't be there long. Casual flirting was as close as she could afford to get.

She'd dropped the barely charred cigarette on the cobblestone sidewalk and crushed it under the heel of her black Carel boot, trying to stamp out any attraction to Malcolm along with it. Instead, the stiletto had promptly snapped off. Just as she lost her balance, wobbling and stumbling ungracefully, Malcolm had appeared—golden, muscular, delicious-smelling—to steady her. His dark eyes had glittered in the lamplight, although he was evidently too gentlemanly to laugh out loud at her awkwardness. "My car is right here," he'd said in a wonderful, liquid-gold rumble of a voice, gesturing toward the street, "and I'm going to have to insist on giving you a ride home, if only for the safety of other pedestrians."

Before she'd realized what was happening, he'd scooped her up in his arms and strode easily toward a waiting limousine. Then she was ensconced in the warm, leather-covered back of the car, and Malcolm was handing her a flute of champagne.

Elodie's head popped through the curtain of the dressing room, curls bouncing like springs. "You look gorgeous," she cooed, interrupting Jane's reverie and bringing her crashing back to the reality of the boutique: flimsy clothes, ludicrous price tags, and a saleswoman who clearly knew she wasn't dealing with her usual clientele, as she'd been chatting on the phone incessantly since the two of them had walked in. "Your sexy American will never know what hit him."

"I wish," Jane admitted honestly. "At least then we'd be even." She'd done her share of dating, naturally; you couldn't be a curvy twenty-four-year-old blonde in Paris without getting asked out one or two million times a day. But she'd never understood what people meant by "chemistry" until she met Malcolm. Even the air around him felt heady and intoxicating, and she simply couldn't get enough. Her resolve to keep a safe distance had lasted all of two minutes once they were alone together in his limo, as had, in fact, her resolve to keep *any* distance between them whatsoever.

Then she had been on the sidewalk, and the car was a pair of red lights vanishing around the corner, and the streetlight above her head had blown out with a rather spectacular shower of sparks that seemed to capture her frustration quite perfectly.

Luckily for the city's electrical grid, we spent every night after that together, Jane thought ruefully. She and electronics had always had an uneasy relationship: lights flickering, computers crashing, photocopiers spitting out reams of chewed-up paper, Mètro trains breaking down when she was in a hurry. Fortunately, her relationship with Malcolm was nothing short of blissful. They'd spent three weeks eating (when necessary), sleeping (barely), and making love more or less constantly, until Malcolm had regretfully announced an unavoidable business meeting in Italy. But tonight he would be back, and had suggested they try to maintain their composure long enough to have an actual date. And, apparently, it was going to be a rather dressy occasion.

Jane stepped out of the dressing room to examine herself in the full-length mirror on the main floor. She scowled in frustration at the embroidery along the hem. "I'm so last season it hurts."

At the counter, the saleswoman, a thin and rather pinched-looking blond woman in her mid-thirties, laughed as if on cue. She lowered her voice to a hush, no doubt whispering about her fiscally challenged customers. Jane blushed, and then mentally kicked herself for blushing.

"Men don't notice things like that," Elodie told her soothingly, but Jane remained stubbornly un-soothed. Maybe the guys Elodie knew didn't, but Malcolm wasn't any ordinary man.

Although he was quite casual about it, Malcolm was loaded. The only child of a wealthy family in Manhattan, he was an art dealer out of passion, not necessity. His car, coat, voice, suits—*everything* about him—oozed the kind of wealth and breeding that an orphan from French farm country could barely imagine. Jane knew that she couldn't possibly manage to dress to his level, but at the very least, she could avoid embarrassing herself. She picked at the hem. *Maybe.*

"The black one wasn't bad," Elodie reminded her, holding up an admittedly boring, but affordable strapless gown with a tired silk flower bobbing at the waist.

"Mesdemoiselles?" the saleswoman said, finally hanging up the phone with a clatter. "Excuse me," she went on in heavily accented English, surprising Jane. The woman had barely seemed to be aware that she had customers at all, but apparently she had been listening in between gossipy phone calls. Jane had always spoken English at home with her American-born grandmother, and Elodie was the daughter of a British diplomat. They enjoyed getting to speak their first language too much to care about being mistaken—frequently—for tourists in Paris. The saleswoman nodded her blond head to the back of the store. "I believe that there is something perfect for you in our new collection. It is not supposed to be for sale yet, but . . ." Her long-fingered hands curled expressively in the air.

Jane's heart sank: perfect would be nice, but she couldn't even begin to guess what perfect would cost. "Thank you," she began slowly, feeling heat rise to her cheeks, "but I was really just look-ing . . ." She trailed off, unable to find just the right excuse. From her perch, Elodie held up the black dress brightly.

"But a Monsieur Doran called," the saleswoman told them briskly, and Jane's head snapped up. *Malcolm.* "You are Made-moiselle Boyle, yes? He has instructed me to charge anything you like to his account. *Anything.* And this, I think you will like." She smiled, which seemed to strain the tight muscles of her face almost to the breaking point, then clicked her way to the back room.

"And he's generous, too," Elodie sighed, wrapping a Beaujolais-colored scarf around her neck and pursing her lips at the mirror. "Here I've been wasting my prime dating years on French boys when there were men like that just a tiny little ocean away!"

Before Jane could respond, the saleswoman returned, hold-ing out a gorgeous dress in sapphire chiffon. Jane gasped. The elegantly pleated bodice plunged to a deep V, and the folds of the long skirt cascaded down to Jane's toes. It was truly extraor-dinary.

The cash register's drawer slammed open of its own accord with a ringing crash, and all three of them jumped. "*Cette fichue chose; c'est la quatrième fois . . .*" The saleswoman stormed away, muttering darkly at the misbehaving register, leaving Jane with an armful of whisper-soft chiffon that cost approximately as much as her monthly rent.

"Try it," Elodie whispered excitedly, and Jane practically skipped behind the curtain to do exactly that.

Two

By that evening, Jane's confidence had completely evaporated. She looked doubtfully at the address in her hands for what had to be the thousandth time before stepping out of the taxi in front of 25 Avenue Montaigne, which just so happened to be the iconic Plaza Athénée. *Thank God I'm dressed right.* She took a deep lungful of the humid winter air, and smiled at the uniformed doorman who ushered her deferentially into the impossibly magnificent five-star hotel. The lobby was a sumptuous mixture of marble, velvet, and crystal that set her teeth on edge, and Jane felt a pang of longing for the clean lines and simple track lighting of her studio apartment.

She fought the urge to panic and instead focused on her image in the mirror across the lobby. Her pale blond hair was swept loosely into a low knot, and she'd opted for minimal makeup. Her gray eyes looked wide and innocent; the blue of the dress set them off nicely—and showed a tantalizing stretch of creamy dé-colletage. She looked sexy, but tasteful . . . almost as though she belonged here.

Of course, she also looked a bit vain, since standing there, over her reflection's shoulder, was Malcolm. Watching her watch herself. Perfect.

She turned and pressed her lips to his, wiping the amused smile off his face. She inhaled deeply; she had forgotten how delicious he smelled. His spiced-champagne scent made her feel half-drunk already.

"You look good enough to eat," he whispered in her ear when they broke apart, and she had to fight off a sudden impulse to point out that he could easily skip dinner and do just that.

A real date. Like civilized people. In chairs.

As if he had read her thoughts—the second, less scandalous set of them, anyway—he took her arm and led her into the restaurant. He held a white-silk-cushioned chair for her, and she sat carefully, scooping and arranging the full skirt of her dress in a futile attempt to keep it from creasing or pulling.

"God, I missed you," Malcolm's deep voice rumbled, and she forgot all about the chiffon. The candle at their table flickered, making his deep, dark eyes glow orange. "Those were the six longest days of my life."

"I missed you, too," she told him softly, and she meant it. She couldn't quite explain it, but whenever she was around Malcolm, every part of her body hummed, desperate to be touching him. But at the same time, her mind felt peaceful, calm, as if it were perfectly happy to step out of the way and let her body take over. She was glad that their table was tucked in a private corner of the room, at least ten feet from the nearest other couple; an entire meal in public suddenly seemed like an awfully long time to avoid doing or saying something embarrassingly intimate.

"The auction house delivered my vase today," Malcolm told her conversationally, unfolding his crème-colored napkin and placing it on his lap. She smiled automatically—of course he would make this easier with small talk. She felt her mind adjust itself to match the lightness of his tone.

"They did?" Jane said teasingly. His carbon-dated tastes had been their very first topic of conversation. "Let me guess: you'll put it in some corner where no one will bump into it by accident, and then go tell all your friends how yours is two centuries older than theirs?"

He laughed. "You know, I didn't think France gave passports to people who weren't fanatical about preserving history. We're surrounded by people who haven't changed their traffic laws since horse-drawn carriages were the cool new hybrids. How did a serial renovator ever manage to slip through airport security?"

"I looked surprisingly innocent as a baby," she answered. On their second date (they'd made it as far as her tiny kitchen table), she'd confessed that she was actually an American citizen, too, although she had lived in France with her grandmother since she was ten months old.

A white-jacketed waiter appeared just then with glistening flutes of champagne and two small glass bowls of radish foam with caramelized leeks.

Jane cocked a suspicious eyebrow. It smelled good, but it looked like shaving cream. "You know, they don't eat foam in Alsace. This is strictly a pretentious Parisian thing," she joked as the waiter glided off.

"Tell me more about your farm," he suggested, taking a sip of the effervescing wine.

"You mean my own personal juvenile detention center?" She poked her bottom lip with the prongs of her fork. Malcolm's eyes shifted for the briefest moment. "You don't want to know about that."

"I want to know everything about you." His toe touched hers under the table, and a shiver ran from her pearl-painted toenails all the way up to her spine. She thought about all the luxury rooms in the floors above and had to clutch her chair to keep from dragging Malcolm upstairs. But that was the whole point of the evening, she reminded herself: to stay out of bed long enough to exchange more than pillow talk.

"Well, Gran keeps a fully stocked bomb shelter," Jane admitted with a wry grin, feeling the warmth of the champagne begin to spread outward from her stomach. Six years away from her childhood home had given her the ability to see some humor in her unusual upbringing . . . as long as she didn't linger on it for too long. "She was convinced we would one day be under siege."

Malcolm laughed. "That sounds a little paranoid."

Jane smiled and took another sip of champagne. Her grandmother was more than paranoid, but it wasn't entirely without merit. Her daughter—Jane's mother—and son-in-law had died in a car crash in North Carolina just ten months after Jane was born. The woman was so petrified of losing her granddaughter, too, that she'd moved her to her home in a tiny village in France and barely let Jane out of her sight. And when that had been completely unavoidable, Gran had sent her faithful dog, Honey, along to watch over her. "She was very . . . protective of me."

The delicate sounds of a Mozart sonata filtered down from hidden speakers, and the waiter wordlessly refilled her water glass.

"Well I guess we have that in common then," Malcolm said. A few tables over, a couple dug into goat cheese salads and fresh bread. "What's your grandmother's stand on antique art?" he teased, wriggling an eyebrow comically.

Jane smirked. "The woman has the absolute worst taste—even worse than yours, Mr. Quaint-French-Whatever. She has all these awful china plates on the wall and everything's huge and floral and heavy. She can't hang her hideous knickknacks and depressing oil paintings to save her life, so they're constantly slipping and falling and breaking, and she was convinced that I was going around knocking them down myself. It didn't even matter that I was in my room or outside; she always thought it was me. Let me tell you, though: if just hating those things was enough, then I broke every last one just by looking at them."

"Now that's quite a talent," Malcolm said, an unreadable expression in his eyes.

"Wouldn't it be? I could redecorate without lifting a finger." Jane chuckled, lifting a polished fingernail in demonstration. "It would certainly make my job a lot easier. Madame Godinaux has me running all over the city to pick up light fixtures and furniture. I don't know how she thinks it'll all fit into one house. I'd love to be able to get rid of a display nook or six without leaving fingerprints."

Malcolm leaned forward, his gaze suddenly intent. His abrupt intensity made her breath catch in her throat. "You're amazing, Jane. Do you know that?" He reached across the table and grasped her hand. "I had this whole plan in place, but . . ." he trailed off, shaking his head ruefully.

Jane's heart started pounding, and her skin sizzled at his touch.

"Jane, I've always believed that when you meet the one, you know it."

Jane glanced around, sure that her heartbeat must be echoing through the whole room.

"I'm not a patient man," Malcolm continued, "and a month is already too long." He set a small box covered in deep blue velvet on the table between them like a challenge, and gave her one last long look before snapping it open. Set on a platinum band, the diamond—an emerald-cut solitaire of at least five carats—sparkled fiercely in the candlelight. "Jane," Malcolm said, his voice throbbing with passion, "you're the one. I don't want to spend another day away from you, and I don't want to wait. Please," he added, but there was no pleading in his tone, "Jane, say you'll be my wife."

The room spun fast. Jane's heart was in her throat and her cheeks flamed, as though the heat had been turned up full-blast. Marrying Malcolm would mean leaving France behind: her job at Atelier Antoine, her adorable apartment in the fifth arrondissement with its charming view of Notre Dame from the fire escape, her friends, her entire life . . .

The choice was easy.

"Of course. Of course I will." She held out her left hand so he could slip the ring onto her finger. It fit perfectly.

Three

JANE SANK LOWER IN THE BATHTUB, THE BUBBLES TICKLING HER collarbone. She lifted one lazy hand out of the water and turned it over: her engagement ring sparkled wildly even in the muted light. She stared at it, trying to convince herself that the evening had really happened. There was the evidence, certainly: the ring itself, for one thing, and then also the fact that she was lounging in a massive marble tub with a panoramic view of the Eiffel Tower, for another. But as soon as Malcolm had left the suite to pick up a quart of salted-caramel ice cream—Jane's favorite—a feeling of unreality had set in.

She glanced involuntarily toward the door; it was too soon for Malcolm to be back yet, but she couldn't help hoping anyway. She had objected to his going out—wasn't that what the hotel staff was there for?—but he had been too intent to talk down. He had insisted that this was the sort of thing that fiancés did, and Jane, who had never had a fiancé before, had been hard-pressed to argue otherwise.

A curl of steam rose off the water, and outside a crow landed on the roof across the street. Jane wondered if it should bother her that she seemed to be adjusting to Malcolm's lavish lifestyle of concierges and penthouse suites so quickly, but she inhaled the steam and brushed the worry aside. Why shouldn't she be comfortable? It was her lifestyle now, too.

There would be loose ends to tie up, of course. She had an apartment lease to terminate, and friends to say good-bye to. She began mentally tallying her projects at work, all in various stages of completion. *And my very first solo client,* she thought, feeling a tiny pang of regret, but she was a talented architect, and New York was a perfectly good place to be that . . . especially with some newly acquired family connections to smooth the way. *I'll have a family,* she thought happily, and wiggled her toes to watch the ripples spread.

Even when she had lived with Gran, she'd felt alone. Gran loved her, certainly, but in the old woman's nervous mind, "love" seemed to mean "worry," pretty much to the exclusion of anything else. Even if the standoffish villagers in their Alsatian town had wanted to be friends, Jane wouldn't have been allowed to spend time with them unchaperoned. She hadn't even been allowed to attend the half-timbered school in the center of town, and Gran would come looking for her if her market shopping took five minutes longer than usual. Gran had never been willing or able to explain what it was that she thought was so dangerous in the outside world, but her determination that Jane should never encounter it had formed a wedge between them, and every passing year had driven it deeper. Jane, beside herself with frustration, had left the little gray farmhouse nestled at the base of the foothills the day she'd received her letter of acceptance to the university. She had not gone back once in the six years since.

The sconces lining the bathroom wall flickered, the shadows shifting like the branches of ancient trees. She'd have to tell Gran she was leaving, Jane realized, shivering a little in spite of the steam. They had exchanged a few stiff and awkward letters over the years, but the farmhouse didn't have a phone. A visit felt more appropriate now—and, of course, Gran would want to meet her fiancé. But it would be so cold and dark this time of year...

Gran might be happy for her, she reflected; stranger things had surely happened. She wouldn't be thrilled about Jane moving all the way across an ocean. She had never even approved of Jane's move to Paris, referring to it unfailingly as "when you ran away," and Jane really wasn't looking forward to breaking the news that she planned to leave the country entirely. But Gran's main concern had always been Jane's safety, and no parent (or grandparent) could ask for a better protector than Malcolm Doran. He was kind, caring, attentive, and had the resources to take very, very good care of her. All that aside, he was madly, desperately, head-over-heels in love with her, just as she was with him.

As soon as Jane lowered her hand back under the water, a low, scratching sound snagged through the silence, interrupting her reverie. It was a small noise: a scrape of metal on metal, but in the silence it sounded hard . . . and close. The bathroom lights abruptly flashed and died. Water splashed around her, and moonlight streamed in through the windows, turning the room as flat and cold as Alsace's landscape in wintertime. It took a few moments of listening to her heart pounding before she noticed that no light was coming in under the door. Somehow, the entire suite had gone dark.

Then she heard another sound. It was soft at first, but as it drew closer, the steady fall of shoes on carpet became unmistakable.

Someone's here.

Jane felt panic bubble up in her throat. There was no way Malcolm could be back yet. He'd only been gone ten minutes. She had just enough time to wonder if the panoramic windows behind her could be opened before the door of the bathroom swung toward her. In the deep shadows on the other side, there was an even deeper shadow in the unmistakable shape of a very tall man.

Jane shrieked, and tried to stand up, but her feet skidded on the slick bottom of the tub. She fell back heavily into the bath, smashing her elbow hard on the marble and sending soapy water racing across the floor.

"Jane?"

She froze.

The Eiffel Tower's festive hourly sparkling lit up the sky, as well as the face of the intruder. "Malcolm, you scared me!" She sighed and cradled her elbow, feeling too foolish for words. "I wasn't expecting you back so soon."

"Clearly." He chuckled. "The power went out right after I came in. No wonder you're jumpy." He moved quickly to the side of the tub, offering a hand to help her up. She noticed a frosted carton of ice cream in his other hand. "There's nothing to be scared of," he told her gently. He folded her tightly against him, and her shivering subsided in his warmth.

"There is one thing, actually," she murmured against his chest, remembering the wide, gray landscape that had invaded the room just ahead of Malcolm's steadying presence.

He drew away sharply. "Did something happen? Are you hurt?"

Her heart melted at his immediate concern. "Nothing like that," she assured him quickly. "I was just thinking that I'd like to see my grandmother before I leave France. And I'd really like you to meet her." She held up her left hand and wiggled her fingers meaningfully; the diamond threw the glittering tower lights around the room like merry, blue fireflies.

She had expected him to relax a little at her explanation, but he remained in the same posture: holding her stiffly away, a line of worry creasing his forehead. They stayed that way for a few tense moments, and then he seemed to finally register that she was truly okay.

"Of course," he agreed hastily. "We could go for Christmas, if you'd like." With that, he pressed his lips to hers and slid his hands lightly across the slick, wet skin of her breasts. She moaned softly. "I feel overdressed," he added, smiling into her cheek.

Agreeing wholeheartedly, she unbuttoned his shirt with the speed of frequent practice. His perfectly creased black pants followed easily to the floor while Jane kissed the golden skin of his chest, inhaling his spiced scent the way a drowning woman would inhale air. *Maybe I should be scared,* a tiny part of her brain told her. *This can't be normal.*

Then his fingers found her, stroking expertly, and she could feel him hard and ready in the darkness between them, and she shut off the thinking, worrying part of her brain entirely. With a wolfish grin, Malcolm lifted her by the hips and set her down on the counter next to the sink. She dug her nails into his back as he entered her, and wrapped her legs around his waist, trying to pull him as deeply inside as she could. He braced himself with one hand against the mirror, and with the other he began to stroke her again, so when they climaxed, it was together.

The lights came back on as he carried her to the bed, kissing her sore elbow tenderly. It seemed as though every lamp in the suite was glowing—far more than she remembered turning on before—but Malcolm tapped the master switch beside the bed, and she was asleep almost as soon as the room was dark again.

four

"You know, I've never actually seen you drive," Jane pointed out as Malcolm slid behind the wheel of the rental car. It was Christmas Eve, and their flight had landed in Strasbourg ahead of schedule. From the air, the highways had looked reassuringly clear, but that wouldn't help them much if Malcolm was as uncomfortable in the driver's seat as he looked. "Are you sure you don't want me to drive?"

"Don't be silly," Malcolm insisted, fumbling with the keys. "Just because I have a chauffeur or three doesn't mean—huh." He gave the gearshift a dubious look. "Is this a manual transmission?"

"Out," Jane laughed, giving him a little shove as she hitched up her belted gray coat and slid across the seats. Once he was settled on the passenger side (looking a little chagrined, she thought), she started the car and began making her way to the parking lot's exit. "It's still a good two hours away," she told him, feeling oddly giddy, as though her nerve endings were firing off at random.

"Are you okay?" he asked, buckling his seatbelt and giving it an experimental tug. "You haven't been yourself since we boarded the plane."

I'm not really sure, Jane thought, trying to suppress a shiver. "It's just that when I left home, I really, really didn't plan to come back," she explained.

"I thought we were talking 'quaint French farm village' here," Malcolm said. "What could be so bad about that?"

Jane forced a laugh; it came out as a nervous, high-pitched sound. "That's why I don't date Americans. You all think Europe is some kind of theme park—as long as you can go back to your glass high-rises with the never-ending supply of hot water, France is just *adorable*."

"You object to your hometown on architectural grounds?" Malcolm's eyebrow was skeptically high.

"Of course! And of course not *just* that," she admitted. "My relationship with my grandmother is . . . complicated."

She frowned and changed lanes abruptly to pass a truck that was struggling on the incline. She knew that "complicated" didn't really capture the years of conflict and strain between her and Gran, but that part of her life was over now. All she wanted to do was focus on her future with Malcolm. *Just have to make it through this one little errand first, and then we're home free.*

"I know a thing or two about complicated families," Malcolm replied, startling her out of her thoughts.

"Oh yeah? Did your mother ever chase the neighbor kids off with a broom, or read your diary and then yell at you about what you'd written?" At age nine, a precocious and very bored Jane had entertained herself by imagining an illicit affair between their neighbor Monsieur Dupuis (a thin man with an extremely long black beard) and Madame Foucheaux, the butcher's wife (a round and rosy woman who seemed to have a meat cleaver perpetually in hand). Every time she had seen them together, she'd imagined a whole secret communication happening. The neighbor would say, "Half a kilo," and Jane would hear: "Meet me at six so I can ravage you again." When the reply came, "Like this much?" to Jane it would sound like "Make it seven."

She had written down every last lurid detail. When Gran had found the diary, she'd screamed herself hoarse about the evils of gossip and what happened to little girls who told vicious stories. Jane shuddered as she remembered the thunderstorm that had rolled in while Gran yelled. Although she never would have said so out loud, Jane always thought that Gran had the same kind of luck with the weather as Jane herself did with electronics. Crashing thunder had been the soundtrack to *Jane's in Trouble* for her whole life, and even now she couldn't hear a storm coming without flinching.

Malcolm shook his head. "Well, no. Then again, I didn't keep a diary, so . . ."

Jane let out a mirthless laugh. "Smart boy."

"How did your boss take the news that you were leaving?" Malcolm asked, and Jane forced her mind to change gears.

"Much better than I expected, actually." Elodie had scowled around the office, referring to Malcolm as "that kidnapper," but as soon as Jane had said, "I'm in love," the renowned Antoine of Atelier Antoine had squealed with pure French *joie*. Within moments, he had gone racing through his Treo, e-mailing her contact after contact in Manhattan. Just that morning, she'd spoken to a bubbly-voiced woman named Pamela, who was ecstatic to meet Jane. Apparently, Jane's overseas experience was crucial to Pamela's business plan. "I have a promising lead at Conran and Associates; they're in the Village somewhere," she told Malcolm. She hoped that sounded right. Didn't New Yorkers on TV talk about "the Village"?

"That's great." She could hear his supportive smile, and she made her lips curve upward in a matching one.

They rode that way for a while, talking about everything and nothing, passing from flat fields into a thick tangle of trees, whose greedy limbs seemed to reach out to swallow the road.

Within moments, the sky was largely invisible. *Ten in the morning and it might as well be nighttime. Welcome home.* The air felt almost too oppressive to inhale. She opened the window a crack, hoping that it would help, but cold wind whipped around the car, making her ears and fingers numb, and she had to close it again. They rode the rest of the way in strained silence.

When the red, black, and white sign for Saint-Croix-sur-Amaury appeared, Jane gripped the steering wheel tight. Within moments, they would be in the village's tiny center, where the shops huddled together like old friends along the main route—the only road in the town large enough to rate a name of its own. Farther along, there would be the patchwork clusters of farmhouses, surrounded by amber, green, or brown fields, depending on the season. Gran's place was even farther beyond that, down a long dirt track that was headed determinedly toward the mountain. Gran's house, unlike the others, stood completely alone.

"We should bring something," Jane announced suddenly, trying not to hear how flat her words fell in the car's silence.

As a Christmas present for her grandmother, she'd wrapped a warm wool shawl in metallic green paper, but she suspected that after six years and with no warning, a hostess gift was probably warranted. "She's big on manners." Gran may never have been friendly or even neighborly, but she had always insisted that Jane observe proper etiquette.

"There's a flower shop over there." Malcolm pointed to a tired-looking building on the right. Dark tracks of a century's worth of rain snaked down the stone façade, making it seem as though the upper windows were crying.

Jane nodded, and jerked to an unsteady stop by the curb. The road was so narrow that the ancient black Mercedes behind her had barely enough room to squeeze by.

Locking the car doors behind them, Malcolm and Jane entered the store. It took a moment for her eyes to adjust. The tiny shop was overflowing with flowers—tulips, peonies, delphiniums, and rows and rows of waxy green fronds. The low beams of the ceiling seemed to press down on them, and the air was thick with growth.

"These are fine," she said randomly, grabbing the first wrapped bunch she passed and handing them to Malcolm. He nodded amiably and carried them to a pitted wooden counter that held an ancient-looking cash register.

"Is strange," a creaky voice said from behind her. The accent was thick to the point of being unrecognizable, but it was English. Jane spun to see an old man sitting on a stool just inside the doorway, a high-crowned hat shoved down low on his forehead. Tufty eyebrows poked out from under the brim like opportunistic shrubs.

"Strange?" she prompted. "*Quelque chose d'étrange, Monsieur?*"

"Normal people come one time," he explained, pressing dog-gedly on in English in spite of Jane's native accent. *French pride,* she thought with a mental eye-roll. *Half of them refuse to speak English ever, and you can't get the other half to cut it out.* "They do not again," the man elaborated. "Saint-Croix is not good for the touring."

"Do I know you?" she asked, confused. Was he a friend of her grandmother's? The man didn't look like he'd remember what he had for breakfast, never mind a face from six years ago. Behind her, Malcolm quietly thanked the shopkeeper for the flowers.

Jane peered a little more closely at the old man's parchment-skinned face, trying to make out any familiar detail. Malcolm materialized by her elbow, and the man's watery eyes flicked be-tween their two faces. Malcolm pressed her elbow a little more urgently, and she let him steer her out of the shop.

"Was he bothering you?" Malcolm asked her, an edge of anxi-ety in his voice. Jane felt a small twinge of satisfaction at his re-alization that her "quaint French farm village" wasn't exactly picture-perfect. "What did he say?"

"It was nothing," she assured him. She turned back once more to look at the old man, but his stool beside the door was empty, and there was no sign of him anywhere.

five

THE FIRST THING JANE NOTICED WHEN SHE PULLED THE CAR
into the long dirt driveway was the wide-open gate. "That's not
right," she muttered. Gran was a firm believer in physical barriers as well as social ones, and Jane couldn't remember ever
seeing the gate standing open. As if to compound the strange-
ness, a loud, hoarse noise came from the stand of trees that separated the little stone house from the road. Jane's eyes widened
as a rangy German shepherd came bounding across the Boyles'
land, barking furiously.

"Honey?" The dog stalked closer more slowly now, mouth
twisted into a snarl. Its fur was matted and rough-looking.

"He doesn't seem to recognize you," Malcolm pointed out
tensely as the dog crouched low to the ground, as if ready to
pounce.

"I don't recognize him either," Jane explained. "But he might be new. My grandmother always names her dogs Honey. She said she got tired of thinking up names."

"Maybe it's a stray?" Malcolm suggested.

Only Gran would never let her own dog get so skinny—or so aggressive. Jane fidgeted with the window, making sure that it was tightly closed. "Let's just get to the house. I'm sure she'll have heard the racket by now." She pulled the little car up the slope of the drive, feeling her jaw relax slightly when the dog bounded off into the trees, away from the house.

Jane parked to the right of the dilapidated porch, whose white paint was peeling off in long strips. The house was dark, and there was no answer to Jane's timid knock on the weathered wooden door.

Her stomach churned and her toes started to tingle. Lips pressed into a tight line, she pushed the door; it opened easily. The air inside the house felt stale and cold. Jane shivered. "Malcolm, something's not right."

"Maybe she's traveling." Malcolm's voice sounded far too loud in the house's stillness. Goose bumps rose on her forearms.

"She doesn't travel," Jane told him flatly, but she felt a spark of hope. *Maybe she does now,* she thought wildly. *Or she's moved, and we're trespassing on some stranger.*

She drifted down the front hall, taking stock of the familiar reproduction of Matisse's "Red Studio" on the wall and the worn-out Persian runner. But when she reached the low-ceilinged living room, where four-year-old Jane had built forts from over-stuffed pillows and hand-knit afghans, she knew for sure Celine Boyle hadn't gone on vacation or moved out. Her grandmother was right there, sitting on a floral chintz-covered chair, her hands folded primly on her lap. The skin of her fingers was gray, and her eyes stared through Jane, a white film covering her dark pupils.

"Oh God." Jane instinctively held her breath, afraid to know how the air around her would smell.

"Jane." Malcolm appeared at her side and gripped her elbow, trying to pull her from the room. But Jane couldn't feel her feet, couldn't move, couldn't believe this was happening. She tried to speak, but her words couldn't make it past the lump that had lodged itself in her throat. She felt like a ship whose moorings had come loose; her mind floated free and unattached. Her grandmother, the woman who had raised her, her only anchor in the world, the one constant, was dead.

"Jane, we need to go outside. We have to call someone."

"No phone," Jane said automatically. "She never had anyone to call." Her voice sounded hollow, as though it was someone else's. "You have to go to the neighbor's."

"We'll use my cell," he told her, his voice uncharacteristically snappish. "But let's do it from outside." She didn't move, and he was pulling at her arm again. "Jane, I'm not leaving you here."

Jane wondered why it mattered. She had already seen the body; there were no mysteries left in this room to protect her from. Malcolm could stay, go, talk, be silent . . . she just wanted to be here. Through the fog, she realized she had been away from this house for an unforgivably long time.

Jane heard Malcolm rummaging through his jacket for his cell phone, and closed her eyes, waiting. Her heart counted out the seconds she knew it would take him to give up on getting any kind of signal. And then she heard his curse—a low, soft sound that barely moved the heavy air—confirming that he had realized just how far away they were from the rest of the world. "I'll be *right* back with help," he told her firmly, and she wondered distantly if she was nodding, or acknowledging him at all. Either way, he stepped away from her side, and then the familiar snick of the door told her that she was alone with the dead body of her last family member in the world.

Gran's vacant eyes stared straight ahead, and Jane suddenly imagined that the woman could see her somehow. *If anyone could* . . . Gran *had* always seemed to be watching her, even when she wasn't there. Jane abruptly turned and walked down the hallway.

She paused in the small doorway to the kitchen. It was as if time had passed the farmhouse by, holding the wood structure constant while the rest of the world spun by. The same rough red curtains lined the leaded windows; the same curling but relentlessly clean linoleum covered the floor; the round breakfast table boasted Gran's favorite blue-glazed vase exactly in the middle. The flowers in it were brown and shriveled. She guessed that they had been daisies, but it was hard to tell. They had clearly been dead for a while. The thought made Jane wince, and she left the kitchen without another glance.

She climbed the stairs and passed Gran's room (bed neatly made, hospital corners and all), shutting the door on impulse to indicate its owner would not be back. There was only one place left to go now: the door at the end of the dark, narrow hall.

Her old room felt brutally familiar and painfully small. Dark wooden beams held up the low adobe ceiling, and a water stain shaped like an elephant marred one of the white walls. Teenage Jane had done what she could with the space: mirrors bounced gray light around the room, the furniture was the simplest she'd been able to get her hands on, and the surfaces were entirely free of knickknacks. But the steep gray foothills of the mountain still loomed outside the only window, blocking the sun, and trapping her inside the darkness.

Everything the same . . .

Actually, Jane realized with a start, everything was not the same. On the far wall, right next to the watermark, Gran had hung a small, round mirror set in thick, dark wood. *She had to know I'd hate it.* Jane approached it curiously. *Why would she put it here?* Gran may not have shared Jane's tastes, but she had never interfered with this room. Other than this one anomaly, it didn't look like the place had been touched in six years, except to rid it of dust. Jane slipped her fingers behind the unfamiliar thick frame before she could even imagine what she was looking for.

"Ow!" Her hand struck something sharp, and she jerked it out again.

She watched a drop of blood well up on her finger for a moment before reaching behind the mirror again, more carefully this time. Her fingers hit something hard and crisp, an envelope. It was marked "Jane" in her grandmother's unmistakable cursive, and bulged oddly in the middle.

The heat in the hallway hissed on and the mournful yowl of a dog floated through the window. "What did you leave me, Gran?" Jane whispered as she opened the envelope. A yellowed piece of stationery fluttered out, along with a silver ring that flashed in the muted light before settling into Jane's palm. She blinked. For a moment, she could have sworn the ring was engraved with antique carvings, but when she ran her fingers over it, she saw that it was entirely plain: just a smooth silver band with beveled edges. *Kind of my style,* she registered with vague surprise. She slipped it on her left middle finger and held it up to examine it more closely.

A violent shock tore through her hand, as though she'd stuck it in a live outlet. "What the—" Jane reached to tear the ring from her finger, but the silver object began to vibrate and hum. Jane's eyes lost focus, and the edges of the room took on a weird, hazy glow. *Take it off!* her mind ordered frantically. The tingling flood of energy took over her arms, snaking through her veins like a shot of adrenaline, and there was nothing she could do to bring her limbs in line with her mind's increasingly desperate commands. A burning pain flew down her torso and through her legs, pricking her skin as though she were being set on fire from the inside. She inhaled and tried to scream, but it was too late: the pulsing energy had reached her throat, and her vocal cords were as frozen as the rest of her.

Images from nowhere flickered along the whitewashed room: a horse reared back with an armor-clad knight on its back; a ringletted child in Victorian dress pulled a trapdoor closed behind her; seven stars traced an ellipsis around the earth; a ship cracked and sank below a clear blue sky. A pale woman with sad eyes and a crown of leaves watched from the corner, twisting her long-fingered hands together.

Jane felt herself torn in a hundred directions at once, unable to move or speak or even think. The invisible fire that held her still seemed to also be dragging her apart, and a more specific, familiar burn began in her chest. She had just enough time to wonder how long it had been since her last breath, when suddenly she was ten years old again, deep in the muddy water of Monsieur Pennette's pond. She kicked for the surface, but the murky gloom and suspended tangle of flora made it impossible to tell which way was up. Gran had warned her almost daily to stay away from the water, but Jane had been desperate to see what lay beneath the lily-padded surface. As her lungs rebelled and her body went limp, she'd wished with all her strength that Gran would dive in and save her. And, just like magic, Gran had appeared. She had dragged Jane out of the dank standing water, and lectured her the whole way home about doing as she was told.

Now Jane was drowning again, this time in heat and darkness, but there was no Gran to pull her to the light. In the very last instant before she passed out on her bedroom floor, Jane's mind succumbed to the fiery energy, and in that instant, she understood everything.

Six

JANE PULLED HER BODY UP INTO A SITTING POSITION AND RAN an absent hand through the disastrous tangle of her blond hair. Her muscles felt loose and rubbery, as though she'd just run a marathon, and the world looked overly bright, the way it did when she awoke from a deep sleep. She turned her left hand curiously; the silver ring sat perfectly normally on her finger, looking as harmless as a declawed kitten. Her hand was trembling, yet her breathing was steady, her mind detached.

The scrap of stationery that had fallen out with the ring was a few inches from her knee. She unfolded it with care; there was no real hurry now that she knew what was inside. The date was six years old, but the ink was barely faded.

My dearest Jane,

I am so very sorry, but there is no way to say this gently: you are a witch. So am I, so was your mother, and so are many others around the world. Magic is real and powerful and all too ready for the taking. I have spent my lifetime hiding myself, my daughter, and then you from those who would kill to steal this terrible gift from us.

You left for Paris last night, and this morning at dawn I put the most powerful protection spells around you that I could. You are as safe as I can make you without telling you the truth about who you are. I simply cannot bring myself to do that, even now, even if in my bones I feel I should. When you were born, your mother, my darling Angeline, made me promise to never share our secret with you. She wanted to raise you as a normal girl, just as she had always wished to be. I had hoped to someday persuade her of the value of our heritage, but when she died, I had no choice but to honor her wish.

Still, I fear it is a mistake. I feel my age a little deeper in my bones every winter, and when I die, my spells will die with me. I don't know what you will do then, or how you can possibly be ready, and I do know that people will be looking for you. I have to hope that this last gift of mine will be enough to keep you safe then.

Jane: you are powerful. Extraordinarily so. I have seen what you can do: the words you hear that haven't been spoken, the things you move that haven't been touched. The enclosed ring will add to your abilities, enhance them, make you as powerful as your enemies are desperate to be.

If you are reading this, then I am dead, and that means that

*you are in danger. Please, please find a place to hide and learn
how to use your gift so you can keep yourself safe. And under no
circumstances tell anyone the truth about who you are; you'll
never know whom you can trust.*

   *I am so proud of you, my Jane, and I only wish that I could
have done more to help you.*

                              I love you, and I always will.
                                             Gran

Hot tears pricked at the back of Jane's eyes. "I have seen what
you can do: the words you hear that haven't been spoken, the
things you move that haven't been touched." *The lights I blow out
or the cash registers that I break?* She had spent her entire life mis-
interpreting the world around her: believing that Gran was too
strict, that violent weather was a coincidence, that she, Jane, was
just "unlucky" with electronics. She had heard thoughts, blown
circuits, called Gran to her when she was about to drown in the
neighboring farm's pond. There were no accidents . . . just powers.

A small part of Jane—the part that allotted 10 percent of her
paycheck to savings and only allowed herself three cigarettes
per week—resisted. Magic was preposterous; witches were old-
wives' tales. But the rest of her, the vast majority of her, couldn't
force itself to question something so obviously true.

She closed her eyes, barely able to process the sound of the
wind howling past the leaded windows or the creak of the bed
under her weight. She was a witch. And now she was going to be
hunted, tracked, sought after, unless she hid away from the world,
as her grandmother had . . . or died, like her mother. The pain and
betrayal and loss of it all hit her like a brick wall, mingling with

her new power, until Jane began to think that she really might explode.

No wonder Gran was always so jumpy. No wonder they had had a bomb shelter, code words, crisis plans. No wonder Gran had seen enemies everywhere. Jane shuddered: could the world really be so dangerous? She had lived on her own for six years with nothing worse than the occasional blown fuse, and she had taken that as proof that Gran was off her rocker. But what if that was because Gran had cast a protective spell around her? *What if Gran was right?* Was living a "normal" life impossibly reckless?

"It can't be," Jane whispered to herself. Dangerous, sure, but crossing the street was dangerous. She couldn't live in fear now just because she knew the danger's name. She couldn't wind up alone with bear-trap nerves on a farm in the middle of nowhere. There had to be another way to handle this gift—this burden.

From what felt like light-years away, she registered the sound of the front door creaking open. Heavy footsteps sounded, and several voices filtered up from the front room. "Jane?" Malcolm called, but her throat was too thick with emotion to answer.

"Jane?" Malcolm said again.

Jane's eyes flew open; Malcolm stooped in the narrow doorway of her bedroom. She surreptitiously shoved the letter into her jeans' pocket. "You're so pale," he murmured, moving to fold her into his arms. For a moment, she was almost surprised that he recognized her; it felt impossible that she could still look the same when so much had changed.

But I need to be the same. She concentrated on that thought as hard as she could, trying to force her mind to work in spite of the battering it had just taken. At first it rebelled, but after a long moment, a decision began to form. She wouldn't be like her grandmother. She wouldn't shut herself away, hoping to hide from disaster by closing herself off from the world.

"Jane?" Malcolm's dark eyes were gentle and worried, a trace of a frown on his full lips. Danger, magic, mysterious enemies . . . it was hard to imagine all those existing in the same world as Malcolm. *He'll never know that they do,* she told herself fiercely. *I'm not losing anyone else. I'm not giving any more ground.*

"You're all I have now." She took his hand, a tear slipping down her cheek. "You're my family."

He took her left hand and kissed the diamond on her ring finger. If he noticed the smooth silver ring beside it, he didn't say anything. He just laced his own fingers between hers and led her back toward the door. "Always and forever," he promised.

Seven

"We'll all miss her, dear," Monsieur Dupuis said. Jane couldn't help but notice he was holding Madame Foucheaux's hand. She thought back to Gran's apparent overreaction to the "fictional" romance in Jane's diary, and wondered how much—if any—of it had ever been in her imagination. "And I promise to take good care of Honey." Honey had never warmed up to Jane and Malcolm, but a few good meals and a thorough brushing courtesy of Gran's neighbors had turned him into a generally pleasant and eminently adoptable dog.

"Thank you," Jane said, her eyes downcast. A black thread was unraveling from the sleeve of the cheap black dress she had chosen randomly from Saint-Croix's sole, dingy department store. *One more thing coming apart at the seams.*

For the past few days, she and Malcolm had feverishly prepared for Gran's funeral. The coroner had discreetly (but a little too eagerly, as if he had a penchant for gossip) informed them that between Gran's age and the cold, it was impossible to establish exactly when her heart had stopped. It didn't matter, though. She was gone, and knowing exactly when it happened wouldn't do a thing to change that.

The macabre story of the dead widow in the farmhouse had piqued plenty of interest around the area, and everyone in town had turned up for the funeral mass. Every last villager was now standing in the receiving line at the small stone church, offering Jane condolences in one breath while waiting hopefully in the next for a crumb about Gran's tragic demise. Jane wished that at least one of the so-called "mourners" would have bothered to check on her grandmother in the last month, if they were going to act all caring now. Then again, Jane herself hadn't stopped by in six years.

"I'm so sorry for your loss," Madame Martine, a local artist who fancied herself eccentric, murmured. Jane gave her and her tie-dyed headscarf a wan smile. A headache was blooming behind her eyes, growing stronger with every "sorry." The ancient church, damp and musky, echoed with words—both said and unsaid.

Perhaps if she'd come back sooner . . .

Such an odd lady . . .

Jane rubbed her temples, longing to block the voices that seemed to wander through her head at random.

. . . wonder how much the house will go for . . .

. . . girl was gone for so long . . .

. . . killed her . . .

If my child ever leaves like that . . .

The *idea* of mind-reading, as it turned out, was much more

appealing than the actual experience of it. The magic from the ring still pulsed through Jane's body, throbbing uncomfortably at unexpected moments. She didn't know how to control her powers, and disembodied thoughts came in unpredictable, vivid flashes. She couldn't even pinpoint whom they belonged to, and could rarely hear more than a snippet before her mind skipped away to eavesdrop on someone new. She felt perversely glad to be in mourning: no one would expect her to behave completely normally at a time like this. Her confusion, distraction, and startled responses to unsaid words didn't seem too terribly out of place, even if they felt cringe-inducingly noticeable to her.

"You poor dear." Madame Sandineau grasped her fingers, and Jane nearly gasped aloud at the influx of unwanted information that flashed in her mind: namely, that the sinewy fromagière hadn't showered since Tuesday in order to conserve hot water. Jane felt a rush of vertigo as she watched herself through Madame Sandineau's thoughts.

She carefully disengaged herself from the woman's strong grip. That grasp confirmed Jane's suspicion that her powers were amplified when she touched people. She couldn't see a way to get out of that completely, what with the receiving line. She sighed. Her feet hurt, and the cheap dress was making her legs itch. *I'm supposed to be able to move things without touching them,* she thought glumly, longing to scratch them red. *That would be a little more useful right now than the stupid mind-chatter.*

"Are you doing okay?" Malcolm whispered in her ear. "Do you need to take a break?"

Jane shook her head, grateful for his comforting presence by her side. "It'll be over soon enough." Malcolm had been unbelievably attentive since their horrible discovery in the little old farmhouse, and if such a thing were possible, she'd grown to love and need him even more in the last eight days. Each morning he'd brought her breakfast and held her when she cried, and each night he'd stroked her hair until she fell asleep. He'd hired a team of movers to ship all her belongings to his parents' house in New York, where they'd be staying until they found their own apartment, and he'd insisted on paying for the entire funeral. She hadn't had a thing to worry about except for her grief . . . and her stupid, willful, uncontrollable magic.

Malcolm's attentiveness had made her even more resolved to hide her new secret from him, and so she had flushed Gran's note down the toilet as soon as she was alone. She ached when she watched the familiar handwriting disappear, but she already knew the contents by heart—and besides, Gran herself had warned Jane to hide the truth. Destroying the physical evidence was an unavoidable first step.

Unfortunately, the flickering lights and finicky heater in the squat little church strongly suggested that Jane wasn't hiding nearly as well as Gran would have liked.

Suddenly, goose bumps rose on her arms and she got the chilling feeling of being watched. Looking up, she saw an old man with papery skin and wiry eyebrows in the back of the church. He was glaring at her, and she realized with a start that he was the strange man who was at the flower shop the morning they arrived in the village. She stiffened.

Malcolm lightly touched her back, but Jane couldn't look away from the old man's dark, unwavering eyes. A stab of rage pierced her mind, and a violent jumble of images that she couldn't quite make out—a letter-opener maybe? a barking dog?—flooded her mind. She winced, and felt Malcolm squeeze her hand in concern.

The magic subsided as quickly as it had come, and when she regained her bearings, she saw that the old man had left.

It doesn't matter, she told herself firmly. He *doesn't matter.* Soon she and Malcolm would be thousands of miles away. She didn't have to worry about deciphering the secret feelings of some stranger from her hometown; she had to worry about protecting her fiancé from finding out that he was in love with a mind-reading freak.

"Please talk to me if there were a thing I can do. I loved your grandmother greatly," the local constable said, resting his hand on Jane's shoulder. He'd known her since she was a baby, and had always insisted on practicing his English with her—even, apparently, at her grandmother's funeral. Jane fought the urge to snort, but it was quickly overshadowed when another voice, male this time, filled her head.

. . . killed that nice old woman herself for the inheritance. Those city girls are all the same—wouldn't lift a finger for . . .

Jane winced and snatched her shoulder from the tight grip of the beefy, iron-haired constable. Suddenly she couldn't stand being in Saint-Croix for another moment, couldn't stand to hear another thought about what a horrid person she was or about her grandmother's gossip-worthy reclusiveness. Most of all, she couldn't stand to be so near the place that had filled her with this loathsome power.

She tugged Malcolm's impeccable black cashmere sleeve. "We have to leave," she told him. "Now."

She wanted out of the village, out of Alsace, and out of France entirely. She was done being Jane Boyle, mysterious, ungrateful American orphan; that chapter of her life couldn't be over soon enough.

Malcolm nodded, considerate as always, and she felt a tiny pang. Even though he would never know that she was deceiving him, she would work as hard as she possibly could to make it up to him. "I'll take care of it. Meet me at the car."

She turned and began to push through the crowd, muttering "Excuse me" in defiant English, and ignoring the shocked—and angry—looks from the congregation.

She emerged outside into the gray daylight, a little breathless. The old man from the flower shop was waiting across the narrow cobblestone street, and he didn't look any less furious than he had before. A matching fury began to stir in her. How dare he? How dare he insult her grief and intrude on her mourning? Couldn't he spare an hour or two to respect the dead rather than glare at the bereaved? Jane was seized with a sudden impulse to cross the street and make him explain himself. Just as she was about to step off of the curb, Malcolm came up behind her and looped his arm through hers. "This way," he reminded her, kissing the top of her head, and the hard knot of her anger began to melt away.

She walked arm-in-arm with him to the car, leaving the angry old man—and everyone else in Alsace—behind her for good.

Eight

Eighteen hours later, Jane was a continent away from the funeral, Saint-Croix-sur-Amaury, and her past, and staring straight at her future. From the view in the airplane, the New York City nightscape had been all glass skyscrapers and neon lights. But now, on the Upper East Side and firmly on the ground, the city looked like something else entirely.

A sharp January breeze played around her ankles, and Park Avenue was deserted as far as the eye could see. Jane clutched her canvas bag closer to her chest. Wasn't this supposed to be the city that never slept?

Malcolm thanked Yuri, the family driver, and the silent hulk of a man nodded curtly before pulling away from the curb, leaving them alone. Jane studied the heavy stone archway of the Dorans' house. It struck her that, squatting gloomily between 664 and 668, the building shouldn't really have been numbered 665 at all.

She had never been superstitious, but she felt a sudden rush of gratitude for whomever had decided that the carved stone façade was just too forbidding to tack on a sinister number; it would have been creepiness overkill.

The greenish-gray building easily rose eight stories from the street, but there was nothing graceful or sleek about its height. Instead, it seemed to almost be looming over the sidewalk, even though her inner architect, which tended to see things in blueprint form, insisted that it was vertical. The windows, although moderately sized, were set deep back into the thick stone. She wondered how much daylight could penetrate the fortress. *House,* she corrected herself sternly. *Home.* But it didn't look especially like either.

Malcolm typed a short code into a discreet keypad to the right of the entryway, and a massive wooden door swung open on silent hinges. Of course, despite the house's archaic appearance, it would have an electronic key system. *Perfect.* Jane hadn't had an uncontrolled surge of magic since she'd left Alsace—she'd drugged herself into oblivion on the plane so as to keep it in the sky where it belonged—but it was just a matter of time.

They stepped through the enormous arched entryway into the foyer.

"Mr. Doran," wheezed a tiny, white-haired man in a black uniform with gold trim. His eyes looked bleary with sleep, and Jane guessed that her own probably looked about the same. "Welcome home."

"Thanks, Gunther," Malcolm replied. "This is Jane, my fiancée." Gunther nodded deferentially before retreating silently into the shadows behind them. The lobby was ostentatiously large; Malcolm's extended family could clearly afford to waste as much prime Manhattan square footage as they liked. The marble floor gleamed and the gilded moldings along the ceiling had been expertly restored—assuming they had ever even fallen into disrepair. It was clear the Dorans were not interested in understatement.

Jane stifled a yawn as she stepped into the mahogany-paneled elevator. According to her silver-and-turquoise watch—a gift from Gran on her twenty-first birthday—it was eleven p.m., which would make it five in the morning to her jet-lagged body.

"Are you sure your family is still up?"

Malcolm had seemed sure that his family would be wide-awake and waiting for them, but she was really beginning to hope he was mistaken. She was anticipating a chilly reception at best: the farm-country orphan, to whom New York's most eligible bachelor had proposed after one short month, was bound to come under scrutiny. She was fully prepared to win them over, but it would be easier after a full night's sleep had cleared the jet lag and the drugs from her system.

He tapped another code into the elevator keypad and closed the gold metal gate behind them. The button for the sixth floor lit up immediately. "Don't worry, they'll love you," Malcolm reassured her, as if reading her mind. She smiled wryly at the thought of them having his-and-hers superpowers. *We could fight crime.*

The elevator smoothly rose, an arrow clicking off floors two and three. Malcolm's Upper East Side manse, he had explained during their layover in Paris, had been in the family since the end of the nineteenth century. Over the years, it had been divided and subdivided, and it currently housed three branches of Malcolm's family. The Dorans occupied floors six through eight, while Mrs. Doran's cousins and their adult children lived on the floors below.

"Do a lot of families live together like this in New York?" Jane had always heard that Americans moved out of their homes the moment they could. She had imagined that she would fit right in here, but perhaps rushing off to live on one's own wasn't such a chic thing to do when it came to UES brownstones.

Malcolm shrugged. "We're a tight-knit bunch. We just renovate when we need to change the divisions." He grinned. "Plenty of work for an architect with the right connections, now that I think about it."

Jane smiled. *Sure—think they'd let me tear it down and start over?*

The elevator bumped to a gentle stop on floor six, and the doors hissed open.

"Jane! I'm so glad to meet you!"

Jane nearly jumped out of her skin. Waiting on the other side was the tallest woman she had ever seen. Jane knew that Mrs. Doran had to be at least sixty, but she could have passed for forty. Glossy, gray-streaked brown hair fell softly to her shoulders. Her crisp charcoal-gray cashmere sweater made her eyes look positively smoky and showed off her trim figure.

She pulled a dazed Jane into a hug, then shot a sharp look at her son. "It's about time you brought her home." She clapped brightly. "Now come say hi to everyone. We've been *dying* for you to get here."

Mrs. Doran spun on one high-heeled boot and made her way down a low-lit hallway covered with a plush Oriental runner. Jane was too shocked by the woman's warmth to do anything but follow. *"Random Nobody Snags Heir to Billions; Matriarch Is Glad"?* They turned a corner, and Mrs. Doran threw open two heavy doors to the parlor, revealing a sea of eager faces. "Guess who's finally here!"

Three, six, eight, eleven . . . Jane's head spun as she tried to count the grinning faces and raised glasses; there were just too many to take in at once.

"So nice to meet you, dear," a woman Mrs. Doran's age cooed. Her silver hair was pulled back in a pinched bun and she was dressed in a powder-blue boatneck dress. Like Mrs. Doran's, her eyes were dark as pewter. "I'm Cora McCarroll and this is my sister, Belinda Helding." She gestured to a woman completely identical to her, dressed in severe black. Belinda's eyes flicked dismissively over Jane, decidedly less interested than her sister's.

"Nice to meet you," Jane nodded. Malcolm had mentioned that Mrs. Doran's cousins were twins—both widowed—but she hadn't been prepared for them to be so thoroughly indistinguishable.

In her fuzzily jet-lagged state, the whole family, in fact, was beginning to blur together. Cora and Belinda seemed to have about a dozen sons apiece, some with families of their own, and only a few people made any impression on her tired mind at all. ("Will you friend me on Facebook?" pleaded awkward young Ian McCarroll, and Jane hoped that her indulgent laughter was all the discouragement he would need.) Malcolm's father was a stately old gentleman with steel-colored hair and a vaguely distant air, who all but blended in with his armchair; Jane got the impression that his main role in family events was to nod along while sipping his scotch.

An investment banker she eventually placed as Blake Helding sidled up and grasped her hand lecherously. "If I'd known they built 'em that way in France I'd have traveled more," he slurred, earning himself a cold glare from wife Laura-with-the-implausible-Bergdorf-highlights.

"Oh," Jane replied awkwardly, hoping he didn't spend much time in the Dorans' apartment. She wanted Malcolm's family to like her, but there were limits. "Ha. Um, if you'll excuse me a minute, I just have to . . ."

Hardly seeming to hear her words, Blake dropped her hand and drifted over to the bar to refill his whiskey on the rocks. Malcolm was now chatting with his mom, and everyone seemed engrossed in their own conversations. Jane used the brief break in introductions to take a long look around the parlor. The room was pentagonal and high-ceilinged. Four of the walls were covered with ivory paper so thick and textured she suspected that it was actually fabric. The fifth, though, was a massive sheet of unpolished white marble, covered in carvings too small to make out from across the room. She approached it and realized that the etchings were names, connected by a complicated web of lines.

A family tree, she guessed, and checked the lowest branches for familiar names. She found Mrs. Doran almost immediately in the dead center of her generation's row, and impulsively reached out to touch with her fingers the line that led to Malcolm's name. Just before it reached him, though, it branched. She frowned. Malcolm had called himself an only child, but Jane's fingers traced across the record of a sister. *Annette,* she read silently. She had been born six years after Malcolm, and next to that date was another one, six years later. She had died when Malcolm was only twelve. Her heart ached at his loss, and then a little pinprick of hurt vibrated through her. Why had he never mentioned something so important? *But you're keeping secrets from him too,* a little voice in the back of her head pointed out. And Jane realized that she couldn't imagine how much it must have pained him to lose his little sister. Swallowing some of the dwindling champagne in her glass, she decided to not mention her discovery until Malcolm was ready to tell her about Annette on his own.

She was about to step away when an unusually smooth, rect- angular patch to the right of Annette's name caught her eye. It was too polished to be a natural flaw, and it was the only one on the entire wall. Had it been a mistake?

"We take a great deal of pride in our heritage and tradition." Lynne Doran appeared suddenly at her shoulder, and Jane jerked her hand away from the wall.

"I see. It's quite remarkable." Jane's own family tree would be nothing more than a small sapling dwindling down to one lone name. *Two*, she reminded herself. She had Malcolm now.

"We can trace our family all the way back to ancient Egypt," Lynne said, the pride obvious in her voice. "*They* traced their an- cestors through the female line, and you can see that we've done the same."

"Interesting." Jane appraised the generations listed on the wall, and quickly understood what Lynne meant. Though presumably the males had married and had children, offspring was recorded only for daughters descended from Ambika, the very first woman on the tree. All of the male lines simply disappeared.

"It's common sense, really," Lynne went on. "It's the only way you can be sure."

Jane twisted the sequins on her canvas Vanessa Bruno tote: she should have known the welcome was too warm to be true. This was Lynne's way of letting her know that she'd not see her name in marble anytime soon. "Mrs. Doran, I—"

"Goodness, dear!" The tall woman threw her head back in a full-throated laugh. "You can't call me *that*. Just imagine what people would think! 'Mom' is probably out of the question, but you *are* going to be my daughter soon . . ." Her peach-lipsticked lips pressed together thoughtfully. "Why don't we try 'Lynne' for now? And we'll think of something new when there are grand-children to consider." Lynne's dark eyes assessed Jane from head to toe so shrewdly that Jane cringed a little. "I do hope there will be some girls, of course. As soon after the wedding as humanly possible." Then she swept away magnificently, leaving Jane staring after her.

Now that's not someone you meet every day. Jane shook her head at the bubbles rising in her champagne glass. The whole evening had been too strange for her to keep up with. But, she realized abruptly, it had all been the normal kind of strange. She had made eye contact, shaken hands, and kissed cheeks with at least a dozen people, and none of them had set off an unpleasant mind-reading episode. She mused on the anomaly for a brief moment. The magic seemed to flare up the most when she was tense or nervous, which she certainly had been tonight. Had the Dorans made her feel more comfortable than she realized? Or was it the lingering aftereffects of drugging herself? Whatever the reason, she was grateful for it. She couldn't have handled knowing where Lynne's mind had gone when she'd mentioned her wished-for grandchildren.

At that somewhat catty thought, Jane immediately felt guilty. Lynne had been welcoming beyond her wildest dreams. Of course she would be intense about grandchildren: she'd lost her only daughter, which had to be particularly earth-shattering, given her pride in female heritage. Because Annette had died, the Doran line—as per the tree on the wall, at least—would end with Lynne.

The somber reflection weighted down Jane's already heavy

limbs, reminding her just how tired she was. Malcolm was in a heated conversation with Rolly McCarroll (or was that Andrew?) nearby. She tapped lightly on his arm and, with an apologetic smile, drew him a few feet away. "I think I need to sleep," she whispered.

Lynne Doran reappeared abruptly at her side. "Of course, dear. I'm afraid I'll need to catch up with my son for just a bit longer, but Sofia will show you to your and Malcolm's suite. And Jane, we must schedule some time to chat soon. Lunch tomorrow? I'd love to get to know you better."

Jane thanked Lynne and followed the black-uniformed maid to the hallway. She looked back once and took in the odd collection of people inside—her brand-new family.

Nine

SOFIA TURNED OUT TO BE A TINY MAID WITH IVORY-COLORED
skin and slightly bulging eyes that gave her a permanently nervous look. She padded silently down the hallway on sensible
shoes, giving Jane the impression that she was following a ghost.
The girl came briefly to life when she showed Jane her suite:
the bathroom with its heated tile floor, the walk-in closets with
gentle track lighting, the staff call button—and, of course, the
ubiquitous keypad that controlled the privacy lock. Jane worried
a little about having so many important things in one place that
she could potentially blow up, but the worry was brief: she was
too tired to so much as power a lightbulb, and tomorrow would
just have to work itself out.

Jane dropped her bag on an overstuffed velvet chair and
took in her new pad. The wallpaper was the same rich ivory as
the living room had been, and the deep chocolate-brown of the

wooden floor glowed darkly in contrast. The effect, however, was spoiled by a multitude of Oriental throw-rugs, most of which favored the red-and-gold theme of the canopy bed. The bed itself was a work of art, although Jane usually preferred her art a little less suffocating. Carved animals, flowers, and mythical creatures adorned each of the four posts, which rose nearly to the molded ceiling. Heavy brocaded curtains hung around the bed, matching the red and gold of the Pratesi duvet. The room felt as though it came from a different era; it reminded her of a medieval birthing room she'd once seen in an illuminated manuscript.

Everything will look better in the morning, she reassured herself. The sun would stream in through the east-facing windows and make the highlights in the dark wood glow. She might even be able to catch a glimpse of Central Park from here, an almost suitable replacement for her familiar corner of Notre Dame. She would find the kitchen, sip an espresso, and try her first authentic New York bagel. Malcolm would read the paper . . . preferably the real estate section. And, in a perfect world, he would find the perfect apartment listing—a converted loft somewhere downtown with bone-colored hardwood floors and keys that actually turned— and they would spend a delightful afternoon poking their heads into California closets and testing water pressure.

She stuffed her tired limbs awkwardly under the duvet. As soon as her head hit the feather pillows, she felt the last of the day's tension begin to melt out of her muscles, and then she felt nothing at all.

Jane awoke with a start several hours later, unsure what had jolted her from her sleep. The memory of voices hung heavy in the air, as though she'd just been talking to someone. But she'd been so deeply asleep that she doubted she'd been dreaming. Blinking in the unfamiliar darkness that pressed in on her from all sides, Jane fumbled on the wall for the light switch, but found only heavy, textured wallpaper. *Of course. Nothing so practical as a switch on the wall for people who decorate like it's 1803.* Sitting up, she reached out and flicked on the Tiffany-glass bedside lamp. Dusky light spread through the room, and Jane groaned.

The first thing she noticed was that Malcolm's side of the bed was empty and unrumpled. The second thing was the disturbance that had woken her up: a soft babble of voices somewhere in this maze of the house. Was the party still going on? She felt as if she had been sleeping for hours, but it was still dark outside. Her internal clock felt just as uprooted as the rest of her; it could just as easily have been noon as midnight.

She held still, listening intently. It quickly became clear that the voices weren't normal party chatter. Their rise and fall was clear and rhythmic, one unified chorus rather than the random white noise of separate conversations. *It sort of sounds like . . . chanting?*

A chill ran down Jane's spine, her body wide-awake now. She slipped out of bed, her feet sinking into the thick Oriental rugs scattered between her and the door. The hallway was pitch-black, and she didn't even know where to begin to look for a light. She left her bedroom door open so the dim lamplight would spill out into the hallway. She tiptoed cautiously, running her fingers along the thick fabric wallpaper to help guide her. *See Jane. See Jane walk. See Jane walk into an $18,000 knickknack from the fifteenth century.*

The noise seemed softer now—someone had probably put on a CD too loudly—and she was tempted to grope her way back to her cozy featherbed and lay her head on those wonderfully fluffy pillows. She knew that if she just went back in, closed her door, turned off the light, and burrowed under the covers, her cold toes buried deep in the still-warm sheets, she would fall back asleep instantly . . .

Just as her body was poised to turn back, the chorus of voices swelled again, coming from the right, away from the parlor where the party had been however many hours ago. *Huh.* She felt her limbs shivering nervously, and she carefully spun herself in the direction of the noise, like the pointer on a Ouija board. She started forward purposefully, and promptly crashed into something warm and solid.

"Jane?"

A scream died in her throat. "Malcolm!"

Note to Self No. 2, she thought wryly, remembering her scare in the bathtub back in Paris. *From now on, that terrifying thing in the dark is pretty much guaranteed to be Malcolm.* As happy as she was to have someone to share her life with, it was apparently going to take some getting used to.

Holding a finger to his lips, Malcolm led her back to their bedroom and shut the door. "Out for a midnight snack?"

"It's that early?" Jane peered down at her watch on the Louis XII end table, wondering why she hadn't just thought of that in the first place.

"Well, it's nearly one now." Malcolm shrugged off his sweater. He threw it over the chair carelessly and ran a hand through his hair tiredly. "The party just broke up. You were a hit, by the way."

"I thought I heard . . . chanting or something." As soon as the word "chanting" left her tongue, Jane blushed. It sounded so foolish. The notion of über-wealthy Upper East Side socialites engaging in a little late-night chanting was even less likely than the idea of Lynne buying a cocktail dress at Wal-Mart.

Malcolm pulled back the covers on his side of the bed, his lovely dark-gold waves of hair gleaming in the lamplight. "Sometimes the wind whistles through the attic. When I was younger, I used to be convinced a ghost lived up there."

Jane shook her head. "See, this is why I like modern architecture. The houses are too new to have ghosts."

He sat down on the bed and held out his arms to her. "Come to bed, darling. You've had a hard week followed by a very long day. I promise that tomorrow everything will be better."

Jane fell willingly into his warm arms, and his soft lips began to trace the line of her collarbone. "Things are looking up already," she whispered, feeling him stir against her. He looked up at her long enough to smile, then disappeared under the red-and-gold duvet, kissing his way down her body until he reached the most advantageous position from which to dissolve her stress with his mouth. Feeling some energy return to her under his attentive tongue, she pushed gently at his shoulder, signaling him to turn so that she could reciprocate.

Lynne would be so disappointed, she thought idly a little while later, once his slowed breathing indicated that he was asleep beside her. *No chance of grandkids tonight.*

Ten

Just as Jane had predicted, morning light did wonders for her new home. With the sun shining in, the cluttered bedroom looked less gloomy, and even a little bit less intimidating. It definitely helped that this time, when she woke up, Malcolm was there, with his long, golden torso bare until where it disappeared invitingly under the thousand-thread-count sheets. His long-lashed eyes opened while she watched him, and his lips curved up into a happy, unguarded smile.

She began to reach for him automatically, but her stomach rumbled angrily, suggesting that her appetite for food was more urgent than her appetite for anything else. "Is there a kitchen in this place?" she asked hopefully. "Or is it true that New Yorkers live exclusively on takeout?"

"A little of both," he replied cheerfully, swinging his legs out from under the covers and treating her to a delicious view of his muscled derrière. "There is a kitchen, but we mostly use it for eating takeout." He went into the bathroom and turned on the water. "The staff cooks, but the rest of us burn water, so . . ." he yelled over the hiss and spray of the shower head.

Jane reached for an Egyptian cotton robe hanging from the bathroom door, but then reconsidered: even if kitchens were robe-appropriate in most houses, she vaguely recalled passing a study *and* a library on her way to her room last night. The Dorans probably preferred their guests to wear something a little more formal than sleepwear. She rolled out of bed and stumbled toward the bathroom, which was already shrouded in a thick cloud of steam.

A tanned hand snaked out from behind the shower curtain, and she squealed happily as Malcolm tugged her into the shower with him. The water pressure was spa-massage worthy, and Jane's determination to focus on breakfast wavered briefly when Malcolm began to lather soap gently on her bare skin. But he apparently had eggs and bacon on the brain, since he was tender, but also brisk and efficient as he ran his hands all over her body. When they had finished, he gave her a playful push. "Now get dressed, you temptress, you. I won't have the tabloids running stories on how I starve you."

She grinned at him and wrapped a fluffy towel around her body, but a seed of doubt was working its way into her mind. *Tabloids?* Malcolm had mentioned that his family was in the spotlight of Manhattan society, of course. And she had known that he had been photographed for his entire life, that every accomplishment and mistake had been documented for the public. But she had never really considered that the same scrutiny might be extended to Malcolm's wife. *She* wasn't an heiress, a party girl, or a household name. She wasn't anybody; there was no reason for anyone to care what she did.

Except that now she was going to be the wife of a somebody, and that was going to be the end of anonymity for her. *Caesar's wife must be above reproach,* she reminded herself. *But Caesar's wife is a witch, so now what?* Being photographed by everyone from *Vanity Fair* to *US Weekly* probably wasn't what Gran had meant when she had told her to hide. She shivered a little as she remembered Gran's letter: *"People will be looking for you."* People who had had much more practice hiding their magic than she did, people who would notice the slightest oddness about her immediately—and who might expose her to the Dorans . . . to Malcolm.

She shut down that train of thought abruptly and shook the tension out of her shoulders. There was nothing she could do about media attention, and anyway, it hadn't even started yet. Maybe they wouldn't be all that interested in her, and her magic had been reassuringly quiet since they had left France. She could gloss over her family background if anyone asked, and as long as she kept smiling and didn't knock out the power, everything would be fine.

That decided, Jane glanced around for her suitcase, but then her mind adjusted to what it had absorbed last night: the hangers, racks, and shelves of the closet were already filled with her clothes . . . as well as some she could swear were brand-new. She clasped her hands together in delight and did an impromptu little twirl before settling down to the very serious business of choosing the day's outfit.

A floaty white blouse, charcoal-gray pencil skirt, and retro string of pearls later, Jane found herself clicking down the halls after Malcolm.

In spite of his earlier concern for her hunger, he evidently couldn't resist suggesting that they take the long way to the kitchen so that she could see more of the magnificent house. That included a closer view of the gallery, with paintings dating back to medieval times; the sitting room; the library, with its floor-to-ceiling shelves and handy rolling ladders; but not of the study, since the door was closed. "My dad hangs out in there sometimes," Malcolm explained in a clipped tone, and Jane, recalling Mr. Doran's whiskey glass and bleary eyes from the night before, didn't press for details. Nor did she ask how one family—even a sizable and close-knit one—would manage to use a living room, a den, a family room, a dining room, *and* a parlor. She was glad that she had gone for a more conservative, dressy outfit than she might have normally chosen for a breakfast at home with her fiancé. She might be overwhelmed, but at least she looked like she belonged.

Their tour wound to a merciful close in the kitchen, which Jane immediately identified as her favorite room of the house so far. It was spacious and airy; copper pots and kettles hung everywhere and dark green marble covered the countertops. Unlike the stuffy, tapestry-coated formal dining room next door, it was a room more about substance than style, and, contrary to Malcolm's claims about only eating takeout, there was certainly plenty of substance. It contained every food Jane could possibly want: fresh fruit, pre-sliced vegetables, organic yogurt, hand-pressed pasta, and even brie flown in from Paris. It also contained a note on Lynne Doran's monogrammed stationery.

"My dear Jane," she read to herself while Malcolm tried valiantly to crack an egg. *"Please join me at 21 Club at one o'clock. I look forward to getting to know all about you!"*

"Your mother seems *extremely* pleased that I'm here," Jane began cautiously.

Malcolm shrugged, tossing the shards of his demolished eggshell into the trash, and pushed the staff call button. "She's always wanted a daughter," he explained, and Jane bit her lip, remembering the mysterious name on the wall. The long-dead sister, the only daughter in her generation. *Annette.* "Besides," he went on, and Jane blinked back into the moment, "she knows that I'm happy. What more could she want?"

Jane nodded. She was so used to Gran's overbearing overprotectiveness that she probably couldn't recognize a normal family dynamic when it was right in front of her. No doubt she would soon wonder how she had ever gotten along without such an involved and caring mother-figure.

Sofia shuffled into the kitchen, her wide eyes downcast. "Thank God," Malcolm declared grandiosely to the tiny maid. "You're just in time to save me from wrecking the place in an attempt to impress Jane. Would you whip me up one of those wonderful omelets of yours—sausage and peppers, please?"

He nodded encouragingly toward Jane, who found herself tongue-tied. Her usual breakfast was a cup of coffee—maybe with a croissant from her corner bakery if she had extra time. "Um, the same for me, please?"

Malcolm clucked his tongue and shook his head disapprovingly. "You hate peppers, Jane. Relax, you can have anything you want! Even that weird German ham you insist is better than bacon." He held his palms up, as if the very idea was beyond him.

Jane felt her gray eyes go wide with hope. "Speck? And . . . um, maybe tomatoes?"

"Cherry, grape, plum, beefsteak, or green zebra, miss?" Sofia asked in a neutral tone as she pulled a butcher-paper packet from a pile of similar ones in the refrigerator. Even from where she was standing, Jane could see that it was clearly marked SPECK. She felt suddenly warm and comfortable all the way down to her toes.

"Whatever's on top," she smiled, and then jumped as her handbag seemed to come to life, rattling across the floor.

Malcolm looked at her oddly, but she quickly placed the bag's strange behavior, and reached in to draw out her iPhone, which was apparently in the midst of a seizure. The number wasn't in her contact list, but it was in Manhattan's 212 area code. "Hello?"

"You've landed!" a vaguely familiar bubbly voice squealed. "Jane, this is Pamela! From Conran and Associates. Antoine's friend?"

Jane tried to reply, but Pamela, in spite of apparently hoping for a response, did not seem to be inclined to pause long enough for one.

"Things are moving *fast* down here, so we need you to come in ASAP. Are you free today, two-ish?" Pamela finally paused, but Jane was so caught off-guard that she didn't manage to speak in time. A horrified gasp came through the phone's speaker. "Ohmigod, you're still available, *right*? We so urgently need to get this international division off the ground. You *have* to at least come in and hear my offer. Jane! Don't commit to anyone else yet. Are you free at two?"

"Three," Jane blurted finally, forcing her voice out into the tiny space allotted. "I can come at three."

"Thank God. Forty-nine West Fourth, three p.m."

The line clicked dead before Jane could say another word. She stared at the phone in her hand; the screen went dim. "I seem to have a job interview," she announced thoughtfully. Then she caught up with the rush of Pamela's words, and smiled happily. She had hoped to hit the ground running, so to speak, but things were moving even faster than she'd expected. And having something that got her out of the house, something that was just hers, would be a great way to keep from obsessing about reporters, witches, and fitting in with her new family-to-be.

"That's great, honey!" Malcolm kissed the side of her head and set two sunny omelets onto the rough-hewn breakfast table. Jane noticed that Sofia had disappeared discreetly, passing the credit along to the man who couldn't break an egg, and she marveled at how incredibly useful it must be to have good help for all the little things. No wonder Malcolm had always struck her as so self-assured, so comfortable in his own skin. He had truly led a charmed life.

And now I'll have one, too, she thought, cutting into the tender froth. *And a family, and a home, and, it sounds like, a job just waiting for me to come and accept it.*

Things were most definitely looking up.

Eleven

"HAS LYNNE DORAN ARRIVED YET?" JANE ASKED 21 CLUB'S HOST-
ess. The restaurant was old and dark, and very English in feel. A
bizarre ceramic jockey, similar to the ones lining the fence outside, stared forebodingly at Jane as if it were warning her away.

That's silly, Jane told herself—and the jockey—firmly. *Lynne's
been niceness itself.* But on the short ride down to 52nd Street, her
high from Pamela's unexpected phone call had pretty much
evaporated as she had begun to catalog the myriad ways that
she could screw up a one-on-one lunch—accidentally answer-
ing an unspoken question, knocking the next table over, causing
a freak power outage. Nothing like starting off the mother-in-
law–daughter-in-law relationship with an actual bang. And that
wasn't even counting all of the nonmagical ways that she could
screw things up: mentioning exes, bringing up religion, raving

about the wrong restaurants, designers, celebrities, politicians. Asking about Annette.

"Follow me please," the petite brunette hostess told Jane, tucking a menu under her arm and escorting her to a prime table right by the window. Lynne's brown hair was loose around her shoulders as it had been the night before, but she had traded her cashmere ensemble for a crisp pink button-down. Her taupe shoes and clutch coordinated in an understated way, and Jane was fairly sure that they were both Ferragamo. Her sapphire earrings were the size of walnuts.

"Oh good, you're here, Jane," Mrs. Doran said brightly, folding her hands lightly on her lap. Beside her was a stack of magazines— *Martha Stewart Weddings, Brides, New York* magazine's wedding issue, and even the Monique Lhuillier lookbook.

Alarm bells went off in Jane's head and she felt a sudden impulse to beg the hostess to rescue her, but the girl had already retreated back to her post. With no escape plan in sight, Jane sank into the wooden chair opposite Lynne, trying not to notice that it looked as though a wedding planner had exploded on the tablecloth.

Lynne's perfectly manicured nails beckoned to a white-clad waiter. "We'll both take Caesar salads and the sole"—she glanced thoughtfully at Jane's hips for the briefest moment—"grilled, I think. Dressing on the side. *Everything* on the side. Thank you!"

The waiter disappeared almost before Jane could open her mouth, but it stayed open in shock all the same.

"You do *like* sole, don't you, dear?" Lynne's eyes were dark, like Malcolm's, but the color was somehow less warm, less liquid. "It's something of a specialty here."

"Sole is fine, thank you," Jane replied dutifully. Eyeing the magazines, she guessed that there would be plenty of battles ahead to choose from—grilled fish wouldn't even make the top twenty.

"How did you sleep, dear?" Lynne went on, barely acknowledging the response. "Are you settling in all right?"

"I think so," Jane offered timidly. "Thanks again for welcoming me into your home."

"Malcolm told me about your grandmother." Lynne patted Jane's hand sympathetically, giving her a conversation whiplash. "Such a shame. How are you holding up?"

"Oh, fine thanks." Mrs. Doran's hand lingered on Jane's fingers for the briefest of moments. Jane stiffened, bracing herself for a flash of Lynne's thoughts at the contact, but none came. *Thank God.* A teeny part of her dared to dream that she'd left her magic behind when she'd left France. *It could be an Old World European thing. Why not?*

"Have you made any plans for the day?" Lynne asked solicitously, releasing her hand. A woman in hot-pink wedged boots walked past their window, wrangling four poufy Pomeranians. "That's Topsy Donovan." Lynne leaned forward conspiratorially. "She claims her daughter married an Italian count, but I have it on good authority that he's actually a dry cleaner out in Queens."

"Oh." Jane blinked. "I do have plans this afternoon, actually," she replied after a moment, deciding to stay with the safer topic. She doubted a granddaughter of a reclusive witch ranked much higher on the social scale than a dry cleaner. "I was really hoping to hit the ground running and build my life here as quickly as possible." *And not look like such a gold-digger, in case this is where the conversation is going.* "So I have an interview this afternoon with Conran and Associates down on West Fourth Street. It's a small firm, but they're doing some really innovative things in the . . ." She trailed off, uncomfortable. Lynne's dark eyes were wide as saucers and she was staring at Jane in apparent horror. "I—I'm sorry," Jane stammered. "Is something wrong?"

"You mean a *job interview*?" The peach-lipsticked mouth gaped. "Why on earth would you want a *job*?"

Jane floundered. She'd assumed Malcolm's family would be *thrilled* that she wanted to continue working. She had half-expected them to insist on it, along with an eighty-page prenup that Lynne probably had stuffed in her little taupe clutch.

"I like architecture," Jane heard herself say softly, and cleared her throat. "I love being an architect," she announced more firmly. *There. That's better.*

Lynne continued to stare at her until the waiter reappeared with two dainty porcelain plates of Caesar salad. Without sparing a glance in his direction, Lynne reached out one French-manicured hand, and the waiter deftly slid a plate of lemon quarters under it just in time. As Lynne began to squeeze the juices onto her salad, a subtle whiff of anchovies mixed with her confusion, making Jane feel faintly nauseated.

"Jane, dear, I don't think you fully understand the amount of time, work, and commitment that being a part of this family requires." Lynne's voice was soft, almost hypnotic. "Just think of the wedding alone—you simply won't have time for anything else until that's done with. And even then, you'll be busy with charity work, social events, networking . . . Malcolm has his art hobby on the side, but his *real* job—his first obligation and top priority—is the business of being a Doran. And I fully expect that, devoted as you are to my son, it will be yours, too."

The words "being a Doran" bounced hollowly around in Jane's head as she pushed a piece of romaine around her plate with her fork. She hadn't thought yet about changing her name. She had actually never known what her father's last name was. Her birth certificate and passport said Boyle, and her grandmother had always pointedly ignored the question.

Jane bit absently into a lemon wedge. The tartness puckered her lips, and her heart turned at the thought that Gran would never get to meet her new family. She would probably have loved Lynne's womyn-power family tree. Or, given their extreme social differences, perhaps the two matriarchs would have fought to the death. That possibility seemed a little more likely: the world couldn't be big enough for two such formidable women.

"Well I am committed to that, obviously," Jane began, "but—"

"Lovely," said Lynne, looking pleased, as if Jane had signed some kind of contract. "And that starts with the wedding, which, given our position, will be the event of the season. Now, I know that a lot of girls buy into the whole 'June bride' thing, but God knows you won't want to be *showing* on your wedding day. So I think a March—"

"Mrs. Doran!" Jane gasped, too shocked to care about interrupting. "You think I'm *pregnant?*"

Lynne shrugged. "It's 'Lynne,' dear. And I do know my son, Jane, and if you're not now, it certainly won't be long." The peach lips curled up in such a knowing way that Jane's jaw fell open. Jane tried briefly to form a response, but she couldn't think of a single civil answer to such a horrifyingly inappropriate remark.

"So," Lynne snapped, apparently satisfied that Jane wasn't going to put up a fight. "*Early* March, then, because anything delivered less than eight months later is just plain tacky. Now."

She shuffled through one of the stacks of magazines. "Let's talk flowers."

"Calla—"

But before she could get the "lilies" out, Lynne was off on a tear about Chrisobel Santos's orchids versus the "carpet of roses" that Twig & Vine had managed to create on the ceiling at Blake and Laura's wedding.

". . . which may sound like overkill but it was really just the loveliest effect because it positively *rained* petals all evening . . ."

Jane closed her eyes against the resurgence of nausea. Maybe she *was* pregnant. Or perhaps she was just allergic to her soon-to-be mother-in-law. What had happened to the warm, understated Lynne of the previous night?

Jane tried not to think about the fact that she'd spent the last six years of her life trying to get away from someone who controlled her every move. But then the conversation turned to dresses.

"Now I know Vera Wang is the first thought for most people, but really, I've never thought anyone over a size two should even bother." Lynne pushed the stack of magazines at Jane. "Do take a look. I've folded down some pages and we can get an appointment to try on anything you like."

January's *Manhattan Bride* fell open to reveal a hoop-skirted, lace-covered confection, and Jane felt air hiss out from between her teeth. She took a shuddering breath, trying to stay diplomatic. "That's really beautiful, but I actually was picturing a more . . . modern gown."

She began flipping through the pages, looking for an example of what she meant, but there didn't seem to be anything that couldn't have moonlighted as a costume in *Marie Antoinette*. Everything had at least seven layers of netting, some sort of boning up top, and yards upon yards of bows and ribbons. "Something with cleaner lines," she added, flipping faster. "Maybe an empire waist, or even a sheath style."

Lynne waved her hand dismissively. "Honestly, dear, you really won't want anything too *contemporary*—your pictures would look dated two hours after the reception's done." Her mouth softened a bit. "It must be so sad not to have your own mother to share all of this with, but you know, I always dreamed of having a daughter who would grow up and be . . ."

She trailed off. A few tables over, a pair of red-faced men laughed riotously at some joke. Two blond girls who looked like sisters leaned over a different table, gossiping and comparing manicures. For a horrible moment, Jane thought that Lynne might start crying.

Jane closed her eyes, silently chastising herself for resenting a woman who had lost her only daughter. She didn't care that much about the wedding itself—she cared about whom she was marrying. And as for the few things she *did* care about—like her dress and having a job—she would just have to get sneaky.

She snapped her eyes open and smiled innocently. "Lynne, I feel so lucky that you're so willing to help, especially since you have such exceptional taste," she said. "I'm just so grateful because I could definitely use some guidance."

Lynne beamed, and Jane chose her next words even more carefully. "In fact, it makes me feel so at ease with the planning that I'm confident that a job—one with reasonable hours, of course—won't get in the way at all. If I had to work out every single detail of the wedding from scratch it would be one thing. But I clearly have such wonderful help." She resisted the temptation to bat her eyelashes; that would probably be overdoing it.

Lynne speared a stalk of asparagus rather viciously, but her forehead remained smooth and unconcerned. *Pick your battle,* Jane silently urged her, suddenly wishing that mind control were one of her powers. *Which one do you want more?*

Lynne deftly maneuvered the fork into her mouth without ever looking away from Jane. Their eye contact felt so intense that Jane half-expected beads of sweat to break out on her forehead. It seemed as though Lynne's irises were growing, filling with blackness like stormy waters into which a squid had emitted ink. Lynne blinked, and the black disappeared—if it had never been there at all. Jane rubbed her temples. Damned jet lag.

"Well, if you think you can handle it," Lynne said, looking the picture of a concerned mother. "I just want you to be happy."

"Perfect," Jane said, trying not to sound giddy. "I should actually get going, but maybe later this afternoon we could talk about the location of the ceremony?"

Lynne nodded. "That sounds lovely. And I have a list of caterers at home. We should review it as soon as possible."

"Tonight," Jane promised. *See? We can get along just fine.* "And thank you. For the help, and for lunch, and for just being so . . . welcoming." She smiled. "I really couldn't have wished for a kinder family to marry into."

Lynne's peach smile was wide and sincere-looking. "We're so happy to have you. Now run along—you wouldn't want to be late."

You don't need to tell me twice, Jane thought. She air-kissed Lynne good-bye, then pushed her way out onto the bustling street.

Twelve

AN HOUR LATER, JANE WAS PERCHED ON A SLEEK BLACK POD CHAIR in the offices of Conran and Associates, trying to ignore the painful blister forming on her right pinky toe. She'd walked up and down the street three times, her suede boots getting less and less comfortable with each pass, before noticing the understated brass C&A plaque on what she was sure was an apartment building.

"So." Pamela Bronsky, the managing codirector of the firm, looked from Jane to her résumé and back again, her almond eyes hard behind thick brown frames. Her glossy brown hair was piled on top of her head in an odd-looking update of a beehive, and Jane guessed that she considered it an artistic style. She began to second-guess her decision to leave on her blouse, pencil skirt, and pearls ensemble from that morning. She had deemed it business-like enough for a job interview (especially with someone who sounded desperate to hire her), but maybe it was *too* businesslike? Clearly, she had done something to put Pamela off because in person, the architect was nowhere near as breathless and bubbly as she had been on the phone. It was as if Jane had walked into someone else's interview, and that someone was apparently annoying and underqualified.

Pamela clicked the top of her maroon metal pen a few times. "I see that all of your experience is foreign."

"Well yes," Jane said, leaning forward, aiming for a tone and demeanor that screamed *Hire me!* "I interned for Atelier Antoine in Paris; I joined them right out of school. From there I became an assistant, and had just been promoted to designer when I moved. I would love to have the same kind of ground level–up experience here—"

"Of course. But you see, we don't really have any international projects at the moment."

An automatic room freshener emitted a puff of vanilla-scented air into the office with a hiss. Jane leaned back, puzzled. *I know. That's why you wanted me.* "Well, that's an area where I think that I could be an asset to you," she said instead. *Just like you said— in that new international division that just has to get up and running?* She heard herself prattling on about the cultural differences between America and Europe, giving Pamela a miniature sociology lecture that she couldn't seem to switch off. By the time she had gotten to the issue of table manners, Pamela looked openly bored, and Jane forced herself to wrap it up. "As someone with a foot in both worlds, so to speak—"

"Do you, though?" Pamela pushed her glasses up on her nose and stared at Jane.

Jane stopped abruptly, straightening the cuffs of her Elie Tahari blouse before she could remind herself not to fidget. "I'm sorry?"

"Do you actually have 'a foot in both worlds'?" *Click, click, click,* went Pamela's pen. "Your schooling is French, as are all of your professional credentials, and you've been in this country all of a day. Have you even looked into becoming licensed in New York? I don't believe that your school is accredited here, and the process could take months even if you *are* eligible. Which I don't believe that you are."

Jane inhaled, stung. She hadn't expected to have a license just handed to her, of course, but that didn't mean that she couldn't be an asset while she worked toward one. That was fairly standard in an architectural office. She glanced at the downtown skyline visible through Pamela's charmless square window. An ambulance flashed its way down the street, the pitch of its siren rising and then falling as it passed them. The stuttering whoop was familiar to her only from movies; it was completely different from the steady, two-toned bleat of French sirens. Jane felt a wave of homesickness, but there was no point in nostalgia. She wanted a life with Malcolm, and that life was here. She would just have to fight for it a little harder than she had thought, was all.

Jane perched herself at the very edge of her chair, bracing herself, for an awkward moment, on its Space Age lip before finding her balance. "My understanding from when we *spoke*"—she couldn't stop an edge from creeping into the word—"was that you were looking for someone to liaise with *potential* international clients." There was a long pause.

. . . just take a hint, Mrs. Soon-to-Be Doran . . .

"Excuse me, what was that?" Jane asked. She was nearly sure

that she had never mentioned Malcolm to Pamela—and certainly not by name. She had wanted to at least *try* to find something on her own, without any of the preferential treatment that a soon-to-be Doran would surely get. She'd wanted her new connections to be something to fall back on, not rely on exclusively.

Pamela's French-manicured fingers rifled absently through the papers on her desk. "What was what? Look, I'm sorry. You're simply not the right fit for us. But I see that you're wearing an engagement ring. Take some time off. Do cake-tastings and bridesmaids' brunches and spa days or whatever." Oblivious to Jane's suddenly narrowed eyes, Pamela leaned forward. "Honestly, I *wish* that I'd had that kind of freedom when it came to planning my wedding. The DJ was a nightmare." She twirled a felt-tipped pen through her fingers. "You're really very lucky, you know."

Jane forced a tight smile, gripping the strap of her distressed-leather handbag. She tried not to think about its contents—the plans for Madame Godinaux's renovations, the office building she'd helped design near the Bastille; Pamela hadn't asked a single question about Jane's portfolio. "That's so kind of you to think about my interests," Jane hissed between clenched teeth, but Pamela seemed not to notice her tone. Instead she continued to nod, glossy brown nouveau-beehive bobbing absurdly, clearly relieved that Jane was finally catching on.

And catching on she certainly was: Pamela was unaware of her slip, Jane realized, because it had been a nonverbal one. *So much for leaving my magic in Europe,* she thought wryly, but most of her mind was occupied with a much more pressing mystery. How did Pamela know who she was marrying . . . and what did it have to do with this bizarre farce of an interview? She thought about asking, about trying to figure out some subtle approach that would get her more information, but Pamela's face was shuttered. She had already moved on to a stack of what looked suspiciously like résumés. "I'll just see myself out," Jane announced resolutely, standing.

She stalked out of Pamela's office with as much dignity as she could manage, although she yanked the glass door shut behind her so hard that it rattled ominously in its frame. She tried to control her breathing as she threaded her way through the scattered desks in the main office, but she was too keyed-up to keep her face from flushing crimson. A bulb in an Art Deco shade flickered wildly, and something behind the receptionist's desk let out an ear-piercing beep. Jane jumped.

"It's okay," the mousy receptionist told Jane, although she was clearly just as shaken by the sudden blast of noise. Her small, squeaky voice perfectly matched her looks. "It's just the intercom from the street. I guess it's on the fritz. *Again.*"

She frowned and fiddled with some buttons on her desk as Pamela stormed out of her office, hands over her ears. "For God's sake, Sally, I thought we had that damned intercom fixed." She stopped short when she saw Jane still in the office. For a tense moment, Jane waited for the other woman to say something to her—to apologize, even—but instead Pamela just spun on her stacked heel and slammed her office door behind her nearly as hard as Jane had. "Call that worthless repairman back and do *not* take no for an answer!" Pamela's voice rang through the door. The receptionist hunched obediently over her phone.

All at once, for the first time since she'd learned that she was a witch, Jane was glad for her powers. She closed her eyes and let hot rage wash freely over her. When she felt good and out of control, she forced her body forward into the stairwell right on cue for the speaker to emit an extra shrill, extra long *beeeep*. A crash came from the office behind her, and she heard at least two voices shouting.

Oops.

Thirteen

JANE TURNED UP THE COLLAR OF HER CREAM-COLORED WOOL coat against the sudden gust of wind that blew down Park Avenue. She had been walking since her sorry excuse for an interview. Taking the subway while angry would guarantee some kind of train malfunction that would just raise her blood pressure even more, especially now that she knew that her magic was still rattling around in her body. The lingering sense of triumph over her intercom prank had vanished somewhere around Union Square, and since then she had just forced one foot in front of the other, trying to keep from thinking too hard about the whole fiasco.

Even walking in New York was different from walking in Paris, she'd realized quickly. Rather than navigating a lunatic maze of triangular streets until she found herself face-to-face with a surprise Mètro entrance, she felt drawn along by the city's endless straight avenues and convenient right angles. She was mildly surprised when she realized that she'd already reached the low 30s; it barely felt like any time had passed at all.

She didn't know what she was more depressed about: the dramatic reemergence of her powers or the fact that Lynne had clearly sabotaged her interview, a realization she'd had as she passed through the arch of Washington Square Park. *Why did I tell her the name of the firm I was interviewing at?* she berated herself, although she never could have guessed that Lynne would actually call the firm. She'd known the Dorans were influential, but tanking her in less than an hour with nothing more than a name to go on took a type of influence she couldn't even imagine. She had been told that New York was all about who you knew. Ironically, now that she had hooked up with people who knew absolutely everyone, it was working miserably against her.

A cab rushed past, nearly clipping her as she crossed 37th Street. The MetLife building loomed in the distance, and she was overcome with an enormous sense of loneliness. She missed the easy camaraderie of her office-mates, missed having inside jokes and the kind of silliness that only comes with girlfriends. Malcolm was wonderful, of course, but he couldn't possibly replace her entire world all on his own—and it seemed that his mother might object to her attempts to fill her new life with anything else.

More than anything, though, she missed Gran, which surprised her more than a little. She had always thought of herself as an orphan, a runaway, someone from a difficult past. But regardless of their many conflicts, Jane had always known for an absolute certainty that if she'd ever needed someone, if the sky was falling, if she had nowhere else to go, that Gran would be there waiting. Maybe not with open arms, exactly, but at the very least with a glass of pastis and a comfortingly dense slice of stöllen. *And with love,* Jane admitted. It was easier to see that now that she knew why Gran had been so stiflingly overprotective, although that thought led her to another painful one.

I wish she had told me.

She twisted the smooth silver ring on her middle finger, tracing its beveled edge. Gran's final letter had been typically brief and to the point, and it left Jane with many more questions than it had answered. She "had power," but she didn't know how to use it—or how *not* to use it. Surely Gran would have known why Jane heard some people's thoughts but not others', or how she could avoid knocking the lights out when she was annoyed. *And she could have told me about my parents.*

Jane knew that her parents had died in a car crash when she was ten months old, skidding off a narrow mountain road in North Carolina during a flash storm, while Jane was at a neighbor's house. Until Gran's letter, she hadn't even known the truth about why her parents had left France to begin with, and now she counted the many other things that she didn't know: what her mother had *really* been like? Had she truly met Jane's father ice-skating, or was that just a cover for some witchy encounter? Of course, that also raised the question of whether her father had known the truth about his wife's magic—and whether he'd accepted it. Had she used her own magic openly, or hidden it, like Gran? And what happened when she'd gotten angry? Did she explode fuse boxes, like her daughter, or bring bad weather, or something else entirely?

Jane's heel caught in a crack in the sidewalk, and she nearly fell as the horrible thought occurred to her: *Did she raise storms? Were she and my father arguing about something while they were driving? Was the accident just "one of those things," or was it one of Those Things?* But everyone who could give her answers was gone.

On 45th Street, a cloud of acrid smoke hit her, and Jane realized she was starving. *Grilled sole indeed,* she grumbled silently. And she hadn't even managed to finish the thing, her jaw had spent so much time dropping open during her strange lunch with Lynne. She stopped at an aromatic street vendor's cart, bought a hot dog from a stocky man with an incomprehensible accent, and pulled the napkin away greedily as she resumed her uptown trek. It was shockingly good, and she fought down the temptation to buy another one at 51st Street.

By 60th, her energy was flagging, the tingling in her feet had upgraded to a burn, and she was nearly ready to admit defeat and hail a cab for the rest of the way, but she knew she would be too embarrassed to tell the driver that she was only going eight blocks. Jane reflected that Lynne wouldn't let a little thing like that stop her . . . but then, Lynne would have just had her creepy driver pick her up in the first place. *I clearly have a lot to learn about "being a Doran."*

She hitched her handbag up a little and resolutely marched to the gloomy front door of 665, silently cheering when she remembered the code—and managed not to zap herself. She waved halfheartedly at Gunther, who looked as though he'd just as soon keep napping, and rested her head against the cool paneling of the elevator for as long as she could before its doors opened again.

Fortunately, they opened to reveal the one thing that she wanted to see most: Malcolm, grinning his easy grin, dark gold hair charmingly tousled, cream-colored linen shirt revealing a tempting triangle of tanned skin around his collarbone. "You look like you've just run the marathon," he told her.

"Well, I was only walking," she admitted. "But it was from West Fourth and I get extra credit for doing it in heels."

His smile widened. "You could use a martini and some authentic homemade Creole gumbo."

She accepted the arm he offered and they began limping down the hall. "Make that martini a nice chardonnay and I'm sold," she sighed. "French, remember? Speaking of which"—she glanced at him suspiciously—"you're not Creole. And since when do you cook?" Other than the eggs that morning, she couldn't remember seeing Malcolm eat anything but room service or restaurant fare.

"I don't," he admitted shamelessly. "But I *do* have access to an excellent chef, who could probably arrange it so that I'm stirring something whenever you happen to walk into the kitchen."

She smiled. "How about I just agree to give you the credit, and you convince this chef to send the gumbo to our room? I'm not up for a formal dining experience."

"Deal."

Twenty minutes later, they were cozily snuggled into overstuffed armchairs next to a roaring fire, the spicy smell of Cajun soup heavy in the air. Jane wiggled her toes with a happy sigh.

"Better?" Malcolm asked with a raised eyebrow.

"This is the life," she replied. She hesitated for a moment, but the heat from the fire was working its way in and the heat from the wine was working its way out, and between the two she was feeling bold. "Except—and I don't mean to sound like one of *those* fiancées—I'm not sure that your mother and I are getting along so well." Then the story came pouring out: lunch, the awful wedding dresses, the interview, and Jane's suspicions about what had gone wrong. She tried to keep her version of events as fair—and unmagical—as possible, but by the end of it, she couldn't tell whether she was downplaying things or being melodramatic. She twisted a lock of limp, pale hair around her fingers and waited for Malcolm's verdict.

He looked concerned. *Because he agrees about Lynne, or because he thinks that I'm criticizing Mommie Dearest?* she wondered nervously. But although he looked sincerely sympathetic, his response was ambiguous. "That sounds awful. Mom gets a little enthusiastic, but she usually comes back down to earth, so you shouldn't worry too much. The perfect job will turn up. Then we'll have a wonderful wedding and live happily ever after."

"I *do* like the sound of that," she admitted, stretching her toes out toward the fire. She turned her head just in time to catch him staring appreciatively at her legs, bare now under her old cotton robe.

With a wide, wolfish grin he leaped from his chair and swung her up into his arms. "It just so happens that I can think of some other things you might like," he whispered, his breath warm and seductive on her neck.

He crossed the room in two long strides and set her down gently on the red-and-gold duvet. His lips moved across her collarbone, and she felt her back arc as the last of the stress of the day melted from her mind. It felt as though her skin was on fire at every point of contact, and she twined her fingers through the golden waves of his hair and gave herself over to burning alive.

fourteen

"JANE!" LYNNE TRILLED, SHATTERING JANE'S MORNING-AFTER calm. She had hoped to find the kitchen empty again, but there was Lynne, large as life and twice as fashionable in what absolutely had to be vintage Chanel. "This was waiting when I came in."

Lynne handed Jane an ivory card, which matched her long, ivory nails perfectly. It contained a record of a phone call from an Archibald Cartwright at the Museum of Modern Art. There was no real message, just a return number.

"Who is this?" Lynne asked, curiosity shining in her dark eyes.

"No clue," Jane replied honestly. After yesterday's interview debacle, she probably would have answered the same even if she had known. The less Lynne knew the better. "I guess I'll have to call him back."

"Do let Sofia make you something first, dear. Does she know how you take your eggs yet? She's not what you would call a fast learner." That last remark was accompanied by a sharp glare at the tiny maid, whose eyes bulged a little extra in fear.

"Yesterday's were perfect," Jane blurted, unable to resist defending the anxiously hovering girl, even if it did earn her a scathing eye-roll from Lynne. She pretended not to see, and pulled her iPhone out of her purse while Sofia spun gratefully toward the oversized La Cornue faux-antique range.

To her surprise, Archibald ("Archie, please!") Cartwright was the director of human resources at the MoMA, and he declared that Jane would be "absolutely perfect for a job that just opened up here." It was only part-time, but he'd heard that she had spectacular qualifications, and perhaps it could lead to more responsibility down the line. "How do you feel about special-event planning?"

"Event planning?" Jane repeated numbly. Where would he have ever gotten the idea that she was "spectacularly qualified" at party planning . . . or even particularly interested? "Where did you say you got my name from?"

Lynne craned her neck like a cartoon vulture. Jane instinctively shielded the phone with her palm.

"Oh, honey! The whole town's buzzing. Besides, I've got my sources . . ." Archie chuckled.

Sources? Jane glanced at Lynne out of the corner of her eye. Not her, certainly . . . but maybe Malcolm had believed Jane's suspicions after all. A warm glow spread through her chest.

"I know it's a bit different from what you've been doing," Archie went on cheerfully, "but it offers a great opportunity to network in Manhattan with all sorts of fabulous people—including local architectural luminaries."

"That does sound exciting," Jane admitted. And given that

Lynne had (almost definitely) torpedoed her last interview, it would be helpful—maybe even necessary—to make some contacts of her own. True, throwing parties for one of the premiere modern-art museums wouldn't be exactly the same as dazzling the curators with her drafting skills, but who was to say that one thing couldn't lead to the other? She was surprised at the thrill of excitement that ran through her. *Parties, art-lovers, and a chance to get out of the house for something non-wedding-related? Thank you, Malcolm. Note to self: this totally calls for that striptease thing he likes . . . possibly even including those ridiculous marabou heels.*

"So you'll come in on Monday? Just ask the ticket-takers for Archie, and they'll wave you through."

"Great. See you then." Jane hung up and turned to Lynne, who was leaning so far over the counter that she was halfway out of her seat. Lynne immediately turned her attention to a stoneware vase containing peach roses that matched her lipstick, trying to cover the fact that she'd been eavesdropping. It took everything Jane had and more to not roll her eyes.

She considered letting Lynne stew in her curiosity—especially since she didn't want a repeat of the Pamela debacle. But Malcolm had picked something that even Lynne would have to like: it was part-time, was basically practice for planning a wedding, and gave her all sorts of opportunities to Be a Doran. Besides, Lynne would obviously find out sooner or later. It would probably be better to enlist her support than to tick her off. "Job. MoMA. Part-time, and event planning," she informed her, ticking off the bullet points on her fingers.

Lynne's peach smile was only a fraction of a second late. "How lovely, dear."

"Yes, it is lovely," Jane inserted before Lynne could get to "but."

"But—"

Jane sighed.

"But you certainly can't work at the MoMA in *that.*" Lynne's nose wrinkled in the general direction of Jane's marine-striped tunic and jeans. "Imagine how people would talk! You'll have to make a trip to Barneys. Sofia, let Yuri know to pick Miss Boyle up out front as soon as she's done eating. And Jane, dear, go ahead and use our account. Just tell the girls to charge whatever you need." With that, she swept from the kitchen, a subtle wave of Guerlain L'Heure Bleue lingering in her wake.

I really never do know what's going to come out of her mouth, Jane reflected.

As promised, Yuri was waiting by the back door of a nondescript town car. Jane was troubled to find that he looked no less intimidating in broad daylight than he had the night she arrived. At well over six feet, he seemed nearly as wide as he was tall, and from the way his shirt cut in sharply just below his ribs, Jane was quite sure his bulk was all muscle. His bald head and apparent unwillingness to speak—ever—completed the impression that this was someone who would normally have a job description much scarier than "family driver."

Bodyguard? she wondered, sliding in through the door he silently opened. *Private security? Guy who hides the bodies?*

"Barneys, please," she said, and the car pulled smoothly away from the curb. It was a short ride to Madison and 61st, but Jane couldn't help but think that every time she looked up, Yuri had *just* stopped watching her in the rearview mirror. *Of course he has to check traffic behind us,* she reprimanded herself. *The drivers here are almost as bad as the French.* But she checked again in spite of herself, and was almost sure that his eyes had just flickered away.

It was a relief to arrive at the red-awninged department store. Jane hightailed it out of the car with a quick thanks and pushed her way through the revolving glass door. Case after case of jewelry sparkled up at her—though she couldn't help noticing that nothing there was quite as magnificent as her own engagement ring. She hustled past a trunk show of antique items from England and the Balenciaga display, and rode the elevator up to the Co-Op on 7.

The moment she stepped out of the mirrored lift, a young woman named Madison swooped in and announced that she would be thrilled to be Jane's personal shopper for the day. She towered over Jane by nearly a foot, but didn't appear to weigh even an ounce more (unless the extra was in her sizable breasts), and her tan screamed, "Ask me what tropical paradise I spent the holidays in." Her chestnut-colored hair looked as though it had been blown-out at lunch, and a set of flawless scarlet nails completed her striking look. A little more intimidated than she wanted to be, Jane squared her shoulders firmly and followed along as Madison led her on a dizzying circuit of the floor.

"Do you already have an account with us?" Madison asked cheerfully, pausing briefly to squint at Jane and pull a size-six Rag & Bone sheath off the rack they were passing.

"It's under Doran." Jane was working so hard to keep up with Madison's extra-long legs she nearly crashed into the girl when she stopped abruptly.

"Doran with a D?" The friendly voice sounded the tiniest bit forced. "Are you a relative?"

"Almost," Jane said, holding out her left hand, where the Harry Winston diamond glittered fiercely. "I'm engaged to Malcolm."

"Oh." Madison's scarlet lips clamped firmly shut for a moment, and she twirled a silver key ring between her fingers. Was that skepticism? Did people try to defraud iconic department stores on a regular basis?

Waves of conflict seemed to roll off the salesgirl, reaching out toward Jane in little electrical sparks. *Oh no.* Jane took a step back. *Control, Jane, control.* Now was *not* the time for a magical light show.

Madison stepped back as well, knocking into a toothpick-skinny woman with perfect caramel highlights. The woman glared at Madison before making her way to the wall of jeans. A security guard in all black stood in the corner, his eyes narrowed as they followed the proceedings.

"I'm so sorry, but I'm going to have to leave you here for just a minute to check on something." Madison practically spit out the words and then vanished without waiting for an answer, leaving Jane to stare open-mouthed at the space where she'd been.

"Lynne said it would be fine to use the account," Jane whispered to no one in particular. Was this Lynne's idea of a practical joke . . . or payback for taking a job without her consent? For one panicked moment, she thought that the security guard was going to come arrest her for attempted theft, but he seemed to just be shifting his weight. *For now.*

"Jane?" A throaty voice broke into Jane's reverie. Jane whirled around to see a thirtysomething woman with pin-straight copper hair bearing down on her with a giant armload of clothes. "I'm Lena, and I'm so, so sorry about Madison's little meltdown. I'll be speaking with her supervisor."

A couple of Nordic-looking blondes giggled by the register, and an iPhone hummed nearby.

"Huh?" Jane had been so prepared to explain about the charge account that no other words came to her.

Lena grabbed a cotton dress off the Loomstate rack without

seeming to register her client's bafflement. Jane trailed along automatically behind her. She couldn't quite make sense of what was going on, but for the moment it seemed to involve browsing. After rounding the Splendid and Nanette Lepore sections, they sailed along toward the private shopping space.

"This room will be yours." Lena ushered her inside a well-lit room the size of Jane's bedroom in Paris. "Try these first." Her fingers grazed Jane's as she handed over a blazer and a pair of supertight suede pants from The Row. An explosion of sparks fired in Jane's brain, and suddenly Lena's voice felt as though it was shouting directly into her eardrums.

. . . Honestly, I don't know when Carlos will stop hiring these children. I know that party girls make good backdrops, but is it worth it if they're going to drag every little personal thing in to work with them? These girls are just too young to have the slightest idea how to separate their jobs from their love lives . . .

Jane gasped and pressed her fingers to her temples.

"Are you all right?" Lena asked, her voice concerned.

The blaring voice in her mind ceased, and Jane was the only person in her own head again. She cleared her throat, trying to get her bearings. "Lena, do you mind if I ask what happened to Madison?"

Lena looked a little chagrined, but opened her mouth to gossip nonetheless. "I probably shouldn't tell you this, but Madison *claims* that she dated your charming fiancé for all of three minutes last summer. She managed to convince herself that they were practically engaged, even though it was probably nothing more than a conversation at some nightclub. And then the real thing shows up—can you imagine? I found the girl hyperventilating in the break room." She handed Jane a featherlight Vince sweater, as an afterthought. "This'll go under the Marc blazer, Jane, and then, hmmm, you'll need a good black bra for that. Hang on, I'll be right back."

Jane slipped the sweater on over her head, then tugged on the blazer. The clothes fit like a dream and looked about a thousand times better than her thrifty attempts to approximate the same looks in Paris, but it was impossible to fully enjoy it. As she examined herself in the mirror, Madison's boobs loomed large—very large—in her mind, followed quickly by her blood-red lips and salon-perfect hair. Of course Malcolm had dated girls before he'd met Jane. But just how many girls? And did they all look like Madison? Her exes paled in comparison to Malcolm. Scratch that. There *was* no comparison. But while hers were tucked safely away in France, his stunning life-size Barbie dolls were scattered all over New York like landmines. *Ugh.*

"Here Jane, try these next." Lena bustled in and dumped a whole mound of clothes on the chair in the corner. Jane sighed and settled in for what was shaping up to be a very long day of playing dress-up.

fifteen

"CHAMPAGNE?"

"God, yes." Lynne Doran sighed waspishly at the waiter. "For everyone, I should think, after that god-awful weather."

Jane resisted the urge to point out that they had been outside for a grand total of thirty seconds—fifteen from the front door to the car, and another fifteen to the door of La Grenouille. The rest of the day had been spent indoors: the library and newly discovered indoor pool for her, the game room for Ian McCarroll, and the den for Malcolm's father. Blake Helding had rounded up all the thirtysomething men for a card game of some sort. His wife, Laura, had her manicurist make a house call, much to the delight of Ian's little sister Ariel, although the rest of the children had favored a wild, five-story version of hide-and-seek.

All three branches of the family had done whatever it took to avoid having to actually step outside in the subzero temperatures and driving sleet, but their reservation at La Grenouille—Jane's "official" welcome party—had forced their hands. Andrew McCarroll had been on the phone for half an hour trying to bribe the executive chef into coming to the mansion to cook for them in-house, but eventually had had to grant that the chef's objections ("ambiance," "supplies," and "sous-chefs"—he didn't bother with "a restaurant full of other customers") were probably valid. Jane suspected that if Lynne had been the one on the phone, they would all be dining in after all, but Lynne and her twin cousins, Belinda and Cora, had locked themselves in the west-facing atrium on the eighth floor with strict instructions that no one should interrupt their "girl time."

And now here they were, all twenty-odd of them, tucked into a private room.

"Isn't Jane sick of French food, though?" Ian piped up from the end of the long, flower-adorned table. He wore a preppy light blue Brooks Brothers button-down and tan cords. "Isn't that what she, like, ate at home?"

Before Jane could mention that her version of French cuisine was hardly five-star, Malcolm saved her the trouble.

"If she's willing to put up with all of us at once, she should get *something* familiar out of the deal." He ruffled Ian's hair and took a sip from his champagne flute. Jane did the same, minus the ruffling. The bubbles tickled her nose.

"It's really lovely," Jane offered sincerely. The cozy space was covered in so many dense sprays of flowers that she had felt as though she had walked into a garden. Recessed French windows led to balconies that were so inviting she could almost forget about the hostile weather on the other side. She had been a little anxious about being the center of attention twice in four days, but the lush private room and champagne had worked wonders on her nerves.

As Lynne prattled on to Belinda about invitations, and Ian told Malcolm about his Fantasy Football team, a crew of waiters delivered to the table artfully arranged plates of foie gras and blinis with caviar. The rich hors d'oeuvres turned Jane's smile up a notch, and she popped a bubble of golden osetra against her teeth with the tip of her tongue. Malcolm patted her knee under the table. Mr. Doran and Blake clinked their champagne glasses, and little Ariel admired her metallic-purple manicure.

"Now Jane," Cora McCarroll announced, setting her fork down decisively. "I hear you start a *job* next week." She managed to pronounce the word "job" with precisely the same mix of confusion and disdain that her cousin typically used, as if it were some kind of family quirk.

The silence around the long table was deafening. In the awkward pause, all that could be heard was the clinking of silverware against china.

"It's event planning," Lynne informed the family with a dismissive wave of her glass.

"I thought she was an architect," Belinda Helding snapped to her twin sister, and then whipped her silver-gray head toward Jane. "I thought you were an architect."

"I was," Jane replied weakly. "I am, I mean. Just not right—"

"God," Laura sighed melodramatically, flicking her blond tresses off her shoulder. "A job? Are we *all* going to be expected to *work* now?"

"No one expects that of you, dear," Blake slurred cheerfully from across the table. Jane felt suddenly, uncomfortably sure that the foot rubbing against her ankle neither belonged to Malcolm nor was there by mistake.

"Thank goodness." Laura dug back into her blini.

"Ariel, stop playing with your foie gras. It's not polite," Andrew said.

Cora's and Belinda's eyes were still glued to Jane as though she were a bizarre museum exhibit. She braced herself, but no one else at the table seemed to register any tension at all.

"So no more architecture?" Cora drawled. Her steely dark eyes were as cold and unyielding as the black Mikimoto pearls on her necklace.

"Now's not the right time for it," Jane said, choosing her words carefully. "But I do really love it. Making a space into someone's real *home* is so—"

"Of course," Belinda interrupted, waving a finger in the air. "You'd like that sort of thing, as an orphan."

Jane's mouth dropped open. In an instant, Laura was up and tapping her shoulder. "I'm going to powder my nose. Jane?"

"Excuse me," Jane murmured. Ariel dropped a piece of foie gras down the back of Ian's shirt. She snickered behind her hand as Ian obliviously continued to shovel risotto into his mouth by the forkful.

"This way," Laura whispered, leading her down a narrow wooden staircase.

"Thank you," Jane whispered as soon as they were out of earshot.

Laura waved her off airily. "They take some getting used to, don't they?"

The two women took the shortest path to the discreet hallway that contained the restrooms, their heels tapping dully on the thick carpet. Just when they came into view of the main dining room, a flash of blue-white light tore through the room, shaking Jane so badly that she dropped her clutch.

Jane swiveled her head frantically to look for the source of the disturbance, but no one else seemed to even notice it. *Am I seeing things?* The flash came again, along with a vaguely familiar clicking noise. This time, Jane spotted a bearded man crouching behind a vase of gladioli, and the disparate pieces of information came together when she saw that he was holding a bulky camera.

"Laura," she whispered, "who is that?"

"Who knows?" Laura whispered back, then seemed to register her concern. "Probably Page Six, but he could be freelance. Just ignore him and look happy. The hostess will escort him out soon enough." She looped her arm through Jane's and pasted a smile on her face until they were in the relative safety of the bathroom.

"Does that kind of thing happen a lot?" Jane asked awkwardly. The marble bathroom was also covered in flowers. A bouquet of peonies drooped from a metal vase and a collection of gold soaps and lotions lined the vessel sinks. Wall sconces cast dim, flattering light throughout the room, but Jane's reflection still looked pale.

Laura leaned into the mirror and applied a coat of Nars Dragon Girl to her lips. "You should have seen the fuss when I was trying to poison my mother-in-law."

Jane's mouth fell open. "You . . . what?"

Laura rolled her eyes. "I seriously don't know where the tabloids get their stories. As *if* any sane person would cross one of those old bats."

Jane snickered.

"But you," Laura went on, dabbing a Jo Malone perfume behind her ears. "You are impressive. I wouldn't trade *both* of the twins for Lynne. Malcolm might have been the hottest catch in town, but the idea of *that* as a mother-in-law could make a girl think twice."

Jane stiffened, surreptitiously checking under the stalls for legs. Laura seemed nice, but Lynne was seriously well-connected—and well-informed. "We seem to be getting along all right," she mumbled.

Laura shrugged again. "Well, good luck with that." She smiled, as if at some private joke, before sashaying to the door. "You're certainly going to need it."

Sixteen

On Monday, Jane hopped off the M3 bus as soon as the back doors were fully open, and looked around. *Well that has to be it,* she thought, and headed briskly toward a square concrete building with enormous MoMA banners running down the front. Her breath fogged out in front of her, crystallizing in the crisp January air.

Lynne had seemed absolutely baffled that Jane wanted to take the bus—why wouldn't she simply use the family's car and driver? But the prospect of even a few minutes with Yuri made Jane adamant. She'd told a narrow-eyed Lynne that she wanted to have all kinds of authentic New York experiences, and commuting to work was one of them. Fortunately, Lynne had decided it wasn't worth arguing about, though she did darkly predict that a few days of having coffee spilled on her by sweat-stained nurses in sneakers would change Jane's mind. Thinking of Yuri's beady stare and thin-lipped frown, Jane was inclined to disagree.

Jane strode through the glass doors of the MoMA, immediately surrounded by a sea of tourists and twentysomethings in school sweatshirts, trying to prove they were still in college for the extra discount. A harried-looking woman in a neon-blue PS 290 T-shirt was trying to wrangle a group of elementary school kids in identical Ts, and a ticket-taker was yelling at everyone to form a line.

The uniformed man at the information desk directed Jane to the HR floor, and she slipped gratefully out of the chaos. Archie Cartwright was waiting at the elevator doors. Jane was surprised to realize that he was exactly as she'd pictured him: tall, reedy, with a beak of a nose and a fringe of gingery hair around his otherwise bald head. *Maybe I've got some magical intuition thingy I haven't even noticed,* she thought optimistically. That power would be both un-scary *and* helpful, unlike her talent for derailing an entire traffic grid with one spark of anger.

As Archie told her about the "absolutely amazing" event they'd thrown last month, she absently twisted her silver ring around her finger. She'd noticed herself doing that more and more.

Jane had thought about getting rid of the ring, of hiding the last remaining evidence of her new power, but she'd found herself inexplicably attached to it. It hadn't done anything supernatural since she had first put it on, but it still felt magical somehow, as though it was one last connection to Gran.

"And we had this terrific Dali exhibit last May . . ." Archie prattled on. In addition to looking distinctly like a red-headed Ichabod Crane (the storybook, not the Johnny Depp version), Archie spoke about a thousand words per minute, and he kept having to wait for Jane to catch up when he had bounded too far ahead on his substantially longer legs. He took her on a whirlwind tour of the museum, and with each step, Jane felt herself feeling more and more at home in her new "office." The airy rooms, the austere cubes, the collection of works of master artists who shared her sense of spare aesthetics. She had to admit that Malcolm had scored a home run—or rather he would later that night, when she thanked him, profusely, for putting her in touch with the very enthusiastic Archie.

The reason for his enthusiasm was soon abundantly clear: he had found the perfect person for the job. Cheerfully adjusting and readjusting his tweed blazer, he explained that Jane's first assignment ("a warm-up of sorts") would be a private cocktail reception all of two weeks away—hosted by the Dorans. Of course, he was "just thrilled" to have an insider opinion, since the Dorans were known for being very particular, and it was just "Such an honor to get to host one of their events, which are always just so fabulous. Oh—" He stopped when they reached a hallway on the fifth floor, and threw open the third door from the elevator. "Tada! Your office!"

With that, he dropped a heap of reports from past events in Jane's arms and left her to settle in. The office was sizable and the furniture was sleek and modern—a Lucite desk sat directly under the large window, and wood shelves lined the walls along with several stainless-steel filing cabinets. A white Mac sat on her desk, next to a phone that had about ten different lines. *Maybe one day I'll even have a friend to call on one of them,* she thought wistfully. She thought of Elodie and their tandem desks at Atelier Antoine, and resolved to send her an e-mail that evening.

As if she had conjured a friend by magic, an elfin face surrounded by a wild crop of red curls poked around her door. "Oh!" the visitor exclaimed when she saw Jane sitting at the desk, her hazel eyes going wide like pennies. "I'm so sorry. I had no idea anyone was using this office!"

"I'm new," Jane explained, standing hastily and smoothing the skirt of her color-block dress. She realized belatedly that the empty white walls and total lack of knickknacks probably gave that fact away all on their own. "Did you need the room for something? I have to check in with security at some point, and now's a perfectly good time." She wanted to get her photo ID taken before her stubborn corn-silk hair began to work its way free of its bobby pins.

"Oh, no," the redhead assured her, biting her lip. She wore a cream sweater and mesh gold earrings. "Actually, I've been eating lunch in here," she admitted. "But I totally knew I was eating on borrowed time." As if she were being pulled from behind, she started to vanish around the doorframe.

"Wait!" Jane exclaimed. The fiery halo reappeared, the eyes inquisitive. "You could still eat here, if you want. I don't know anyone yet, so if you wanted to, you could have lunch with me?" *Wow. I could swear I used to know how to do "friendly" without sounding like a total loser.*

The girl's coppery eyes sparkled, and the corners of her mouth turned up. "That's so nice of—" she began, but seemed to change her mind mid-sentence. "Wait, are you the new special-events person?"

Something in the girl's voice put Jane on guard. She hesitated before nodding.

"Oh. Archie mentioned that you'd be starting." Her tone was flat and her smile remained in place as if it had been stapled there.

"Thanks," Jane replied slowly, unsure of what was wrong. Did she know how Jane had gotten the job? Had Jane replaced someone else? Someone incredibly popular with three kids to feed and whose puppy had just died? *I knew better than to take special favors,* she grumbled to herself.

Forcing a smile on her face, she walked to the door and stuck out her hand. "I'm Jane Boyle." She pretended not to notice how long it hung in the air before the girl shook it. Her hand was clammy, but luckily her thoughts did not flood Jane's mind. Jane had a feeling they wouldn't be too pleasant.

"Maeve Montague. Um, it was really nice to meet you, but I've gotta run before my soup gets cold." Maeve waved a heavy-looking white paper bag in her left hand and then abruptly disappeared around the doorframe again. Jane could hear her footsteps thudding down the hallway. It sounded as though she was almost running.

Jane sat heavily on her Aeron desk chair and fought down a wave of disappointment—surely it was unreasonable to assume that Maeve would be dying to become best friends simply because they were coworkers.

She spread over the desk the reports Archie had given her and picked up the floor plan from the previous year's Speak Out for Autism mixer. According to the write-up, it had promoted mingling beautifully, but had failed to provide a discreet way to get fresh ice to the third bar, forcing it to shut down before eleven p.m. Determined to avoid a similar tragedy at her future-in-laws' soirée, Jane began penciling notes onto her map of the Modern restaurant and the adjoining sculpture garden, thoughtfully drawing potential traffic jams.

Time passed quickly, and she was pleasantly surprised to discover that she enjoyed the work. Of course, it probably helped that Lynne wasn't involved in the planning process quite yet, but until then, it was nice to feel competent. After she'd brainstormed possible themes—Surrealism, black-and-white, primary colors—and drawn up a preliminary guest list based half on donors and half on celebrities, she called it a good morning's work.

Setting her notes aside, she ventured off to find the security office. Within minutes, she'd gotten hopelessly turned around and found herself stuck on the fourth floor with no idea how to get any farther. Wandering around the maze of offices in the hope of just randomly coming across an elevator, she rounded a corner and felt the impact before she even saw the person on the other side.

"God, I'm so sorry," Jane blurted, eyeing Maeve, who was now sitting awkwardly under a heap of papers, covered in coffee that Jane could only hope was lukewarm. "I'm so clumsy and I wasn't even looking," Jane said, trying to collect the scattered papers from around the dazed redhead. "Are you okay?"

The girl nodded, looking a little dazed, and brushed futilely at a coffee stain on her cream-colored silk wrap sweater. "It's really fine. I was blocking the whole hall. I'm sorry."

Jane stared at her, mouth hanging open in shock. "You're sorry? Are you crazy? Right now I owe you a coffee, dry-cleaning, and what looks like about an hour's worth of photocopying. Just tell me which you need first."

Maeve shook her head stubbornly, and struggled to her feet, pretending not to see the hand that Jane held out helpfully. "Don't worry about it. You should really just focus on your own work. You have some *very* important clients—and family members—to keep happy." Her words sounded angry, but her eyes were frightened. Jane stood there, completely bewildered, as Maeve backed away and darted off down the hall. Her second rapid exit of the day left Jane stunned, but with a slightly clearer idea of why this stranger might already have a problem with her.

And the Dorans strike again.

Seventeen

THE SOHO BAKING COMPANY WAS A LONG AND NARROW SHOP, with tempting displays of decorated cookies and cakes in the shapes of keys, little jewel boxes, and even a house. It smelled like vanilla and heat, and Jane felt tension draining from her shoulders that she hadn't even known was there.

It didn't stay gone for long.

"Mrs. Doran!" the apple-cheeked baker cheered sycophantically, nearly knocking Jane down in her rush to shake Lynne's hand. She seemed to reconsider at the last moment, perhaps because Lynne didn't look inclined in the slightest to lift either fur-lined gloved hand from her couture-clad sides. The baker slid to an uncertain halt, and for an awkward moment Jane half-expected her to bow.

"I'm Hattie," the baker settled for instead, shoving her frizzy brown bangs off of her flushed forehead. "We are just so excited to have you consider us for your wedding. Please come in."

Whose wedding was that, now? Jane wondered grouchily, unwinding her scarf a little more roughly than necessary. Hattie hadn't so much as glanced her way since they walked in. Also it wasn't even noon on Wednesday, but it was already the third wedding errand of the day. Jane's feet hurt, and she was irritated at having been ignored by the florist, the printers, and now Hattie.

And being ignored only reminded her of exactly how friendless she was. Jane was fairly sure that Maeve Montague was actively avoiding her. She kept seeing flashes of wild red hair disappearing around corners, and one time she could have sworn she heard footsteps approaching, and then rapidly receding when she began to open her office door, a lingering whiff of a Nina Ricci perfume in the air. It was getting ridiculous.

"We have less than two months," Lynne announced authoritatively, dropping her gloves on top of her crocodile Hermès purse. "You're hired. Let's talk decor."

Jane frowned. *I thought you got to taste cake at cake-tastings—and that's tastings, plural.* She had actually been looking forward to that. But it was useless to resist. She hadn't been in Manhattan long enough to care about the actual wedding site, and if Lynne wanted Hattie's cake or fountains spewing roses, then Jane would live with that. It was the image of the horrid, Little Bo Peep wedding dress that had been haunting her dreams, and she was saving all her energy for that particular fight. *And if I get some goodwill by letting her hire Hattie because of the "fabulous" tiramisu petit-fours at the Ross girl's baby shower, so much the better.*

While Lynne and Hattie entered a heated discussion over the

merits of rolled fondant versus piped icing, Jane wandered over
to the pile of glossy sample books in an alcove near the window.

"I can help you with those," a husky but feminine voice whispered from behind her shoulder. Jane jumped a little, and turned
to see a wide pair of amber eyes looking at her with concern.
"I didn't mean to startle you," the owner of the eyes rushed on,
pushing a thick tangle of black hair over her shoulder. She seemed
to be about Jane's age, with skin nearly the same tawny color as
her eyes. "I'm Dee," she added, although her nametag read DIANA.
"Can I help you with the books?"

"Sure," Jane replied. "Thanks." *Not that it'll matter much what I
find.*

As if Jane had said the last part out loud, Dee glanced toward
Hattie and Lynne, her eyebrows knitting together. She looked as
if she were weighing the pros and cons of reminding her boss
that the bride herself was out of the loop, but Jane shook her head
meaningfully.

"It's not her fault," Jane whispered. "It's the other 'her.'" She
nodded toward Lynne, hoping that the gesture was appropriately subtle. Raising her voice a bit, she picked up a book from
the table. "Are these just for weddings, or other events, too?" she
asked, loudly enough to be heard. "I'm putting together a cocktail
party, and I've seen some gorgeous special-event cakes, but I'm
not sure I want anything too traditional." Out of the corner of her
eye, Jane saw Lynne shudder, and she smirked. The more Lynne
thought Jane cared about the silly details, the more Lynne would
think she was winning important concessions. Besides, it was a
little fun.

"You'll want to take a look at this one," Dee told her confidently, handing Jane a book labeled *Evening Elegance*. "It has a mix, but they're all for very sophisticated events."

"Thanks." Jane began leafing idly through the book, although she barely registered the richly colored close-up confections on its pages. She smiled wryly at Dee as the words "absolutely *nothing* involving ribbons" drifted over to their alcove. "Oh, your necklace is tangled," Jane said, pointing to the silver pendant that appeared caught on the neckline of Dee's black top.

"Crap," Dee whispered, stuffing it inside her shirt. Jane froze, hand in midair, feeling awkward. "Oh, sorry," Dee grimaced. "It's just that I'm supposed to keep it hidden at work. It's a pentacle— you know, a Wiccan thing." She slipped it out again and waved it just long enough for Jane to make out a circle containing a five-pointed star. "Apparently it might scare off the target clientele."

"Wiccan—like, witches?" Jane's voice sounded unnaturally high. Somehow her least favorite things—wedding planning with Lynne *and* magic—were converging in one quaint little cake shop. Throw in a chainsaw murderer and it could be a real party.

"That's the basic idea."

Jane studied Dee's wild black waves and wide amber eyes. In her letter, Gran had made the world of magic seem dangerous and secretive, and she'd stressed that Jane's own safety depended on staying hidden. Then again, Gran was something of a paranoid survivalist. Was it possible that some witches—say, of the more daring, SoHo variety—just walked around wearing dark eyeliner and pentacles in plain sight? And how was Jane supposed to tell the difference between the wannabe witches and real ones? Was there such a thing as a witch-dar?

"So, um, do you do spells?" *Nice, Jane. Subtle.*

Dee let out a throaty chuckle. "Not me. My coven is into the religion aspect of Wicca, not the other stuff."

Jane nodded, not sure whether she was relieved or disappointed. She certainly didn't want to throw down with another witch in front of her mother-in-law-to-be, but she instinctively liked Dee.

"I'd say edible gold is unequivocally tacky," Lynne pronounced from across the room, and Hattie nodded compulsively.

Dee rolled her eyes at Jane, then fingered the outline of the pentacle beneath her shirt. "There are people who think that anyone can do magic, if they do the exact rituals and concentrate just right."

"Oh really?" Jane asked lightly, feigning detached interest. Outside, a young girl in a bright-red coat pulled her mother to the SoHo Baking Company's window, pointing to a doll-shaped lollipop. "But you don't think it's possible, then?"

"No. Well. Not for me." Dee tossed a look over her shoulder at Hattie and Lynne, as if to make sure they weren't listening. They were the only other people in the shop. She lowered her voice to a whisper. "I do feel that there's magic out there, and I think that some people are born being able to use it somehow. But it's not like everyone can do magic and I'm some freak exception. I think that there are some people who can, and *they're* the exception."

Jane hung on Dee's every word, which eerily echoed the ones in Gran's letter. She felt herself warming to Dee. What were the odds that the first non-crazy person Jane met in New York would be a black-clad Wiccan baker's assistant?

"And it even makes sense from a spiritual standpoint," Dee continued, "because Wiccans believe that magic is natural. My theory is that maybe there's some kind of genetic—wait, what's that?" she interrupted herself suddenly, snapping Jane back to the moment. "Where on earth did you get that amazing ring?"

"Thanks," Jane said, wiggling her fingers automatically; women cooing over her engagement ring was old news already. "It's actually a little scary walking around with it in New—" She broke off. Dee wasn't looking at the massive emerald-cut diamond on her ring finger; she was looking right past that to the smooth silver band Celine Boyle had hidden behind the mirror in Saint-Croix-sur-Amaury.

"Where did you get that?" Dee repeated, her husky voice low and urgent.

Jane opened her mouth to reply, but the voice that cut through the room was Lynne's. "I think that about covers it," she snapped, staring rather intently at Dee. She followed the girl's gaze to Jane's hand and scowled so fiercely that Jane felt a stab of actual fear.

They know, her mind screamed irrationally. *Both of them know.*

Then Lynne's dark eyes caught Jane's, and she smiled brightly. "Time to go, dear. I'll fill you in on what we've decided, in the car." She swept out of the door, her ivory cashmere overcoat swirling majestically around her as she shouted for Yuri.

Jane's pulse returned to normal. She shot a quick, apologetic shrug at Dee and followed Lynne out into the fading daylight. When she looked back through the picture window, Dee was still standing there, staring intently at the silver ring on Jane's finger.

Eighteen

THE NEXT DAY, MAEVE OPTED FOR THE STAIRS WHEN SHE SAW Jane in the elevator, and Jane's annoyance bubbled over. There was no reason for this sort of cloak-and-dagger nonsense. No matter who her future in-laws were, Jane hadn't done anything to merit being treated like a pariah. She devised a plan on the way home from work, and vowed to get to the office extra-early the next day.

"Extra-early," unfortunately, only turned out to be 8:45. Even having sacrificed her peace of mind by accepting a ride from the creepy (but undeniably efficient) Yuri, her multiple stops before work hadn't left her nearly as much of a time cushion as she would have liked. Nonetheless, she scurried into the office, dumped her Burberry-plaid wool coat unceremoniously on her desk, and made a beeline for the fourth-floor hallway where she'd (literally) run into Maeve on Monday.

It took less than a minute to find the door with M. MONTAGUE printed on its label, and luckily the office was still empty. Jane tip-toed inside. The room was nearly identical to hers, although Jane's view was much grander than Maeve's look into the office building next door. *Ah, the perks that come with connections*, Jane thought with a twinge of bitterness. She'd trade her view for a friend in a heart-beat . . . but she wouldn't give up Malcolm for anything.

She arranged the venti caramel macchiato she'd bought on the way in, along with a size-zero ivory sweater she'd picked up from Intermix the night before. She propped a note up against the steaming latte: *"Monday was all my fault, but I can't seem to run into you since! Let me know what to do re: photocopying. —J."*

There, she told herself when she was satisfied that the items looked just friendly enough, and tiptoed back out. She had waf-fled for a while about the last line of the note and, in fact, had a second version in her pocket that left it off entirely. The stack of papers that her coffee had ruined had been considerable, and there was no doubt in Jane's mind that a sincere effort to replace them was a necessary part of her peace offering. It was deeply unlucky, though, that the decent thing in this case involved the prolonged use of an electronic machine.

Jane heard the rumble of the elevator doors sliding open around the corner and her body sprang into action, launching her across the hallway toward the stairwell door. *Worse comes to worst, I drop the papers off at Kinko's or something.* She rushed up the stairs as if someone were chasing her, and arrived in her office breathless, flushed, and feeling more than a little silly.

Time to calm down, Special Agent Boyle.

She pulled her to-do list for the Dorans' party out of the desk drawer and looked for something mindless that might kill a few hours. Fortunately, all sorts of samples—from swizzle sticks to candles to Venetian half-masks—had come flooding in from potential vendors, and mixing and matching them into appealing combinations was just the sort of activity she was looking for.

Shortly past noon, a familiar set of springy curls appeared shyly around Jane's door. They were followed swiftly by a white paper bag—larger than Monday's—which Maeve waved like a flag of truce. "Cream of wild mushroom or Italian wedding?" she asked cautiously, a delicious garlicky smell wafting into the office.

"Mushrooms, please! This right here is a wedding-free zone." Jane grinned, and Maeve eased herself into the chair on the far side of the desk.

"Seriously?" she inquired, hazel eyes dancing. "I thought every New Yorker our age has been planning her wedding to Malcolm Doran since the tender age of four."

Jane snorted, fishing around in the bag until she found a plastic spoon. "That would have been a waste of time," she retorted. "His mother has the whole thing planned out already, down to the brand of water they'll serve. Acqua Panna, of course."

The soup was deliciously rich and the container was huge. Jane wondered how Maeve stayed so incredibly tiny on a diet like this. The three-quarter-sleeve top she was wearing today revealed wrists so fragile-looking that Jane thought they might snap under the weight of her spoon. But there was nothing fragile about her eyes, which remained thoughtful and speculative even behind her cheerful grin.

"They can't make it too easy to ride off into the sunset with the world's most eligible bachelor, can they?"

Jane sensed a challenge underlying the casual tone, but all she could do was shrug wryly. "I'm not stupid; I could tell he was a catch. But I grew up in France and had never even heard of the Dorans until I met him. How the hell was I supposed to know that everyone here acts like they're royalty?"

Maeve pitched forward in her chair, clearly stunned. "You really didn't know about them? You're not from one of the—" She looked confused to the point of incoherence, and bit her lip hard before apparently deciding how to proceed. "Your families don't know each other?"

Jane frowned, twisting a purple swizzle stick between her fingers. Maeve looked floored by the idea that Malcolm might have chosen someone the Dorans hadn't prescreened. Were subtly arranged marriages a thing in Manhattan society? If so, she should cut Lynne a *lot* of slack from now on. She might be overbearing and controlling, but at least she hadn't told Malcolm whom to marry.

"Total strangers," Jane confirmed, shrugging. She considered adding that even though she'd only met Malcolm a short time ago, it felt like they'd known each other forever, but decided it would sound cheesy. Maeve was just barely warming up to her— no need to scare her away so soon.

"Huh." The tiny redhead slid the plastic spoon back into her soup, pushing meatballs around in the broth. "We go way back with them," she said thoughtfully. "They have a history of marrying within a certain circle."

A sobering thought occurred to Jane: had Maeve been interested in Malcolm? She clearly expected him to marry someone more familiar . . . perhaps someone such as herself? "I hope I didn't disappoint anyone in that circle too much," she said carefully.

To her relief, Maeve didn't seem to register her implication in the slightest. "I bet you did," she replied carelessly, "not to mention every social climber in the city who wants to break into it." She shrugged, shaking her shoulders restlessly as if she were chasing tension off. "Look, it's none of my business, but watch your back with that family. You don't want it to be your closet they're hiding the bodies in. Or for it to be *your* body they're looking to hide." She smiled, but her eyes stayed serious.

"Oh, they're not so bad," Jane said, feeling a twinge of guilt at having complained about Lynne, which was something she had really been trying not to do. Besides, the way that Maeve kept saying "they" made it seem like she was including Malcolm in her assessment of the lot, which didn't seem fair at all. Even Lynne, for all her faults, didn't really rate the title of "sinister body-hider." Maeve had probably just spent too much time gossiping with salesgirls at Barneys. *She'll come around if she gets to know how Malcolm is with me. No one could ask for a kinder, more loyal man.*

She ate another spoonful of soup and listened as Maeve moved the conversation to the MoMA, giving her the lowdown on everyone from the security guard to the tour guide who was convinced that he was Leonardo da Vinci reincarnated. "He seriously wanted to sue Dan Brown!" Maeve exclaimed.

Jane laughed as Maeve did the security guard's impression of the Vitruvian Man, feeling warm and full from the soup—and from the realization that she had just made her first friend in New York.

Nineteen

THE BEST PART OF PLANNING THE DORANS' COCKTAIL PARTY, Jane soon found, was that it gave Lynne something to talk to her about, other than the wedding. Even with the color/theme decision hanging over their heads like an absurdly trivial ax, Lynne had spent their entire lunch focused on gift bags for the party. It was so refreshing that Jane had decided to walk the seventeen blocks to the MoMA, oblivious to the January wind that whipped her charcoal Theory slacks against her legs.

She arrived flushed, her pale hair wavy from the wind, and settled in to make her phone calls: Kate Spade for the bags themselves, and then Kiehl's, Ralph Lauren Home, Stolichnaya, Anna Sui, Teuscher, Blumarine, and Argento Vivo—for the goodies to fill them. She had always been uncomfortable about asking for special favors, but after a week of the words "Mr. and Mrs. Doran" being followed by "Anything you want, darling!"

in deliriously happy tones, it was getting much, much easier. In fact, those calls were so pleasant that they more than made up for having to explain to the baffled caterer, in no uncertain terms, that it was unacceptable to serve anything that could be described using the word "satay," per Lynne's latest edict.

The afternoon flew by (it helped that there was no printing, photocopying, or faxing involved), and when she exited the museum again, she noticed that the wind had turned biting. *Definitely a bus evening,* she decided. Against all odds and contrary to her usual luck, there was an M3 just pulling up to the stop. It had plenty of empty seats, the lights all worked, and there didn't seem to be any crazy people on board. *And people say this city is tough.* Jane smiled to herself.

When she arrived home, the gloomy inside of the Dorans' mansion caused her good mood to waver a bit (even in spite of Gunther's decidedly cheerful snoring). She sidestepped the paneled elevator in favor of the staircase tucked behind it, hoping that raising her heart rate would counteract the effects of too much tapestry. The nondescript wooden door on the sixth floor accepted the same code as the elevator and, as an added bonus, let her in right next to the kitchen. Snagging an apple from the blue-and-white bowl on the center island, she wandered slowly down the hall, wondering if Malcolm was home yet.

While she appreciated his ambition—especially in light of the family fortune that made it totally unnecessary—lately it seemed as though his work ethic was getting out of hand. He had had to fly to California for an auction series over the weekend, and had been gone by the time she woke up every morning since, leaving nothing but a trace of warmth and his lingering spiced-champagne

scent to confirm that he had ever been in the bed at all. They had
sat across from each other at the rather stiff, formal family din-
ners at night, but she was beginning to miss the easy rapport they
had in private . . . not to mention the explosive chemistry. It was
getting to the point where she was considering leaving him an
extremely detailed and explicit note that explained in vivid terms
exactly *what* she missed.

She was so focused on his absences, in fact, that at first, when
she heard his voice filtering down the hallway, she thought she
must be hallucinating it. But there it was again, louder this time,
as if he were walking and talking—or perhaps shouting. She realized with a start that she'd never heard him yell before.

A second voice rang out—it was unmistakably Lynne's, and
carried a low, dangerous note that made Jane shiver. The two
of them were obviously arguing, but she couldn't make out the
words. The voices were heading toward her fast. Not wanting to
look as though she was eavesdropping (yet not wanting to miss
a chance to overhear), she ducked into the hall bathroom and
pulled the door shut behind her. It was cool and dark and smelled
faintly of bleach. She immediately felt disoriented and a little
nauseated, but she resisted the urge to turn the light on, in case
it showed under the door. A door swung open and shut somewhere along the hall, and suddenly she could hear them much
more clearly.

". . . everything you asked me to do," Malcolm practically
snarled as the footsteps thumped closer. "When do you start to
trust me a little?"

"When you start to show some judgment," Lynne snapped
coldly. "If I still have to tell you every little thing and hold your

hand every step of the way, then that is *exactly* what I will do until you grow up and stop being so *sentimental*." She pronounced the word the way most people would say "torturing babies."

"In case you hadn't noticed," Malcolm shot back, "my 'senti-mentality' is actually an asset to you right now."

"To *us*," his mother corrected. Their voices were so close now that they had to be right on the other side of the bathroom door. Jane held her breath. "This is a family, Malcolm. And while I appreciate everything you've done so far, you're taking it to an inappropriate level. There is no excuse for forgetting who your true family is, and that's *us*, not that . . . that *girl*."

Jane jumped. They were arguing about *her*?

"'That *girl*' is my fiancée, Mom," Malcolm confirmed in a warn-ing tone. "Which, as I recall, you were absolutely thrilled to hear." Jane bit her lip until she tasted blood. What could she have done to upset Lynne so much? She raced through every moment of the past week. She'd gone along with every single one of Lynne's plans. Well, except for the dress. But Lynne didn't even know about that yet! The voices grew fainter again, and Jane pressed her ear against the door.

"Don't you dare try and change the subject, Malcolm," Lynne hissed, and Jane found herself nodding in agreement. *Stay on track while I can still hear you.*

But then Jane heard the creak of another door opening and then slamming shut, and Malcolm's reply was too muffled to hear. She leaned against the door, her breath rasping in the darkness. Her stomach churned and her head started to spin. Wedding-planning errands, family meals, and run-ins in the kitchen began to swim together in her mind's eye. *What did I do to become "that girl"?*

The lights in the bathroom snapped on. Startled, Jane banged her knee against the marble sink. *I just bumped the switch, no biggie,* she tried to tell herself, but she knew that she hadn't. Her breathing came harder now, her heartbeat out of control, and she could feel the electricity rising in her body, like an anchor that had come unmoored. The lights flickered again and again, and then blew out with a blinding flash, plunging the bathroom back into darkness.

And then her heart stopped completely. Light from the hallway flickered through the crack beneath the door, on and off, on and off, as if a thunderstorm were raging outside. Her power, fierce and wild as ever, coursed through her veins, shooting sparks between the synapses in her brain. *She* was the thunderstorm.

A door banged open somewhere in the house, and she heard Lynne shout something angry and imperious. Footsteps scurried down the hall past Jane's hiding place.

"*. . . as if I were an electrician, but I can't piss her off or my baby won't eat . . .*"

Jane heard the thoughts as clearly as if Sofia were speaking aloud. Hot tears welled up in her eyes. No wonder Lynne was having second thoughts. How could anyone be happy about bringing *this* into their home?

Just calm down. Everything is fine. Malcolm and I will be . . . The bulb in the light fixture to Jane's right—a heavily carved frosted-glass confection—flared briefly back to life, and then died. Before she could draw a breath, the light directly above her head did the same.

A small moan escaped from her lips, and she spun to her left and ran blindly from the bathroom, a trail of flashes and darkness following close on her heels. "Stop," she whispered, "please stop."

The flat-screen television in the drawing room blared to noisy life as she passed by, and she ran harder. In her distress, she didn't immediately recognize the door of her room, and had to backtrack a couple of steps. She shoved it open and launched herself inside, tripping over the fringe of one of the rugs and nearly falling as she slammed the door shut behind her. She kicked off her shoes, then dived underneath the cover of the red-and-gold canopy.

Once inside the brocaded walls of the bed, she began to sob in earnest. She pressed her face into the pillow, trying to muffle the sound. Outside her room, she heard the shouting, running, and slamming of doors continue. The bedside lamp shattered, but the brocaded panels kept her from having to see the effects of the magic she had unwittingly called up. She stayed tucked in the safety of the hanging fabric, and eventually her breathing slowed and the commotion in the hallways died down.

Malcolm did not come to bed all night.

Twenty

JANE WOKE UP THE FOLLOWING MORNING TO HER NOW-FAMILIAR empty bed. She rolled over and rubbed the crusted salt from last night's tears off her face.

A square piece of stationery, thick and cream-colored, lay on her nightstand. It looked like Lynne's, but the handwriting was Malcolm's. *"Dear J: Amazing acquisition possibility in Moscow. Back in a few days tops. Miss you! Love, M."*

"You win again, Lynne," Jane croaked sleepily. She tried to clear her throat, but it was as if last night's crying jag had dried up all of the water in her body.

She had no idea why Malcolm's mother wanted to put distance between them, but she was certainly getting her way in spades. She had hoped that morning would shed new light on the bizarre argument she had overheard the night before. But even with the sunlight streaming in and Jane's mind arguably calmer, it was just as confusing. Lynne was thrilled about the wedding, and was pretty damned convincingly ecstatic about Jane. So what was all that about loyalty and "that *girl*"?

"She didn't mean me," Jane tried out, swinging her legs over the side of the bed. It sounded good, and not so much as a static-shock's worth of magic hummed in her blood when she said it, so she took it further. "So I guess Malcolm has another fiancée. Ooh! Or Malcolm has a split personality, and his other half *thinks* it has a different fiancée and Lynne wants him to snap out of it." She wandered into the bathroom and made a face at her ratty hair and streaked mascara. "The family has tried to keep his affliction secret for years," she went on, warming to her subject and waving her arms theatrically, "but it nearly got out during that turbulent time in college when Malcolm formed a four-man rock band with no one in it but himself."

She smiled a little in the mirror, but it looked forced, even to herself. Whatever was going on with Malcolm and his mother, it wasn't something she could just joke away on her own. They needed to talk, to open up. Or he did, at least. She still had a fairly major secret to keep.

Hypocrite.

The thought made her pause, though. She had a secret, sure, but even she barely knew what it was. She had spent the last few weeks so focused on trying to suppress it—rather ineffectually, she had to admit, after last night—that she wasn't exactly sure what she was hiding from everyone.

She was a witch because the women in her family were, and other mysterious people out there were, too. So . . . what was a witch? Was it just having those uncomfortable random flashes of power that she couldn't control? Or was there more? Witches in stories could do all sorts of amazing things, even if most of them were spectacularly ugly. *So if I'm kind of a fox,* Jane wondered, *does that mean I have less power?* Whatever she had inherited certainly hadn't done much for Gran . . . living and dying basically alone in the middle of nowhere. But maybe that had more to do with Gran than with witchcraft itself.

"Well, then," she told her reflection as she brushed on jet-black mascara, "I guess I need to know more. And with my split-personalitied fiancé out of town, I have some time on my hands."

She felt the faint gravitational pull of her sleek little laptop, but that didn't seem right. Computers were new, and magic was old. Besides, computers had long memories and secret Internet caches. She hadn't been able to bring herself to surf anything but theknot.com since they had arrived. *But libraries have genuine old things. And I'm pretty sure New York has a library or seventy.*

Two hours later, she was cozily ensconced at a back table of the New York Public Library, as close as she could possibly be to the occult section without actually sitting there. The vaulted ceiling and honey-colored wood certainly had the antiquated feel she had been looking for, but other than that she was beginning to feel a little silly.

"Witchcraft," she had said succinctly, when the helpful young man with the skull-faced ring had asked if he could direct her search. He'd burst out laughing, which did nothing to make her feel any less silly. Things had improved, though, when he had explained that his laughter had more to do with the huge size of the category than her request. Once she had narrowed her search down a little ("historical mythology" had a useful ring to it), he had pointed her in the right direction and recommended a few authors. He'd even told her how to shake the photocopier just so, to make it work for free. She had no intention of leaving a paper trail lying around the house, of course, but it was still nice to know.

It wasn't long, though, before the library's wealth of information about witches began to frustrate her. There were so many conflicting stories and descriptions that it was impossible to choose just one that matched her own limited knowledge, unless she was ready to select at random. Had her ancestors made a pact with the devil? Or had they come into the world already able to tap into unseen natural forces? Was it a blessing? A curse? A mutation? None of it sounded any more likely than the rest.

Jane dropped her head down on her pile of open books. *I should have had a plan,* she thought woefully. It had seemed so straightforward: she had imagined a montage of herself rummaging through the stacks, the Dewey decimal system her new best friend. She was even wearing tortoiseshell glasses, although all she had in reality were sunglasses. Out of nowhere, her witchy blood would draw her, like a moth to a flame, to the one passage that would make sense of it all. Or perhaps it would even make a book jump off the shelf. The montage continued until she understood everything she could possibly want to know, without having to bother sifting through any dull, inapplicable information.

The reason that movies *had* montages, she now realized, was that the long version—the real version—was lethally boring.

"Time for a break," she announced. She had said it under her breath, but it still earned her a glare from a white-haired woman in a blue tracksuit and clashing orange earplugs. "Sorry," she mouthed, and headed off in search of the bathroom.

Before she had gone ten steps, her ankle snagged a book on a low shelf. She tripped and crashed sideways, smashing her elbow on the wood paneling. The ear-plugged woman collected her books in her arms and stomped off in silent protest against Jane's not-at-all silent cursing, although Jane felt that she had been fairly restrained under the circumstances. Feeling fed up and just plain childish, she sat down heavily on the floor and worked out a way to rub both her ankle and her elbow at the same time. It was awkward, though, and it didn't make her feel any better, so she turned her attention to the book that had caused her trouble in the first place.

At first, she assumed that it was simply too large for the shelf, and blamed the librarians for not putting it with the other oversized books. But it quickly became apparent that it wasn't really so big . . . it was just hanging out into the aisle because it hadn't been pushed fully in by the last person to peruse it. She turned the book over in her hands. The faded gilt letters spelled out: A TRUE HISTORY OF WITCHES AND MAGICK, BY ROSALIE GODDARD.

Jane's imaginary montage flickered briefly through her mind, and she grinned. Frustration and sore elbow completely forgotten, she opened the book on her lap and began to read it right there on the floor. Soon she had a whole collection of books stacked next to her: in addition to the "true history," there was one about female authors in the seventeenth century, another about New York's high society during the height of the witch hunts—with several passages on Rosalie Goddard's family itself—and two about the histories of mental illnesses and psychology in America.

Rosalie Goddard had written twelve thrilling chapters, in which she made quite a lot of claims about magic. It was real, she had insisted, and hereditary, although the trait only manifested in women. Witches could do all sorts of amazing things . . . including, of course, blend in with regular human beings. Jane, convinced that she was on the right track, forced her way through the more obscure and confusing parts: there was a dense section on seven magical sisters and their children, complicated wars between those seven witch families, and extensive but vague descriptions of how magic was transferred from one person to another.

Every witch was born with some magic of her own, Jane read avidly, although the amount seemed to vary widely. Rosalie suspected that the variation had something to do with astrology, but Jane got lost in the star charts and couldn't follow the author's logic to any kind of conclusion. If the witch wanted more magic—and, apparently, they all did—she had to either inherit it . . . or steal it. It could be transferred from person to person through silver—Jane stroked her smooth silver ring absently—but the exact process was complex. There was a lot of stuff about "right" and "will" and the witch's "last breath," which didn't make any sense, because Gran had kept on breathing for six more years after protecting Jane in Paris.

A note from the publisher was inserted at the very back of the book, explaining that Rosalie's family had tried to suppress her book entirely, and then to pass it off as fiction. When their efforts failed, the Goddards decided their main PR problem wasn't the book at all—it was the author. They shipped Rosalie off to a European mental institution, never to be heard from by the public again.

When Jane finally came up for air, the rectangles of sun on the floor had moved all the way across the room. It was also more crowded than it had been in the morning. Jane blinked at the assortment of elderly people, students, and families that had filled the honey-colored tables, trying to bring herself back to the present.

Between one blink and the next, something changed.

I saw something, her mind told her insistently, but she couldn't think what.

Just then sunlight flashed off of a perfectly bald head across the room, and Jane started, the hairs on her arms standing on end. Even in profile, she had no trouble recognizing Yuri, Lynne's huge, silent driver, who was now striding silently out of the library. There were plenty of reasons why he might have been there, of course. And plenty of reasons he might be leaving now. There was no reason to think that his presence wasn't a coincidence . . . except that, just as he reached the door, he turned back. His beady black eyes found Jane's and narrowed. An instant later, he was gone.

Twenty-one

MALCOLM'S TRIP LASTED THROUGH THE WEEKEND, AND BY Monday Jane was getting downright anxious. She'd left her entire life behind—for what? An absentee fiancé? But as angry as she was, she was even more lonely. His absence was achingly painful.

So when she got a text announcing that he would be back that evening, she was ready to overlook the fact that it was just a stupid mass text message to everyone in the family. She was feeling more than romantic enough for both of them. Her newly acquired event-planning skills kicked in, and in record time she had put together the textbook definition of a romantic evening for two, complete with dinner reservations and a rose petal–covered bed. All Malcolm would have to do was show up.

Malcolm's luggage arrived before he did, and the porter who brought it informed her that he was in the parlor with his father.

Well, of course his parents missed him, too, she told herself, trying not to feel miffed. The porter's eyes flickered curiously across the rose petals on the downturned duvet. "Thank you," she repeated, more loudly this time, and the man took the cue and left the suite. "Okay," she told the now-empty bedroom. "I'll just have to go down there and remind him why men get engaged in the first place."

Unfortunately, when she reached the parlor (now wearing a sexy white-lace sheath that he'd never seen but was sure to love), he seemed to be in a bad mood. Slouched low in a leather chair, crystal tumbler in hand as he stared into the fire, he looked positively broody. Jane kicked an extra sway into her hips to knock him out of it. "Darling, I've missed you all weekend," she said brightly. Malcolm's eyes flicked up at her briefly and then away. "I don't know if you had anything specific in mind for dinner, but the girls at work were really excited about this little French place on 79th and I was thinking that it might be sort of nostal—"

"Actually," Malcolm broke in without looking up, "I have dinner plans. Some old friends, sort of a guys' night out. Another time, though. Absolutely." His dark eyes traveled to his father, who was swirling whiskey idly in a glass, but never rose any higher than Jane's ribcage.

"Um . . . okay," Jane stammered, feeling like he'd hit her in the gut with the fire poker. *Not to mention the fresh blowout, smoky eyes, and Aubade's sexiest push-up bra, all wasted.* "I'll . . . just have Sofia put something together." She swept dramatically from the room à la Lynne, but knew that it was a total waste of the gesture: there were no eyes watching her go.

Jane's heart crashed down to her toes as soon as the bedroom door closed behind her. *Guys' night?* She had yet to even meet any of his guy friends. Suddenly they were so important to him that he couldn't even say hello to her after five days apart? By the time she'd blown out the candles she'd lit, she was more angry than hurt.

She stared at her fully made-up face in the bathroom mirror. "He's got plans? I can have plans. I have friends too—well, a friend, anyway," she told her reflection. She grabbed her iPhone and dialed Maeve, her ankle boots tapping rhythmically on the thick carpet as she paced.

"I actually have plans. But just with my brother!" the chirpy voice on the other end of the line was quick to explain. "You should come! Vento, on West 14th, twenty minutes."

"Done and done." Jane grinned and dropped the phone into a suede clutch. *Maeve is* exactly *what I need tonight.*

The prospect was so appealing that she managed to make it through the subway without any major electrical incidents, although her anger with Malcolm may have been responsible for shorting out an escalator on her way out of the station. *Fluke,* she told herself firmly, shutting out the nastier voice in her head that whispered, *freak.*

From there, it was a quick walk through the icy night to the cozy restaurant, where she easily spotted Maeve's red hair and dropped into the wide wooden chair beside her. "I should probably warn you that I'm a walking curse when I'm in a bad mood, and I am *definitely* in a bad mood tonight."

"Not for long, if I can help it!" Curls bouncing, Maeve shoved her suspiciously complicated-looking cocktail toward Jane before signaling the waitress for another. Jane, better versed in wine than mixed drinks, hesitated for only a moment before she sipped: the flavors were unusual, but they blended into something surprisingly pleasant. It was only then that she noticed the redheaded guy sitting across the table, watching her with an amused smirk.

"So you're the brother, I guess," Jane said awkwardly. He was tall and lean, with close-cropped copper curls and dancing green eyes. "I'm Jane," she finished lamely, adding a half-wave for good measure.

"Harris." He nodded.

She took another deep drink from Maeve's tumbler.

"Bad day?" he asked lightly, eyeing her now-empty glass.

"'Bad' would be something of an understatement."

"And that's why God created truffle pizza," Maeve declared, jamming a menu into Jane's hands. "And alcohol."

The waitress appeared over Harris's shoulder, bearing two more cocktails and a draft beer. "Perfect timing," Maeve grinned, and dinner was off to an excellent start.

Harris, a financial consultant, shared his sister's enthusiastic outlook and quirky sense of humor. Seeing the two of them with their heads thrown back in laughter, Jane had no trouble at all seeing the family resemblance, and she felt a quick pang. Jane and Malcolm were both only children; neither of them shared this type of bond with anyone else.

Our children will, she vowed silently. The lavender-scented cocktail was deceptively mild-tasting, but she was definitely feeling its effects. She'd never really thought about children, but apparently weeks of Lynne's "hints" and a bit of hard liquor brought the idea right to the surface. Of course, maybe she was counting her chickens too soon, given Malcolm's physical and emotional distance.

Screw that, she told herself, gesturing to the waitress for another drink while Maeve cracked Harris up with a dead-on impersonation of Archie from the MoMA, waving her arms around as if they were attached by springs. *I'm young and out with friends in Manhattan. I will deal with my prodigal fiancé when I get home.*

Out loud, she insisted that the other two order dessert with her, and then broached the subject that was now foremost in her mind: "Where can we go after dinner?" She had lived in Manhattan with a tabloid staple for nearly three weeks and hadn't been to a single nightclub. Through the haze of her four cocktails, that suddenly seemed like an absolute crime against nature.

"Ooh!" Maeve squealed happily, her light brown eyes dancing. "We're right by the Meatpacking District! And Harris, don't even think about laming out."

"I'd be a fool to miss it." Harris laughed, his eyes on Jane. His tone was breezy, but his gaze was intense. She felt her cheeks redden, and hoped that the dim light of the restaurant masked her blush. They paid the bill and left, Harris's cool hand resting lightly on the small of her back. His touch was electric, and Jane knew she was probably glowing red in the dark. *Like a little flirting ever killed anyone,* she told herself airily, breathing on her hands to keep them warm. It was nice to have a hot guy paying a little attention to her, especially since her own hot guy didn't seem inclined to do so. *Could be the gin talking,* she had to admit, but she glanced involuntarily up at Harris, whose green eyes glittered back down at her attentively, and she decided she really didn't care.

The club was dark and hot, and Jane had forgotten its coy one-word name almost before she and the Montague siblings were inside. It didn't hurt that as soon as the bouncers had gotten a good look at her, they had been ushered inside immediately, and a red suede–covered booth had been cleared of its disgruntled occupants. Jane sat where the bouncer indicated—all but bowing as he backed away from their little group. She threw a questioning look at Maeve. "Am I missing something here?"

"You may not read Page Six, but they sure as hell do," Maeve explained, signaling to a waiter. "Honey, you're practically famous."

"Tough life," Harris added. His expression was casual, but something in his tone set Jane's teeth on edge.

"Right, because it's every little girl's fantasy to live in the world's creepiest house with her fiancé's controlling family and then have the rest of the world act insane just because she's about to share their last name." A glass of dark liquid appeared at her elbow and she clutched it like a life preserver.

Harris looked genuinely puzzled at her tirade. "Maybe not when you put it that way, but you still have what every girl on this island has been fantasizing about for the last decade or so. Or so all my ex-girlfriends kept telling me," he added, with a self-deprecating smile.

"But that's another thing!" Jane all but wailed, feeling her skin flush with embarrassment. She had almost managed to forget Madison, but suddenly the shiny chestnut hair and tanned breasts were large as life in her mind's eye. "I ran right into some ex of Malcolm's practically the minute I stepped off the plane. I know he must have dated people before—obviously—but there's 8 million of them here. What are the odds that one of the first ones I met used to go out with my fiancé?"

Harris's green eyes sparkled wickedly. "Do you really want me to answer that?"

"Harris!" Maeve shoved her brother. "Jane, ignore him. But it's true that if you were looking for a lifelong altar boy, you missed the mark."

Jane frowned and sipped at her drink. When she looked up again, Maeve had concern written all over her elfin features. Harris refilled Jane's glass.

"Trouble in paradise?" they asked simultaneously.

Jane stabbed a marinated olive viciously with a silver toothpick. The world was starting to spin, the bodies and tables whirling around her like a Dali painting. "No," she answered sullenly. So Malcolm had a past. So he had dated—who knows?—half of the eligible women in Manhattan? Did Malcolm regret proposing to her now that he was home? Was being back on his old hunting ground making him nostalgic? Was that why he was acting so distant—he was bored with her already?

Jane set her glass down on the table, some of the liquid sloshing over the sides. Suddenly the music felt too loud and the crowd of writhing bodies loomed oppressively. A girl in a teal halter dress glared at Jane from across the room. Had she dated Malcolm, too? "Do you think he misses his single life?" Jane asked miserably.

"Better hope not," Harris muttered. "I wouldn't want the Dorans to set that goon on you—what was his name, Mae?"

"Boris," Maeve declared. "Sergei?"

"Yuri?" Jane guessed.

"That's it!"

Jane shook her head, noticing that the room seemed to move a split second slower than her eyes. "He's just the driver." *And the guy who stakes out libraries,* she added silently since she couldn't exactly say it out loud.

"Not according to at least five or six of Manhattan's clingiest bachelorettes," Harris snorted, resting a lean, muscled arm along the red suede of the booth's back.

"It's just rumors," Maeve hurried to add. "Rumors from a few different sources, is all. That if Malcolm's ex—"

"Flavor of the week," Harris inserted.

"—didn't go away quietly, that driver guy would *do* something."

"Scare the hell out of her, at the very least," Harris corrected. "And it's not just rumors. Tamara DeWitt and Madison Avery both swear it happened to them personally."

The second name made Jane sit a little more upright as the jealousy-inducing images from before churned in her head. *Madison Avery—is that Madison from Barneys?* She spun the plain silver ring around her middle finger. *I'd be bitchy too, if someone sent that giant to scare me off. Wait, does someone want that giant to scare me off? What were Lynne and Malcolm arguing about before he left?*

The music changed abruptly to a Discobitch song that had been huge in Paris a few summers ago, and Jane felt a sudden rush of recklessness. Grabbing Harris's hand, she whirled toward the dance floor, feeling the clinging lace of her mini-dress hug her curves as she moved. "Dance with me," she breathed, and Harris's lean body pressed willingly against hers. She felt the same electricity she had when he touched her earlier, except now, with his whole body just centimeters away, it was more of a pulse than a spark.

It felt, honestly, nearly the same as when she touched Malcolm. *Guess it's not just him,* her libido told her smugly. *I just needed to date Americans after all.*

Not that this counted as dating, of course, but she felt like flirting, and Harris seemed more than willing to flirt back. They danced, laughed, and drank; he brushed imaginary hair from her eyes, and she plucked invisible lint from his shirt's collar. It seemed ages since she had felt so attractive, so desired, even though Malcolm couldn't really have been distant for that much more than a week . . . or two. *Just how long has he been pulling away for?* she wondered suddenly. *Where was I?*

And what am I doing now?

With a mumbled apology, she disentangled herself from Harris, whose striped green button-down was clinging to his now-damp chest in an extremely appealing way. She heard that she was slurring her words a bit and grimaced. *I have to remember to ask someone what the hell is in a Black Russian.*

She tapped Maeve—who had easily found a dark-haired stockbroker to dance with—and gestured toward the door, waving good-bye and blowing an impulsive kiss to her and her brother. Seconds later, she was in a taxi heading silently uptown.

Malcolm will come around, she told herself, watching the storefronts fly by in a ghostly parade. *I'll make him. I deserve way better than someone who thinks he's settling for me, and he's got to be smart enough to realize that, too.* Her eyelids felt heavy, but when she closed them, the taxi spun unpleasantly, so she forced them to stay wide-open until she recognized a giant stone mansion that seemed taller, darker, and more sinister than the rest. Even from the street, in what was arguably the least conspicuous type of car in New York, she felt like someone was watching her from the highest windows.

"On the right side is fine," she told the driver thickly. "I'm home."

Twenty-two

JANE TIPTOED TOWARD THE DARK LIVING ROOM, TRYING NOT to bump into anything. Her suede ankle boots felt like blocks of concrete, throwing off her balance and making her clumsy. *It's probably not just the boots,* she admitted to herself as she smashed into a doorknob. *Ow!* She put out a hand to steady herself and felt curious grooves under her fingertips. *The infamous family tree,* she realized.

Her fingers brushed across Malcolm's name, and then Annette's. She stopped short, suddenly, her fingers lingering over Annette's birth year. She would have been twenty-four, just like Jane, if she'd lived.

The house was eerily still around her; not even the whoosh of cabs rushing down Park Avenue could penetrate the double-paned windows in this room. Jane wondered what Annette would have been like if she'd gotten the chance to grow up. Would Annette have been a friend? An ally even, someone she could count on and complain to and ask for advice?

As Jane slid her hand further along the wall, she felt the oddly smooth patch that she had noticed on her first night. She pushed away from the wall dizzily, her mind too wobbly to think the anomaly through.

She navigated the now-familiar turns of the hallway carefully, gasping once when her heel got caught in the fringe of a narrow Oriental rug. When she reached her room, she fumbled in the darkness for the doorknob, but her hands found nothing but empty air. After a moment, she realized the door was already open. *Malcolm's not home yet? It's three a.m.!* Not that she had the moral high ground here, but still—what kind of "guys' night out" *was* this, exactly?

Her eyes adjusted quickly to the dim light from the street filtering through the heavy curtains, and she realized she'd been wrong. Someone was in the room after all, leaning over their bed. *And that thing that goes bump in the night is . . .*

"Malcolm?"

The man straightened and turned to look at her, and she felt her stomach heave in a way that had nothing to do with alcohol. The height was right, and so were the broad shoulders, but even in the near-darkness, she could tell that the man in her bedroom was a complete stranger. His hair was longer and darker than Malcolm's, and while the two men shared the same large frame, this man's build was fleshy and slack, nothing like Malcolm's taut torso and arms. Before she could speak again, he lurched toward the door, his meaty hands reaching for her.

"Get away," she shrieked. She tried to spin on her heel, but it got caught again in the carpet. "Help!"

She'd only made it a few steps before a rough hand closed on her arm, forcing her to a stop so abrupt that she almost fell to the floor. She screamed again, trying to jerk her arm away, but the hand was like stone, pulling her ruthlessly against the man's chest. She drew in a breath to scream, fight, beg, anything, but the air around the man was absolutely foul, and when it hit the back of her throat, she began coughing in choked spasms. She leaned backward as far as she could, fighting for breath and ignoring the pain in her shoulder as it twisted awkwardly to accommodate her still-imprisoned arm.

The moment of clear air allowed her mind to function just enough to come up with a plan. She spun her body as hard to her right as she could, bringing her left arm up to swing at where she hoped the man's face was.

Missed, she groaned silently as she felt her balled fist barely graze his cheek. With a bellow of rage, he tightened his grip on her arm and used it to shove her against the wall. She opened her mouth again, trying to ignore the stench, but just as she did, there was a soft click and light flooded the hallway.

"Charles!" a voice shouted, and the hand circling Jane's arm disappeared—as did the smell.

There was more shouting, and then Jane felt strong hands on her shoulders, holding her up against the wall. She realized belatedly that they were probably necessary, since her knees had gone watery, but she flinched when they got too close to the bruise already forming on her right arm. *Stupid pale skin,* she thought randomly. *Shows everything.* She looked up then, and nearly cried with relief. There, his head bent so low that his dark eyes were only inches from hers, was Malcolm. Still wearing his leather jacket, she noticed, but looking every inch the loving and concerned fiancé.

"Did he hurt you?" he asked, his voice soft enough to be private but forceful enough to rumble the air between them.

She shook her head mutely and glanced over his arm. The stranger had vanished, and Lynne was storming down the hall, two terrified-looking maids trailing behind her.

"I'm okay, but how—who was—" She frowned; she didn't even know what to ask. "I have questions," she finished stiffly.

Malcolm nodded and drew her into their room, shutting the door behind him. She didn't notice that she'd been holding her breath until he switched on the lights and the wall sconces illuminated every dark corner. As the air rushed out of her burning lungs, she realized she hadn't believed that the room was really empty until she'd seen it for herself. Malcolm shrugged off his coat and slumped tiredly into one of the overstuffed chairs, gesturing for her to do the same. "I'm so sorry," he began. He sounded sincere, but Jane didn't move a muscle; she needed to know just what he was sorry for before she could forgive him.

"What the hell was that?" she demanded.

He picked at the nubby fabric of the armchair. The lamp cast a golden halo of light over his blond curls, but dark circles lined his eyes, and his mouth was drawn. He looked exhausted. "There's a lot I should have told you about my family. But when you keep secrets for so long, well . . . I guess it just becomes a habit."

She massaged her sore shoulder and waited for him to continue.

"I used to have a sister, Annette. She . . . well, she drowned when she was six." He smoothed his jeans over his knees. He hadn't met her gaze once, as if it was easier to tell the story without looking at her. "It was . . . awful, and Mom was devastated. I've never seen anything like it. She went off the deep end, actually," he admitted, "and then she tried to fix it."

"'Fix it'?" Jane echoed. "How do you 'fix' a dead child?"

Malcolm inhaled deeply. "She decided to have another baby. She was sure she could have another girl, like she could just replace Annette and everything would be right again." His lips twisted in a horrible approximation of a smile. "You've seen how her family is about girls. On top of everything else, they'd just lost their only shot at carrying on this incredibly long tradition, and she was convinced that she could just make it all better." He frowned. The heat clicked on, hissing through the room like an angry snake.

"She was older by then, though. Even carrying Annie had been a risk. My parents fought about it a lot. Her first doctor said it was too dangerous, so she got another one, and another, and—well, you've seen Mom when she wants a certain color tablecloth. Can you imagine when she wanted a baby?" His dark eyes flickered up briefly, and Jane nodded, picturing Lynne flipping through a book of baby portraits, demanding that her ob-gyn give her the beautiful blue-eyed girl with the dimples.

"So she got her way. Except that there are things that *no* one can control—not even her."

Another shout sounded from the hall, followed by a slamming door. Jane didn't move.

"I was a kid—the medical stuff went right over my head—but I guess that she was taking something experimental, to make sure the pregnancy took. To make sure she got to have her one last shot at a perfect little girl." He looked up, eyes burning with an emotion that Jane couldn't name. "Except that he wasn't a girl. And he wasn't perfect, either."

"Charles," Jane breathed, remembering the shout in the hall-way right after the lights had blazed on. She sank down into the chair next to Malcolm's.

He nodded, looking absolutely miserable. "It was obvious right away that something was wrong. She said it was just one of those things, but between her age and whatever she took, I know she feels responsible."

She is, Jane thought darkly. But it was hard to judge the grief-stricken mother of a dead child too harshly, and she reprimanded herself silently for the thought.

Malcolm shifted in his chair. "Dad wanted to send him to a place—an asylum, I guess—where they could take care of him, but Mom didn't want anyone to find out. She couldn't face people asking about him, knowing about him. She'd been on bed rest for pretty much the whole pregnancy, so if we kept him here, he could stay a family secret."

Jane's jaw dropped open; this time the judgment was harder to suppress. "So no one knew he existed?"

Malcolm chuckled bitterly. "It wasn't even hard to hide. After Annie died, people just stopped asking where Mom was. She had a perfectly good reason to shut herself in, and then a year later she announced that she was done with 'mourning,' and picked up right where she'd left off. Except that then I had a brother living in the attic who no one was allowed to talk about."

A lump formed in Jane's throat. The terror she'd felt when Charles attacked her fell away, replaced with heartbreak for Malcolm's teenage self, for the loss of his sister, and the horrible secret he'd had to carry all these years. "I won't tell," she whispered.

He stared at her as if he didn't know who she was, for a split second, and then blinked back to himself. "I know that. I was just so used to shutting him out by the time I met you that it was almost like he wasn't real. And Mom promised that he was getting care around the clock. If he'd hurt you . . ." He dropped his dark-gold head in his hands.

Jane slid from her chair to his and settled into his lap. "He didn't," she murmured, stroking the waves of his hair. She felt a stab of guilt for questioning his feelings for her earlier. For a brief moment, she remembered the clean smell of Harris's aftershave when she had pressed against him at the club. She winced as the guilt doubled.

"Everything's okay now," she whispered into Malcolm's ear. "I promise."

Twenty-three

JANE AWOKE AFTER A NIGHTMARE-FILLED FOUR HOURS OF SLEEP to an empty bed. She reached over to touch Malcolm's side; it was cold. Her compassion for him from the previous night evaporated, and anger flashed in her veins.

So he tells me this big secret because *it nearly killed me, and now he's gone again?* She struggled out from under the red-and-gold duvet and headed for the shower. *And now I get a full day of wedding planning with Grendel's mother and I have to throw her a party tonight on top of it.* Not to mention that she would have to do all of those things with a throbbing headache, but she had no one to blame but herself for that . . . and maybe Maeve, just a little bit.

Jane had expected Lynne's enthusiasm for wedding errands to wane following the mysterious argument that she had overheard, but Lynne was still going full-speed ahead. And dragging Jane—tired, bored, and confused—along in her considerable wake.

Even on the morning of the Dorans' cocktail party at the MoMA, Jane hadn't been able to wriggle her way out of wedding planning. She had tried to beg off, using the vague excuse of "last-minute arrangements," but Lynne's eyes had narrowed dangerously.

"Something was left until the last minute?" she purred in what Jane knew by now was a deceptively mild tone. "What on earth would have been left until today?"

Faced with the choice between looking incompetent and spending the morning with Lynne, Jane reluctantly decided that she had to pop a few Advil and opt for the latter.

First on the agenda was gown-shopping ("Monique Lhuillier," Lynne had said, staring pointedly at Jane's hips, "and maybe Marchesa?"), which Jane knew was supposed to be the most enjoyable part of the planning. But after ten minutes, it was clear that it most certainly would not be.

"Absolutely not," Lynne snapped when the salesgirl, Andie, appeared with a dress that seemed to weigh less than thirty pounds.

"I love the waistline," Jane interceded. "And the cap sleeves." But the salesgirl vanished again without even looking her way, and Jane sighed heavily. The dress was the one thing that she cared about, the one battle she had decided to pick. Things weren't going anything like the way she had pictured them, though, and she was beginning to worry. Was it possible that, somewhere between the caterer and the photographer and the brass band, Jane had lost her backbone for good? She closed her eyes and took a deep breath; she could remember how to assert herself. She had to. "Lynne, I feel like we have different ideas about what would look best. Maybe if I could try on one of the—"

"Perfect!" Lynne trilled, and Jane broke off, confused. Was it really just that easy? But Lynne's abrupt approval became all too clear when Jane turned to see Andie struggling under the weight of what looked like two of Carrie Bradshaw's wedding dresses rolled into one.

"*No,*" Jane said reflexively.

"Nonsense," Lynne's snake-charmer voice drawled. "You were just saying how it's impossible to tell without seeing the dress *on.*"

Oh, sure, now *she listens.* How could Lynne stay so cool and polished while being so crafty, conniving, and stubborn? It might have been awe-inspiring, if it hadn't been so thoroughly annoying.

"And Jane, dear, you should really nip that dreadful ring-twirling habit in the bud," Lynne said, furrowing her arched (and perfectly tweezed) eyebrows at Jane.

Jane clasped her hands behind her back—she hadn't even re-alized she'd been doing it again. She tried to communicate her desperation to the salesgirl with her eyes, but Andie seemed com-pletely unaware of the conflict unfolding in front of her. "The sample isn't in your size miss but I would be more than happy to clip it so that you can see an approximation," she announced in an inflectionless monotone. There was no obvious reason to think that she *wasn't* actually speaking to Jane, but somehow it was clear all the same.

"That would be lovely, dear," Lynne smirked, shoving Jane lightly toward the curtained-off section.

Jane fought the urge to shake one or both of them while shout-ing "I'm the bride, damn it!" and allowed the girl to maneuver the massive pile of multilayered skirts over her head.

Once it was more or less on, Jane waited for the humiliating clipping process to begin, but the salesgirl appeared to have had a change of heart. "Actually, this one has a corset back"—*Of course it does!*—"so maybe if I just lace that loosely enough . . . there."

All of the air was expelled from Jane's lungs at once. "So apparently 'loose' is a relative term?" she grunted.

"Ooh," the girl cooed automatically, seemingly oblivious to Jane's labored breathing. "I'm sure your mother will love this one!"

"Mother-in-law," Jane corrected sternly. "To-be." *And only if she doesn't send me screaming for the hills in the next month or so, not to mention that Malcolm will have to take some time out of his busy schedule to actually show up to the church.* She glared at her reflection in the three-way mirror: she looked like a Renaissance fair on steroids. Weren't puff sleeves still "out"?

Closing the curtain separating them from Lynne more tightly, Jane lowered her voice. "I was leafing through your catalog, actually, and I saw this really pretty sheath I was hoping to try. In fact, there were a couple of styles that I loved." She held out a scrap of paper where she had jotted down four style numbers, but Andie didn't even glance at it.

"I really don't think that any of those would be formal enough for the event Mrs. Doran described," she droned. *Is there even a human being in there?* "You'll definitely be more comfortable in a more traditional gown." With that declaration, she flung the curtain open, and Jane was treated to the sight of Lynne in a near-swoon.

"I think we're getting closer!" she trilled happily. "But I'd love to see something in a whiter white. She's so pale," she added, a crease forming on her forehead. "Practically monochromatic. And now that I see it on, I'm not sold on the seed pearls. More of the same Alençon lace on the bustier panel would be better, I think."

"I absolutely agree," Andie breathed, showing some signs of

life now that she was speaking to someone other than Jane. She practically skipped out of the room, leaving Jane to glare balefully after her, still trapped in her Disney-princess nightmare of a dress.

Enough is enough. Jane drew herself up to her full height and took advantage of the fact that the many layers of crinoline made her as wide as she was tall. "We need to talk," she declared in her most authoritative tone.

Lynne's eyebrow nearly shot off her forehead entirely, but she gestured for Jane to continue.

"I really appreciate your taste and input," Jane told her firmly, "and for the most part I've been happy to do whatever you suggest. But a woman's wedding dress is a very important and personal thing, and I don't want to rush the decision." *That sounds better than "Back the hell off, harpy," doesn't it?*

Lynne blinked. She seemed to be struggling with this new and confusing information. For a moment, Jane expected a tirade; she could practically see it forming on Lynne's peach-lipsticked mouth. Lynne's hands clenched the pleats of her canary-colored Ralph Lauren skirt briefly, and then suddenly, unexpectedly, released. "Of course. I only want you to be happy," she said so warmly that, for a moment, Jane assumed that she had misheard.

Andie bustled back in, loaded down with books of fabric swatches. Lynne turned her head smoothly. "I believe that my daughter-in-law asked about a dress you brought out. The one with the cap sleeves."

"Oh." Andie stopped short. An awkward beat passed while Lynne stared pointedly, and then the girl caught on. "Right, of course." She dropped the books awkwardly on a bench and all but fled from the room, returning seconds later with the dress in question.

Jane grinned triumphantly as she slipped the A-line sheath over her head. Finally, finally, something was going her way.

Twenty-four

"People are mingling, and she looks happy!" Archie trilled into Jane's ear that evening before rushing off to greet the latest arrival. He didn't bother to explain who "she" was, but considering the way his eyes had been darting to Lynne every three seconds for the last hour, Jane had a pretty good guess.

Jane smiled as she glanced around the Modern, which had been transformed from an upscale restaurant into a chic lounge for the Dorans' cocktail party, and congratulated herself on a job well done. She had gone with an all-black theme, and the only sources of light came from wall sconces and floor lights cunningly shielded under black leather sofas. The darkness of the room stood in sharp contrast to the dramatically lit sculpture garden just outside the floor-to-ceiling windows, lending an overall effect of being "in the audience" while the art took center stage.

The only *really* well-lit space, per Jane's orders, was the ornate and well-stocked bar, which was an exception that the immaculately dressed guests clearly appreciated—especially Mr. Doran.

"I second Archie. This is awesome. And on your very first try!" Maeve played with the sterling swizzle-stick in her Manhattan. Jane eyed the amber-colored drink with suspicion after last night's foray into the wide world of hard liquor. Eighteen hours later, her tongue still felt a little sandy.

Jane smiled a thank-you and sipped at her own, safer choice: chardonnay. Unfortunately, that was hardly much of an improvement, as associations went. An unusually large number of the bar's wines, as the sommelier had proudly informed her, came from within an hour of Saint-Croix-sur-Amaury. "Alsatian wines are our specialty," he declared happily just before quizzing her on the region's average rainfall for every year of her childhood.

Jane's party smile, already shaky at the reminder of her grandmother, fell from her lips entirely when she saw Harris Montague striding purposefully toward them. "Hey, can I try some of that?" she asked Maeve desperately, reaching for the Manhattan without waiting for an answer. It had an unexpected bitter undercurrent, but was smooth and rich and provided just enough of a kick against the back of her throat to allow her to meet Harris's dancing green eyes without flinching.

"Hi there," she chirped with only a tiny bit too much enthusiasm as he gave his sister a quick peck on the cheek. He hesitated for a moment, and then kissed Jane as well. *A friendly kiss*, she reassured herself. *Practically brotherly.* She sipped at her wine again to cool the sudden flush creeping up her cheeks. *At this rate I'll be dancing on the bar by midnight*, her mind scolded, but the flush—which was beginning to creep ominously downward, too—convinced her that some things just couldn't be helped.

She tried glancing casually around the room, but she had barely gotten a quarter of the way before she had to stop and fret. Lynne's cousin Belinda—or was it Cora who was wearing green tonight?—was staring fixedly at her from a dark corner. *A problem already? The party's just started.* Jane moved instinctively toward whichever twin it was, to see what she wanted, but the woman snapped her head away as soon as Jane began to walk. *Rude like Belinda, but I'm almost positive it's Cora.* Jane frowned. Either way, Lynne's silver-haired cousin didn't seem to want her attention after all. She turned back to the Montagues instead, no less flustered than she had been before.

"Are you here as part of the advance guard, or has the family arrived?" Harris asked casually, appearing not to notice Jane's momentary awkwardness.

"All three branches." Maeve frowned into her drink.

"Except for Malcolm," Jane pointed out, unsure of exactly how she felt about that. Malcolm hadn't so much as called since he had explained about his secret brother the previous night. She had hoped that he would at least show up to support her in her event-planning debut, but there was a growing part of her that didn't fully expect it. But how could she sort all of that out and condense it into cocktail-party banter—especially with Harris's amazingly vivid eyes locked on her?

"So *this* is where you're hiding, dear," an all-too-familiar voice purred, and Lynne appeared out of the shadows at Jane's elbow. Her frosty peach smile excluded the Montagues entirely.

Should've gone with a brighter theme, Jane mentally kicked herself. *Or handed out belled collars at the door.* Lynne's bony hand closed around her arm and began to tug. "Come along. You can't just *stand* here, there are people you need to talk to."

Jane shot a desperate look over her shoulder at the only two people at the party she *wanted* to talk to, but they shot her matching helpless shrugs. Jane could hardly blame them. So she smiled and shook hands and made small talk for what felt like hours until Lynne got distracted enough that she could slip back to her friends, whose coppery-red curls stood out like beacons even in the low light.

While Harris teased Maeve about her stockbroker from the previous night (who had a penthouse in the Financial District and, apparently, a foot fetish), Jane glanced around the room again. She smiled automatically at the mayor's wife, who was chatting animatedly with a Kennedy-in-law. Altogether about a hundred people gossiped over cocktails. She had never met most of them in real life before, although some of them had made the news even over in France once or twice. She counted the faces she had seen in photographs, matching names to them in her head.

As she looked, Malcolm's dark-gold waves jumped out from the crowd. *Finally.* Until she saw him, she hadn't been able to admit just how much she'd hoped that he would show up, or just how worried she had been that he wouldn't. But the sight of him across the room made her limbs feel numb, and she ached to be closer to him . . . preferably alone. She started almost involuntarily toward him, but a moment later realized that he was talking with his mother, and neither of them looked particularly pleased with the conversation. Lynne's eyes flicked up and locked on Jane's. Snagged, Jane threw what she hoped was a casual wave and turned in the opposite direction.

Good God, this is a night that calls for a cigarette. At least the cold snap had broken, even if the reprieve was temporary. Parisian winters were much milder than New York ones, but tonight Jane could at least handle the sculpture garden for five minutes. Maybe the chill would even help to clear her head. She excused herself from Maeve and Harris, and made a break for the door.

Out of the corner of her eye, she saw a flash of blue and realized that Belinda Helding was moving on a converging path with her. As her sister had earlier, the old woman turned her head firmly away, but not quickly enough to hide the fact that she'd been staring. *Watching.*

Just then, Malcolm's voice rang out over the muted hum of conversation around them.

"Don't *tell* me what I saw!" he shouted. Every head in the room turned to stare at Malcolm, who was glaring at his mother but pointing squarely at Belinda Helding. She seemed frozen in place, and a quick glance to the other side of the room revealed a green-clad Cora McCarroll in much the same posture.

Lynne didn't flinch before calmly removing her son's martini glass from his clenched fist. "I think that you've had about enough to drink, Malcolm," she announced in a voice low enough to sound like an attempt at privacy, but loud enough to carry in the now deathly quiet room.

Malcolm looked around, bewildered, as he seemed to finally notice that every eye was on him . . . almost all of them, anyway. Jane would have bet anything that at least one of the twins was still watching her, and she instinctively kept her face expressionless.

Lynne held the glass out at arm's length, and a terrified-looking waiter appeared to whisk it away just a split second before she let it drop. "Yuri's out front. He'll come back for us later. I'll call ahead and make sure there's coffee on." The words were maternal, but the tone was one of emotionless command.

Malcolm spun on his heel—quite steadily, Jane noticed—and stalked out of the party without another word. The low hum of chatter began again, and Jane felt more than just the three pairs of eyes on her now. *Who wouldn't stare*, she wondered, *after a TMZ-worthy scene like that?* She wanted to follow Malcolm and make sure that he was all right—and, admittedly, ask some questions as well—but she worried about making his exit seem even more dramatic than it had been already. And . . . would he even *want* to see her, or would he just blow her off again? Did she really want to find out?

While Jane wavered, Maeve stepped directly in front of her, her brown eyes hard. "They were watching you," she murmured, her voice so low that Jane could barely hear it. "They don't trust you. And Malcolm was angry."

Jane seriously considered snapping at her friend to go away. She really didn't need a recap of the last thirty seconds; she needed a Perfectly Rational Explanation. She had taken about as much cryptic behavior as she could stand, and it was getting exhausting. To her horror, Jane felt herself actually beginning to sway in her strappy silver sandals, and she decided that anger at Maeve was energy she really couldn't spare at the moment.

Tears welled up, stinging her eyes, and she grimaced. Smeared mascara would be the icing on a night like this one. "I don't think I've ever felt so much like an outsider in my life," she whispered. "I don't know what they want from me."

Maeve stared at her for a long moment, her eyes searching. Finally they went wide. "You really don't have any idea," she whispered, looking absolutely stunned. Jane shook her head and shrugged, trying harder than ever not to cry. Maeve's lips pressed into a thin line, and her eyes blazed with sudden determination. She opened her mouth to speak, but the voice that cut the air between them wasn't hers.

"Jane!" Maeve flinched and Jane whirled to find Lynne towering over her. Lynne was staring furiously at Maeve, but as she spoke to Jane, her voice regained its usual thrumming softness. "There are more people you need to meet, dear," she said, her eyes never leaving Maeve's face. Under her light dusting of freckles, Maeve looked pale and shaken.

Jane wanted to grab Maeve and yell, "What don't I know?" But Lynne's hand clamped down firmly on Jane's arm, and there was nothing Jane could do but follow her mother-in-law-to-be back into the crowd.

Twenty-five

UNDER LYNNE'S WATCHFUL EYE, JANE GRITTED HER TEETH AND chatted with Ben Jameson (the up-and-coming state senator), Sandy Kovanski (the new *Times*' food critic), and his wife, Bethany (who was from one of the oldest families in New York). During Samuel Robero, Esquire's, seemingly endless description of pending legislation to allow for prosecuting corporate whistle-blowers, Jane thought that she glimpsed Maeve outside in the sculpture garden. But the door felt impossibly far away, especially with Lynne at her side, apparently hell-bent on dragging out each conversation for as long as humanly possible before steering Jane toward the next one.

Lynne had had a point at that first lunch, Jane realized: being a Doran was downright exhausting. She could already feel that she would wake up drained and empty the next morning; an afternoon of calling caterers for April's ASPCA-looza would be about all she could handle. However irritated she was at Lynne, Jane was forced to grudgingly admire the woman. She took her role as matriarch incredibly seriously, and watching her face round after round of inane socializing with unflagging intensity was kind of impressive.

Finally, while Kathleen Houck (heiress to a pharmaceutical fortune) was happily comparing the merits of various hybrid car models, Jane felt Lynne draw silently away from their little circle. *I guess she thinks I finally have the hang of it?* But Jane had no interest in continuing her slow circuit of the room. She counted to twenty in her head, and then excused herself: it was long past time to find Maeve.

Jane had accumulated so many questions during her three weeks in New York that she wasn't entirely sure what she was expecting to hear. The night, the Dorans themselves, was like a strange scattering of puzzle pieces, and she had a feeling that Maeve could make sense of the larger picture.

She headed purposefully to the sculpture garden, but the fierce crop of red curls was conspicuously absent from the clusters of guests scattered around. Jane began to work her way systematically back around the room, but the closest thing she found to Maeve was Harris. *It's a start,* she decided, and had begun to stride toward him when she spotted Maeve at last, walking smoothly out through the front door.

So I didn't get an explanation, and now I don't even get a good-bye? Jane frowned, stung. Maeve's retreating form looked frail and fragile in her emerald-green cocktail dress. Watching her elfin frame, Jane realized abruptly that Maeve hadn't just skipped her good-byes: she had also bypassed the coat check. Unseasonably warm or not, it was still near eleven o'clock in January, and Maeve would freeze with nothing between her and the cold but a thin layer of charmeuse.

"Maeve, wait!" Jane hurried for the door, accidentally bumping into someone's rum-and-Coke along the way. She heard an exclamation as the dark liquid spilled in her wake, but she barely registered the commotion. The short hallway that separated the door from the lobby was empty and dark, but Jane caught sight of Maeve as she drifted outside. She glowed like a torch on the sidewalk, the streetlamps reflecting off her creamy skin. Maeve didn't seem to notice the cold at all; in fact, she was walking slowly toward the street, arms relaxed at her sides. Was she drunk?

That was when Jane noticed another woman—very tall, wearing a smart brown sheath—standing just outside the streetlamp's circle of light. *Lynne.* She had left the party to . . . stand outside the museum in the cold? Jane hesitated in the lobby, confused. It made an odd tableau: two women in cocktail-wear in the middle of the night on a deserted street.

Not deserted, exactly. The light at the corner winked green and a cadre of cars started toward the museum. As Jane waited for Maeve to raise her arm to hail a cab, an odd tingling stirred the fine hairs on her bare arms, as if millions of tiny electric shocks were bouncing through her veins, rooting Jane to her spot on the marble floor. She could see Lynne's lips moving. The sound didn't reach her, but she could see that Lynne was staring at Maeve with a malevolent intensity. In the darkness, her eyes looked like twin tar-pits, black and bottomless. Then Jane felt another surge of electricity dance through her blood as Maeve, arms still at her sides, stepped off the curb into oncoming traffic.

"Maeve, stop!" Jane shouted. Her limbs finally sprung to life and she launched herself outside. "Maeve!"

But her friend just continued out into the middle of the street, her glossy black pumps tapping distinctly over the roar of approaching traffic.

"*Stop,*" Jane screamed again.

Maeve paused in the middle of the walkway, looking luminous, fragile, and, apparently, completely invisible to the driver of the taxi bearing down on her.

Screams rent the air as Maeve folded against the bumper of the car like a piece of tissue paper. Her body slid limply across the hood before striking the ground with a dull thud. It was only then that Jane heard the screeching of brakes and several loud blows of horns. *Too late.* Her thoughts felt slow, disconnected. *Way, way too late.*

Women shrieked, men bellowed, and the entire cocktail party spilled outside. Harris shoved past Jane as he ran toward his sister's collapsed form. She followed him numbly, sidestepping the driver, who was shaking and babbling beside his taxi as if those two tons of metal had driven into Maeve of their own volition.

"She's breathing, thank God," Harris cried, his cell phone in his hand before Jane fully registered his words. In the beat before his call connected, he looked up and saw Jane hovering over him. "Get a doctor," he snapped coldly, and then turned away to give their location to the 911 operator.

Jane stumbled back to the crowd of dazed-looking partygoers milling around in front of the museum. Her carefully crafted guest list swam in front of her mind's eye. *There was Dr. Headly-Kim, and Dr. Tamez, and Dr. Wilson, but I'm pretty sure his PhD was in something like politics.*

"She needs a doctor," Jane croaked as loudly as she could, and was relieved to see a stocky man, bald head shining under the streetlamp, remove his tuxedo jacket and move toward the Montagues purposefully. Maeve lay perfectly, painfully still, and that immobility brought Jane back to the moments before the accident.

Lynne.

Wind whipped around her bare shoulders and the wail of sirens zoomed closer and closer. She couldn't see the tall woman anywhere in the crowd. She realized belatedly that she didn't remember passing Lynne when she had run out to the curb. It was as if Lynne had vanished clear off the sidewalk. But that was impossible . . . right?

Jane's blood hummed through her veins and her silver ring vibrated on her finger, and suddenly she knew exactly what Maeve had been ready to tell her back at the party.

And that Lynne had been prepared to kill Maeve to keep her from doing just that.

Twenty-six

"WHERE ARE YOU?" JANE HISSED INTO HER PHONE AS THE EMTs loaded Maeve into the ambulance.

"Across from the Plaza, in the park," Malcolm replied. He sounded hollow, almost tinny, and defeated.

"Don't go anywhere," Jane ordered. Then she turned to Harris and squeezed his hand as he climbed into the ambulance. "I'll be there as soon as I can," she promised him before striding off into the darkness. His face looked so closed that for a moment Jane was sure he was going to tell her to stay away. No doubt he had connected the same dots Jane had and realized that his sister nearly died because of her friendship with Jane. But he just nodded and let the EMTs close the door behind him.

Jane quickly fetched her coat from upstairs, then, ducking out the fire stairway, made her way to the park. She longed to be in the ambulance with the Montagues, holding Maeve's hand and whispering that everything would be all right. But first she needed to hear the truth, out loud, from the one person who had owed it to her from the beginning.

Malcolm was waiting by the entrance to Central Park, the streetlamp beside him washing him out to a ghostly pallor. At the sight of him, she felt the now-familiar electric thrum of magic building in her blood. He started to speak when he saw Jane approaching, but she held up a hand to stop him. "Tell me," she demanded, her voice as hard as steel. She felt the magic curling through her words, and when he drew in a sharp breath, she knew that Malcolm could feel it, too. "I want to know everything."

He hesitated for the briefest of moments. "Not here," he said, scanning the street around them. He turned and led her wordlessly along an asphalt path until there was nothing around them but trees and a lonely-looking bench. He signaled for her to sit.

"My mother is a witch," he said simply, and Jane felt, more than saw, the lamp closest to them blow out in a brilliant shower of sparks.

"Understatement," she growled. The corners of Malcolm's full mouth twitched up into the shadow of a smile.

He turned serious again as he studied her face in the semidarkness. "You're not surprised," he concluded, and reached for her left hand. His fingers were warm as he traced hers, moving around but not quite touching Celine Boyle's softly glowing silver legacy.

"No. I'm not." Her voice was flat and cold. The pieces of the puzzle were falling into place too quickly now, and too neatly. Lynne was a witch. Malcolm knew that Jane was a witch—had immediately recognized the plain silver band on her finger for what it was. She remembered how he had lifted her hand at the farmhouse after her grandmother died. He must have known, but he hadn't said a thing. Why would he hide his own family history once he saw hers out in the open? Why go to such lengths to keep his identity a secret, once he knew that it was something they could have shared? Unless . . . She lifted her face up toward his with enormous effort. "How long have you known what I can do?"

Two squirrels rustled in the bushes next to them and the barren branches of the oak tree overhead waved in the slight breeze. Malcolm sighed, as quick to read her tone as he always had been. "Her magic—your magic—is genetic. It passes through the female line and pretty much skips the men. So if you have a daughter, she'll be born with magic, and born able to inherit more." His dark eyes bored into hers. "But that wouldn't be true for my own daughter. Unless . . ." He shifted uncomfortably, apparently unsure of how to go on.

Jane thought of Rosalie Goddard, then pictured the Dorans' family tree branching through centuries of women—of witches—before coming to an inglorious end with Malcolm, his male cousins, and poor six-year-old Annette. No wonder Lynne had been so desperate to replace her dead little girl, racing her own biological clock to keep her family legacy going. *She'd have done anything* . . . Jane was abruptly sure that whatever had gone wrong in Charles's brain, it had nothing to do with "experimental medication" and everything to do with misguided magic. She struggled to bring her mind back to what Malcolm was trying to tell her. *His children wouldn't be magical . . . but mine would.* "Unless you had a baby with me," she finished for him. Her tongue felt thick and heavy in her mouth.

He shrugged evasively, dropping his eyes. "Sometimes the

spark can come back after a generation or two, if just the right people match up. Someone like Maeve—"

"Maeve?" Jane asked harshly. She shuddered involuntarily, remembering Harris's shuttered face as he climbed into the ambulance with his sister. Malcolm, misunderstanding her movement, tore off his cashmere overcoat and wrapped it around her shoulders—playing the perfect gentleman, even now. She decided not to protest: she felt cold and empty from the inside out. Now, in some small measure, Malcolm would, too.

"Her father is like me," he explained, and she realized he had no idea that Maeve was currently fighting for her life in an emergency room somewhere uptown. He had missed everything that had followed his strange scene with Lynne. "His mother was a witch, but he isn't and his wife isn't, so his kids aren't. Just like my kids wouldn't be, if I had married—" He bit his lip. *Anyone else,* Jane's mind supplied numbly. *If you had married anyone but a witch.* "The blood's still there in all of them, though," Malcolm went on smoothly, "so you never know for sure." He blew on his hands. "It might have worked. But—"

"But Lynne didn't want to take that chance," Jane finished dully. Lynne wouldn't leave a thing this important to luck; she wouldn't settle for a "maybe" from her firstborn son. After all, Lynne had a position to maintain. Jane's heart began to pound, and electricity crackled to life in her veins. Another lamp flickered and burst.

Her throat was so tight she could barely force out the next question. "Why were you at that auction house in Paris?"

Malcolm dropped his face into his hands. "Because my mom knew you were going to be there." Emotion muffled his voice. "Madame Godinaux is a family friend."

Jane rubbed her temples. She could barely hold her hand up—the silver ring felt like it weighed a hundred pounds. So it had all been planned—right down to her first solo client. She remembered how she and Elodie had sat on her miniscule terrace the night Madame Godinaux called to hire her. They had toasted Jane's career with champagne, Notre Dame looming in the distance.

"Why me, Malcolm? There have to be other witches." *Witches who don't require an elaborate farce of a seduction.*

He sighed again, looking suddenly thinner in the moonlight as his secrets poured out of him.

"Mom was pretty sure you didn't know. It would've been harder with someone who did; it might have even been a fight. Magic can be passed on, but it can also be stolen, so families that have it usually don't get along." He grimaced. "That's another understatement, actually: they spend most of their time in hiding or at war with each other. But Celine was so careful, so secretive, that Mom figured we could just bring you into the family without you knowing about all that."

Easy as that. She thought bleakly about Lynne's inappropriate interest in her sex life—of course it would be better for the Dorans if she had a daughter as soon as humanly possible. *And then they'd make sure I "accidentally" walked off a cliff or something before I figured out what was going on.*

"And I think there was more," Malcolm admitted. "She said something once about your family . . . there were a lot of names I didn't know, but I think that she was saying that they're strong. I think that they had a lot more magic left than most families do these days—maybe even more than ours. Two families have died out completely; an unbroken line of witches like you come from, I guess, is incredibly rare."

"So I was a great choice, a real purebred," Jane spit out bitterly. Then a thought occurred to her. "What if I didn't like you?" Her eyes narrowed. Was there such a thing as a love spell? Had Lynne done something to ensure their chemistry? Her skin crawled just thinking about it, and she scooted to the other end of the bench.

"Magic calls to magic," he explained in what he clearly thought was a reassuring tone. "I may not be able to use it, but half of my blood carries power, and she said it would appeal to you. But blood's not everything; it's just an attraction, just chemistry." He turned to face her squarely, his eyes imploring. "What we have is real, Jane. You can't fake true love."

She felt her mouth set into a harsh line.

"Mom calls it a kind of natural selection," he went on, floundering a little in the face of her icy glare. "The daughters of two magical parents are more powerful than the daughters of just one. Some families tried to take advantage by throwing cousins together—first cousins, even—to try to breed stronger witches, and then there were a few Romeo-and-Juliet-type stories, and then . . ."

"And then there's us," Jane whispered, feeling a chill that had nothing to do with the mist that hung in the trees. "And there's you just letting this happen—*making* it happen! So I could be some kind of brood mare for your psycho mother. Do you have *any* idea how sick you all are?" Her voice echoed along the empty pathways.

He reached toward her, but she jerked away as if his hand might burn her. "*Don't* touch me. I think you've done more than enough of that already."

"Jane, I didn't—"

"Let me guess: you were tricked. Lied to? Manipulated? Magically *compelled*? Good," she hissed, shaking his coat to the ground and wrenching the engagement ring off her finger. "Now you know how *I* feel." She threw the ring at him, hoping that the diamond was big enough to leave a mark on his perfect face, and ran blindly down the path.

"Jane!" Malcolm called.

A series of hisses and pops sounded behind her, plunging the park into darkness, but Jane just kept running.

Twenty-seven

JANE WALKED ALL THE WAY TO LENOX HILL HOSPITAL ON 77TH, focusing intently on the steady rhythm of her heels to keep herself grounded. She kept rubbing at the empty place on her ring finger; only the beveled edge of her grandmother's ring kept the feelings of loss and betrayal at bay.

She couldn't afford to think about Malcolm. If she thought too much about the last two months, she was afraid that she would fall completely to pieces over her sham of a relationship. And there were far too many things to consider right now to let that happen.

Like the fact that Lynne was a witch—a very evil one. Unlike Jane, who messed up lights when she was upset, Lynne tried to kill girls who pissed her off. The power disparity was too glaring to ignore. Lynne had probably passed the flickering-lightbulb stage before she'd hit puberty. Whereas Jane had only been aware of her power for a month, and she'd spent the bulk of that time trying to ignore it in the hope that it would go away.

She laughed wryly to herself. She'd played at being normal, hiding her magic away, worrying that it would cost her her new family. And it turned out that her magic was the only thing that had won her that family in the first place. Her fairy-tale romance with a modern-day prince had been just that: a fiction. She'd been nothing more than a puppet, with the wicked witch of the Upper East Side pulling all the strings.

"*Magic can be passed on, but it can also be stolen,*" Malcolm had told her. Gran had willingly bequeathed her magic to Jane almost six years before she died, and Jane suspected that the "stealing" option was usually a little more fatal, probably involving that "last breath" Rosalie Goddard had mentioned. And, if the overwhelming and uncontrollable rush of magic in the days that had followed Jane's acceptance of the ring was any indication, then she had an awful lot of power to steal. She was a walking target for power-hungry witches, and until tonight she had foolishly assumed that no one would notice.

She could never go back to the mansion, obviously, but she didn't know whom to turn to, whom to trust. Gran hadn't left any clues about that.

Jane reached the hospital at last and stepped into the brightly lit waiting room of the ER. Her eyes locked on Harris immediately, his lean face drawn and pale. He looked as though he was sorely tempted to hit her. "Get out," he growled.

Jane stepped forward and placed a tentative hand on his crisp white sleeve. When he tried to shrug her off, she could tell by the set of his shoulders that he was close to crying.

"I only found out tonight," Jane whispered, feeling him go

rigid at the words. "I know what she did, and I'm done. With all of them."

Harris's eyes went wide and round, as his sister's always did, and he started to step around Jane. She followed his gaze over her shoulder, noticing an older man wearing surgical scrubs waving him over.

"Mr. Montague," the doctor said in a reedy voice. "Your sister's going to be just fine. We have her resting in the ICU for now, but her vitals are steady, and there's no reason she can't be moved out of intensive care in a couple of days."

Jane's breath rushed out of her all at once, and there was no time to recover it before Harris pulled her close and crushed her against his ribs in a wild bear-hug.

"You'll be able to see her in a few hours, but I should warn you that her injuries are extensive. I'm sure you're excited, but try to keep things calm and let her rest," the doctor finished.

"We promise," Harris said solemnly into Jane's hair. "Thank you."

"She's okay," Jane breathed in disbelief, trying to get the information through to her brain.

"Thank *God*," Harris said, letting her go and sitting heavily in one of the sturdy waiting-room chairs. Jane followed suit in the seat beside him. They sat silently while the clock overhead clicked away a few hundred seconds.

"You must be freezing," Harris declared after a while, and Jane jumped a little. She glanced down at her strappy heels, her toes an icy blue beneath her pedicure. Had tonight really started with a party?

"I'm okay." It was true: she was far too wrapped up in her thoughts to feel any physical discomfort.

"Don't be ridiculous." He pulled her to her feet. "You need to warm up. *We* need coffee. And privacy. Now."

Oh, right. I may have admitted to knowing that magic was real, a few minutes back. Jane trailed obediently after Harris down the antiseptic hallways. It was her first time in an American hospital, and it was much more sterile and anonymous than the cramped clinic Gran had taken Jane to when she had broken her arm climbing a tree in their backyard.

After a few twists and turns down seemingly identical corridors, Harris led Jane into the cafeteria. The room smelled of instant mashed potatoes and burned gravy. The fluorescent lighting was dimmed to a flat gray, and the only other person in the room was the chubby man behind the cash register, who rang up their tepid coffees.

Harris located a private nook in the cafeteria and kept his voice carefully low as he explained everything that Malcolm just had. "It's a whole network here, a clique really." He traced a crack in the plywood table with his thumbnail. "We all attended the same schools, went to the same parties. We know everything about the other families—and sometimes even intermarry to keep our powers viable—but we never, ever trust one another."

Jane nodded numbly and took a sip of the coffee. It tasted like sludge.

"The number of eligible witchy bachelorettes had sharply declined in the last couple of generations," Harris went on, "so these awkward alliances have become even more desperately important. Even though Maeve and I are a full generation removed from any kind of magic, Maeve has received six marriage proposals from concerned aunts and grandmothers trying to reignite their line's magic."

"How long have you known all this?" Jane asked, thinking about Gran's letter. She had dedicated her entire life to keeping Jane hidden, and here was a whole society of witches flourishing in New York. After tonight, though, Jane realized that her grandmother probably had the right idea after all.

"Mother explained all this when I was ten," Harris murmured, casting an eye to the cash register. It looked like the old man had fallen asleep. Sure enough, a light snore carried across the otherwise empty room. "She wanted me to understand why my girlfriends' mothers would practically be throwing their daughters into my bed. We had to be so, so careful our whole lives; everything was a manipulation."

"There's so much I don't know," she told Harris, quickly sketching out her background. "I don't know the full extent of my powers, and I can't control the ones I do know about. I'm not even in the same hemisphere as Lynne."

"I can't do magic myself," Harris said, running his hands over his coppery curls. "Maeve never even wanted to learn. She thinks the whole idea is lame. But our grandmother could, and she used to tell me about it. I might know something useful—I might be able to help." He cast his eyes down, looking suddenly shy. "If you want."

Jane blushed: she wanted. She thought about what Malcolm had told her, how magic called to magic. That definitely explained the pull she felt when she was around Harris, the latent sparks. *Damn it.* Was she ever going to get to just choose someone without supernatural help?

Malcolm.

She shuddered. Harris's openness, his clear and honest green eyes, made Malcolm's ability to deceive her even more frightening. How could someone be so two-faced? How could he have lied to her over and over? And it wasn't just with his words, but with gestures, smiles, touches ...

And Malcolm's deception had led to the horrible events of the night, to Maeve lying broken in a hospital bed somewhere above them, fighting for her life.

"Thank you, but no."

"Look." He leaned across the table and grabbed her wrists. "I know what you're thinking. But you can't do this alone."

Tears filled Jane's eyes. "Maeve is here because of me."

Harris shook his head stubbornly. "No, she's here because of Lynne. She's always had it in for us. You were just an excuse, but she'd throw either one of us under a bus just for sport if she thought it wouldn't make headlines."

"Is that supposed to make me worry less?" The corner of her mouth curled up in a bitter half-smile. After a moment, his quirked up in a matching one.

"Seriously." He leaned in closer, his eyes dancing just a little. "Did Mae ever tell you about the spring break when we ran into Malcolm and Blake in Rio?" He launched into an involved story about a nude beach, three underage models, and a taxi driver who smuggled parakeets on the side.

After a few moments, she relaxed under his grip.

"Jane," he murmured in a softer tone, stroking her palms with his thumbs. "I'm just saying that there's history," he went on gently. "You just walked into this, but we've been sparring for generations. My cousin Mary set Blake up to get thrown out of prep school for cheating. Lynne's aunt—the twins' mother—tried to poison my grandfather when he was ten years old. We live with danger and distrust all the time; we're used to it. Mae assumed you were playing her when you first met, but she decided to go along and see where it led. She knew she was getting into something dangerous. It may not have been for the reason she thought, but she knew what could happen."

Jane bit her lip, hard. The metallic taste of blood seeped onto her tongue.

"I can help you. And trust me, you need help," he finished earnestly. He stood up, slid around to Jane's side of the table, and put his arm around her. She rested her head on his shoulder, utterly exhausted.

She had to admit that Harris was making sense. Going it alone would be stoic, to be sure. But was it realistic?

"Stay," Harris whispered into her ear, sending shivers down her spine. *Magic calls to magic,* she thought grimly. She sat up straight and shrugged off his arm.

"I can't stay here, it's not safe for anyone," she said resolutely. "But I will be in touch." She rested her hand on Harris's for the briefest of moments, then stood. Harris looked baffled, and concerned, as she made her way out of the cafeteria. But no matter how appealing Harris's offer of help was, Jane had brought enough trouble to the Montagues already. She would have to go into hiding and build a brand-new life from the ground up. She would have to start immediately . . . and alone.

Twenty-eight

JANE WRAPPED HER COAT TIGHTLY AROUND HER BODY AS SHE pushed through the hospital's large, wheelchair-accessible revolving doors to the street, almost walking directly into the side of a screamingly red Porsche parked in the center of the ambulance lane. The passenger window was rolled down, and Malcolm was clearly visible in the driver's seat. "Please get in," he begged, his voice hoarse.

She backed up determinedly and set a new course for the sidewalk. "Get away from me," she ordered, not bothering to turn around. She felt her shoulders set tensely in her sleeveless dress, and wondered if he could tell she was afraid.

"Jane."

His desperate, pleading tone stopped her short, and she turned to face him before her mind fully registered what she was doing.

His dark eyes were wide and wild, and his jaw was clenched so firmly that she could see the muscles standing out under his skin. In spite of his obvious ability to deceive her—or perhaps because she was so familiar with every facial expression that accompanied his lies—she instinctively recognized this face as a genuine one. Her body responded to it with absolute certainty before her mind could go through all of the necessary calculations to make a decision. She opened the passenger door and slid onto the creamy white leather of the seat, for no other reason than that she was exhausted and didn't know where else to go. Malcolm, not giving her a chance to change her mind, threw the car into gear. They left the hospital far behind in a matter of seconds.

The flat brick and concrete façades of buildings flew by them in a blur until they reached the first red light. The stillness inside the car while they waited for the light to change was painfully awkward, and Malcolm proceeded more slowly from then on, taking advantage of the timed lights on Lexington Avenue so they didn't have to stop again.

"Where are you taking me?"

At the sound of her voice, Malcolm jerked the car onto a narrow side street and cut the engine. When he twisted to face her, his dark eyes were intense. "You didn't let me finish back in the park." His voice was almost a growl. "Jane, I'm in love with you."

She rolled her eyes. She'd fallen for that ploy once, but it was kind of lame to try it again. "Malcolm, I'm exhausted. Did you actually have anything to tell me, or are you just stalling for the hell of it?"

She had to give him points for committing to his line; he didn't even blink at her frosty tone. If anything, the lines of his face became even more sincere. "I know I'm just an asshole who lied to you now, but I need to fix this. I mean it, Jane. I am desperately in love with you, and I can't let anything happen to you."

"So you're delaying my timely escape?" she asked incredulously.

"Jane, you can't just run off with the clothes on your back and no plan." He shook his head. A golden curl landed on his forehead, and he flicked at it in a frustrated way. "She'll catch you, and she'll know you're on to her, and I really don't want to think about what she'll do then."

He had a point. She made a quick tally of the items in her little vintage beaded clutch: Givenchy Maharani Rose lipstick, three safety pins, a metal-free hair elastic, a $20 bill, and her MetroCard. She didn't even have an ID, since she had dismissed her passport as "too bulky." *Genius move.*

"I'm listening," she told Malcolm stiffly, trying to sound as unconvinced as she could, in spite of the huge amount of sense he was starting to make.

"Stay," he said simply, and she frowned. "Stay, and act like nothing's changed."

"But things *have* changed," she pointed out, feeling some of her earlier anger beginning to bubble back up. How could he think that she could just let the night's revelations go? There was only one person who would be served by that, and it wasn't her. Jane narrowed her eyes suspiciously. "And your solution is to go along with Lynne's bizarre plan, except with her victim's consent this time? Your thinking is that I should just give up and do exactly what she wants? How convenient. Why shouldn't I believe that this isn't just some last-ditch con you and your mother cooked up between Central Park and here?"

He seemed to be considering her question for a moment. "Have you ever heard my thoughts?" he asked after a long pause. "Because you could try reading my mind."

Jane shook her head truthfully. "I've never gotten a thing from you."

Malcolm looked thoughtful. "Too bad, but I'm not surprised. Magic is its own security. You won't be able to read actual witches at all, and it seems that I've got enough magic in my blood to make it pretty tough. It would take a lot of power and control, and you're still new."

Jane thought of the soothing mental silence of the Dorans' home. *One more thing about magic I didn't know.* She cursed herself for wasting the past month enjoying the quiet and ignoring her inheritance. Even if she hadn't been able to break through her prospective in-laws' mental barriers, she might have at least learned enough to be suspicious of them. "So I guess your mother can read your thoughts?"

"Why do you think I've stayed away so much? Mom started seeing you in my mind a lot more than she thought was healthy. You're a pretty memorable-looking woman, you know. Especially tonight," he added with a pointed look at her cocktail dress. She kicked herself mentally for registering his compliment with a blush. Now that they were in a tiny, enclosed space together, it was difficult to keep up her icy reserve. He might be a sociopathic liar, but he was also Malcolm.

"She can't get into your head," he continued, "which she hates, by the way. But given what she's seen in mine . . ." His face hardened and he gripped the steering wheel fiercely, and Jane wondered just what sort of things Lynne had been privy too. "Which is why I need to leave. Tonight."

Her first impulse was to scream at him. To yell and sob about his betrayal of her at every level, to ask how he could dump all this on her and then just run away. But her sense of danger trumped her fury: no good could come of Malcolm being around his mother. A cab flew past them on the otherwise empty street.

"Where are you going?" Her own voice was so calm and rational that she didn't immediately recognize it.

"It's better that you don't know that."

"How long?"

"Awhile. I need to plan, to move money, book flights, get forgeries, buy real estate. To get everything ready so that when I get you out of here, it's to a life that's worth having."

"How much time?" she asked again.

"I just want to keep you safe, and I need time to make that happen."

His voice was so intense that she suspended her disbelief for long enough to avoid a cutting response. She didn't have a plan that was better than his, and she certainly didn't have his resources. Besides, her instincts—her damned, faulty instincts—were telling her to trust him.

"We have a perfect excuse to leave New York in just over a month. Together, and with no one asking any questions, or expecting to hear from us for weeks."

"The honeymoon," Jane breathed. They were supposed to be going to Belize. "You want to go through with the wedding?"

In the faint light from the street, she couldn't see if he was blushing, but the slightly strangled note in his voice made her think that it was likely. "I love you, Jane," he repeated, more awkwardly this time. "Enough to leave you after we escape if you can't bear to be around me. But I can't lie to you—not anymore. I want to be with you for the rest of my life, no matter where that life ends up being." Something glinted between them, and she realized that it was her engagement ring. "Losing you, even for just a couple of hours tonight, was torture."

She took the ring from him, turning it curiously between her fingers. She knew intellectually that it was the same ring she'd thrown at him in the park, but she found herself looking for subtle changes—a flaw here, a nick there.

It hasn't changed, she reminded herself, tracing the arc of the band. *I have—and so has our relationship.*

This time around, she and Malcolm would finally have a true partnership: they were in this together, united against his mother. And she certainly couldn't fight Lynne without him.

She met his dark eyes and slid on the ring, feeling the familiar click of it against the plain silver band on her next finger. "I can't make any promises, but we can try."

Malcolm nodded and reached for the Porsche's keys. His fingers trembled.

Impulsively, she reached out and took the keys. "Wait," she insisted. All of a sudden, she couldn't bear to let him leave like that, so cold and formal. *We have to start over now,* she thought as she unbuckled her seat belt. *We have to make new promises. We have no one but each other, and we need to have each other completely.*

She slid her right leg over the gearshift and across his body, following it sinuously until she was straddling Malcolm. The shock was evident on his face, but so was the relief—and desire. She kissed him deeply, savoring the familiar hot-champagne taste of his mouth, and fumbled blindly for a few moments until her right hand found the switch that laid his seat out horizontally. "Give me a real good-bye," she whispered, feeling the shock of their contact running under her skin like an electrical current.

It felt like the hum of magic in her blood, and she felt it harden her nipples even as it spread lower, bringing warmth and wetness between her legs before Malcolm had even had a chance to move. She shifted her hips against him and smiled hungrily as she felt his erection through his tuxedo pants: he was obviously more than ready to do as she asked.

He slid his warm hands underneath the skirt of her cocktail dress. The magic was burning under her skin now, drawing her toward Malcolm like a million tiny magnets. Their pull only relaxed when he pushed into her, and they were as close as was physically possible. She rocked back and forth on top of him, enjoying her thrumming power, until his fingers dug hard into her hips, and they came together while sparks from the overhead streetlamps showered ecstatically around the car.

It was a good-bye and a new beginning, all in one.

Twenty-nine

"... SUBSTITUTE IN *PEONIES*, AS IF THAT WOULD BE REMOTELY acceptable." Lynne dropped her fork onto the porcelain plate for emphasis, and reached for her delicate teacup. The kitchen smelled of eggs, muffins, and turkey bacon, with just the slightest soupçon of black truffle. Sofia wiped down the marble counter and placed another kettle of water on the stove.

Lynne, who oddly (and unfortunately) seemed to like the kitchen as much as Jane did, had been rambling on about wedding plans for nearly twenty minutes without pausing. Jane widened her eyes into what she hoped would be an appropriately shocked expression, but she was only barely following the saga of Lynne's many wedding-related frustrations.

Jane stifled a yawn and gladly accepted a steaming mug of imported Colombian coffee from Sofia before the maid scuttled out of the kitchen. Last night, heavy feet—Charles's?—had shuffled back and forth in front of Jane's door. She'd tossed and turned, trying to decide if it would be too paranoid to move some furniture to block it. And, if not, which of the heavy wooden antiques in the room she could even budge. Malcolm probably could have slid the huge mahogany bookcase across the doorframe, but he had gone straight to JFK after dropping her off at the forbidding stone manse. She had tried to keep reminding herself that she was safer with him away from the house, but as she lay alone in their canopied bed, it sure hadn't felt that way.

"... level of incompetence in this city is astounding ..."

To hear Lynne rambling on about corsages as if she weren't a powerful and bloodthirsty witch was absolutely surreal. The fact that this woman, in her prim, high-necked lace blouse and plum pencil skirt, was a witch at all was surreal. Jane blinked, trying to find any trace of the villainess who had brutally attacked Maeve, but as far as she could tell, the "annoyed socialite" version of Lynne wasn't actually a disguise at all: the two parts of her identity fit together seamlessly.

Jane couldn't help but be the tiniest bit envious despite herself. She'd felt split in two from the moment she had put Gran's ring on her finger and couldn't imagine ever feeling whole again.

"... just swimming in this tacky perfume like some kind of barmaid—can you imagine?"

Jane had lost the thread and settled for a combined head-shake and eye-roll, which worked for an impressive number of Lynne's tirades.

"Naturally Marie-Annick will find someone to replace her, but I simply cannot believe the level of unprofessionalism from a company that's supposed to be so highly ..."

Marie-Annick . . . Marie-Annick . . . It came to her in a flash:

Marie-Annick was the music director for the Brick Presbyterian Church, where they'd be holding the ceremony. And just like that, the detached fog lifted from Jane's mind and her fingers clenched into fists. The morning after steering a two-ton taxi into a one-hundred-pound girl, Lynne was sipping ginger tea and bitching about one of the ceremony musicians' perfume.

Jane wanted to dump the scalding contents of the rattling kettle on Lynne, but considering the fact that the older woman could literally kill her with the blink of an eye, she forced a submissive smile onto her face. To keep her hands occupied, she reached for a bagel half.

"Jane Boyle, what do you think you're doing?" Lynne's tirade ended in a shout, and she knocked the bagel out of Jane's hands.

Jane's heart started pounding and she nearly jumped out of her chair in shock. *This is it,* she thought wildly, looking for something, anything, she might be able to use to defend herself. Her eyes landed on a butter knife and she gripped it rigidly in her left hand.

But Lynne was oblivious to Jane's sudden battle-readiness, busily digging into the bagel half with a teaspoon. When there was nothing left but an empty crust, she handed it back to Jane with a bright smile. "It's a neat little trick, if you have trouble controlling what you eat," she said, her strange, dark eyes examining Jane's waist. "Our last dress fitting is less than a month away, dear!"

Officially the worst prospective mother-in-law ever, Jane decided, using her would-be weapon to spread fat-free cream cheese on her bagel shell. "Thanks," she mumbled, trying to not glare too obviously at the unappetizing result.

"You weren't raised in New York," Lynne declared, her voice

back to its snake-charmer purr, "so I know it's hard for you to understand. But this wedding is extremely important, right down
to the commas in the invitation. We have a position in this city
and every move we make is scrutinized and judged and dragged
through the press in case anyone important missed the live version. Our every move must be calculated, precise. We cannot
afford the slightest mistake."

Jane shuddered in spite of herself. This woman was unbeliev-
able: she was willing to commit murder in order to procure a
magical heir, yet she was worried about the pomp and circum-
stance that went along with being one of the city's preeminent
families. The amazing thing was, Lynne could have instructed
Malcolm to elope with Jane in France and get her pregnant without ever raising her suspicions. But her desire to throw the wedding of the century and to show everyone in Manhattan that her
son was respectably married before impregnating his wife had
led to the very thing Lynne had wanted so desperately to avoid:
Jane catching wind of her plan.

"You seem distracted," Lynne observed as she sliced her egg
whites into perfectly even rectangles. "I hope you're not too upset
about Malcolm leaving again. I can't imagine what could possibly
be considered 'urgent' in the art-dealing world."

Phrasing aside, it was clearly a question—and perhaps even a
test. Malcolm had sent an e-mail to the entire family from the airport, claiming that urgent business had called him away but as-
suring them that he'd be back in time for the wedding.

Chewing her bagel slowly, Jane thought through every angle
before she answered. In Lynne's perfect world, Malcolm would
be uninterested in Jane, but Jane would be blindingly, head-over-

heels in love with Malcolm. So smitten and clueless, in fact, that she wouldn't bat an eye at his sudden departure just one month before their happy day. Her toes curled at how well she'd unwittingly conformed to that insipid role for the past month.

"I'm not worried at all," she answered, forcing a bright note into her voice. "I love that he takes his work so seriously." To her own ears, she sounded positively moronic, but Lynne beamed approvingly.

Then her peach mouth rearranged itself into a stern expression, and she leaned forward a little. Jane's impulse was to lean away, but she swallowed her revulsion and stayed put. "Did he happen to mention to you where he was going?"

Jane shivered in spite of herself. She felt like a mouse facing a snake at feeding time, but Malcolm had assured her that her mind was like a locked vault to Lynne, so she met Lynne's eyes and plastered on her most vapid smile. "Um, Spain I think?" she lied.

"Ugh. I hate Spain." Lynne sniffed. "It's so hot in the summer, and that rioja stuff could strip paint."

Jane, who loved rioja second only to French wines, resisted the urge to point out that it was still January. Instead, she took an aggressive bite of her unsatisfying bagel shell while Lynne sipped her tea. The older woman's glance fell on a glossy, gold-embossed folder in the wedding-planning stack and she fluidly snapped back into gear. "Our head-count has gone up again, so I'll have to fax the caterer. But the bakery didn't have a fax, as I recall"—she flipped through the folder in frustration—"so perhaps you could call."

The bakery. A pair of wide-set amber eyes swam in front of Jane. *Diana. Dee, who thought magic was genetic.* Not as certain a source of help as Harris would have been, but a much, much safer one, given that Lynne had no clue who Dee was. "I was planning on shopping in SoHo anyway," she improvised. "I'll just stop by."

Sofia bustled into the kitchen to check on the boiling water, then quietly left again.

"Fine." Lynne passed Jane the folder and cleared her throat significantly. "Now, are you sure we need to invite that redheaded friend of yours to the wedding? If she gets drunk enough to lunge into traffic on a regular weeknight, just imagine the scene she would make at the wedding!"

The words slammed into Jane with the force of that speeding taxi. She crushed the remnants of her bagel crust in her fist. "She wasn't drunk," Jane hissed, seething.

"I'm sorry, dear, but I saw the whole thing," Lynne replied mildly. "Now I'm not saying what happened wasn't horrible, but really. New York is a dangerous place—she should be more careful."

Rage and electricity spiked hotly through Jane's limbs and the kettle let out a low whine that rose quickly toward a shriek. For a delicious moment, Jane fantasized about having enough power to lift the copper vessel from the stove and bash it into Lynne's smug smile. This bitch so needed to be taken down. But then Sofia rushed in, and Jane was brought back to her senses. *Someday Lynne will get hers, but right now I have to keep my head.*

"You know what? You're right. Disinvite her—and the brother," Jane said briskly, making a snap decision. "We need to make sure that everything goes smoothly."

Lynne beamed, and Jane tried hard not to grind her teeth together. She hated to even pretend to be disloyal, but the only way to keep the Montagues safe was to make Lynne think they weren't a threat.

The decision made, she shoved her chair back and grabbed the folder, exiting the kitchen to the impossibly domestic noise of Sofia pouring another cup of tea for Lynne.

Thirty

HATTIE'S BUSTLING PRESENCE IN THE BAKERY PREVENTED JANE from having any meaningful type of conversation with Dee. Luckily, a crème-fleurette crisis had given Jane just enough time to secure an invitation to that evening's meeting of Dee's coven before she had hastily retreated to fill out her "shopping" cover story. By the time it was late enough to head to Brooklyn for the gathering, Jane had collected an impressive assortment of bags, an activity that had the added advantage of preventing her from thinking too hard about what she was about to do. Two months ago, she hadn't known witches existed, and now she was joining a *coven*, for God's sake.

When she exited the subway in Park Slope, she felt as though she'd arrived in an entirely different city. Quaint little shops lined the streets and no building was taller than four floors. One grocery store even had a street-level parking lot, unheard-of in Manhattan—or Paris, for that matter.

Though it was only seven, the sidewalks and streets were nearly empty. A dark town car turned the corner, and an old woman pushed a grocery cart down a side street. Despite the relative calm, Jane couldn't quite shake the feeling that someone was watching her. *Stop being paranoid*, she told herself sharply, but she hugged her heavy purse close to her chest. She would never again leave the house without her passport, French debit card, and a copy of Malcolm's AmEx—just in case. With another surreptitious glance around, she hurried down Berkeley Place, past a school playground, until she reached Dee's stoop.

A cheerful Dee ushered her inside her one-bedroom. The tiny living room had an accent wall in brilliant red, and a threadbare Oriental carpet reached from corner to corner. There was no couch; instead, a pile of cushions in silk and velvet dotted the carpet. A wrought-iron chandelier boasted four fat, lit candles, and seven more candles sat on a rough-hewn wood bench pushed against the red wall. It looked like something out of a CW show about trendy twentysomething witches—albeit a low-budget one—but Jane reminded herself to keep an open mind. This might be her only avenue to learning more about her abilities.

Five other women were crammed into the room. Dee wove among them, trying not to trip over her own furniture, a plate of warm chocolate-chip cookies in hand. Jane, eager for an excuse not to try to make small talk, snatched one up. It tasted, in a word, magical. "Oh my God, you made these? Would you switch my wedding cake for a giant one of these? I'll take all the blame."

Dee giggled, her amber eyes glittering. "Glad you like it, but the wedding cookie's a no-go. Your about-to-be mother-in-law locked the order, so you're stuck with vanilla-and-orange-blossom sponge cake with cognac buttercream and all the fondant doves we can roll in one kitchen. And, of course, 'absolutely nothing that looks in any way like a cake-topper,'" she added, doing such a flawless impression of Lynne that Jane flinched.

A girl with spiky brown hair and a long batik tunic laughed. "Man, I hope the guy's worth it."

"I don't think they *make* guys worth that," a tall blonde with a lip-ring teased, slipping an arm around the spiky-haired girl's shoulders. "But to each her own." She grinned at Jane. "I'm Kara, and this is Brooke, and feel free to ignore me if it's true love and all that."

Jane smiled faintly, but didn't quite know what to say. "The wedding is just a charade so we can flee the country" was hardly an ice-breaker, but it was difficult to summon a genuine-seeming rush of enthusiasm for her upcoming nuptials.

Fortunately, at that moment Dee called them all over to the circle of cushions, and Jane hovered uncertainly at its edge. "Come on, Jane," Dee urged. "It's just a meditation, nothing scary."

"I don't want to intrude," Jane mumbled, perching tentatively on a red silk pillow with faintly Indian-looking embroidery. *Or blow the fuses, or die of boredom, or anything else obnoxiously conspicuous.* But the faces of the other women were uniformly welcoming and pleasant. She smiled back at them shyly.

"We've been looking everywhere for a seventh person," Kara whispered from a cushion beside Jane's. "It's a magic number." She winked, her lip-ring glinting in the candlelight.

"Everyone, please close your eyes," Dee intoned, and Kara

clamped her lips together and shut her eyes in exaggerated compliance.

Jane obeyed as well, and inhaled deeply. The smoky flower-and-ashes scent of the incense scratched her throat and made her feel light-headed.

"The Circle is gathered; the Circle is cleansed." Dee's voice was so husky Jane didn't recognize it at first. "We call on the guardians of the Watchtower of the North, and we bring an offering of Earth to the Circle to remind ourselves of the life that flourishes beneath our feet. We call on the guardians of the Watchtower of the West, and we bring an offering of Water to the Circle to remind ourselves that blessings come to us from every source. We call on the guardians of the Watchtower of the South, and we bring an offering of Fire to the Circle to remind ourselves of the passion that brings warmth and destruction in equal measure. We call on the guardians of the Watchtower of the East, and we bring an offering of Air to the Circle to remind ourselves that we are connected even when we do not touch."

Jane's conscious mind registered skepticism at the words, but the rhythm of Dee's invocation relaxed her muscles and slowed her breathing. At the very least, a relaxing evening's meditation would do her some good.

"We meet in the presence of the Horned God and the Moon Goddess," Dee went on. "She who exists as the Maiden, the Mother, and the Crone. We take her into ourselves as we pass through these stages, and become complete in ourselves. We begin as daughters but carry on as sisters, and we are each the greatest blessing to the others as we move along the paths of our lives. Please join hands as we begin our meditation."

Jane reached out blindly, but had no trouble finding the out-stretched hands on either side of her. A faint current seemed to run through them when they touched, as if a circuit had been closed. The lightheaded feeling intensified, almost as though she was floating above her pillow.

"We begin in a meadow, just as the sun is setting," Dee crooned, and Jane found that she could see the meadow clearly behind her closed eyes. Waist-high grass rippled in a light breeze, and Queen Anne's lace and yellow dandelions competed with the green stalks for sunlight. "The stars become clearer and clearer as dark-ness rolls across the sky. The sliver of the new moon rises above the horizon: tonight is a time of new beginnings, of refreshed spirits, of renewed power. Tonight is the Storm Moon, the sign that light is returning to balance with the darkness, and that the world is reawakening around us. Tonight we begin again, jour-neying far . . ."

Dee led Jane past a lake covered with waxy lily pads, along a field of wild violets, then through a thick redwood forest where the ground was spongy with moss. The other women were there with her, too, examining mushrooms and oohing at breathtaking waterfalls. The experience was much more affecting than Jane had expected. A more ordinary sort of magic.

"Now I'll start us off on our evening chant," Dee announced, "and then we will continue silently together to seal our ritual."

Jane exhaled softly as Dee slowly chanted a Latin-sounding phrase, then tapered off into silence. The syllables echoed in Jane's mind, taking root as if the words had been there all along.

After two more cycles of the chant, she realized she was no longer hearing the memory of Dee's voice. Instead, she was hear-ing a collection of voices, all chanting more or less together, creating an almost melodic harmony. *Like the wind through the attic at the Dorans',* Jane thought.

Just then, one of the voices faltered, and Jane's eyes snapped open. The girl with spiky brown hair—Brooke—was staring at her from across the circle, her eyes wild. Brooke released the hands on either side of her and fumbled to her feet. Jane instinctively did the same. Curious eyes opened as the disturbance spread around the circle. The chanting noise stopped entirely, and then six pairs of terrified eyes were fixed on Jane.

"Did I do something wrong?" she stammered, trying to figure out why they were all staring at her, but no one moved. *Not staring at me, exactly,* she realized with a start: it was as if they were looking *through* her. She turned, and then she was staring, too, because all of the candles on the wood bench behind her were *floating.* She jerked at the sight, and the candles tumbled to the ground as if they had suddenly been released. One rolled toward a cushion near Dee, who bent slowly, as if she were under water, to extinguish it.

"Um . . ." A girl whose arms were covered entirely with colorful tattoos grabbed her purse. "I forgot I had this . . . um thing? So I'm just gonna . . ." She jumped up and all but ran to the door, followed closely by two of the other women. As if a spell had quite literally been broken, everyone rose to their feet and pushed toward the exit.

"Sorry," Kara said, quirking an apologetic smile at Dee. "Too weird for my blood." She circled an arm around Brooke's shoulder and guided the shell-shocked girl gently toward the door.

Within seconds, Jane and Dee were alone in the apartment, and Jane couldn't bring herself to look anywhere but the floor. "I'm so sorry," she mumbled. "This was a mistake. Please just forget—"

"Are you kidding me?"

Jane glanced up, startled. Dee's eyes were wide, her smile even wider. Her skin shone and sheaves of tangled dark hair fell around her face. "You're one of *them*, aren't you? I was babbling away in the store that day, and this whole time you were one of them?"

Jane's mouth opened, but no sound came out. She felt trapped. She had unwittingly jumped in with both feet and given herself away in front of six strangers. Now, she realized abruptly, there was nothing to do but ask for the help she had come for. "You're right," she forced her voice to say. "It is genetic."

Dee grinned and shoved a cushion at her. "Nifty. Now would you sit the hell back down already?" Her amber eyes sparkled wickedly. "Let's find out how it works."

Thirty-one

JANE'S iPHONE INFORMED HER THAT HARRIS HAD CALLED HER seven times in twelve hours. The first time was to make sure that she was still alive, the second to tell her that Maeve had woken up briefly, the third was to remind her that she should probably get rid of her phone if she was on the run, and the last four just said, "Call me. Please." When the phone rang again for the eighth time, Jane decided to bite the bullet and answered.

Which was how, that Saturday, Harris came to be seated next to her at a triangular table at Book and Bell, Dee's favorite occult bookstore-slash-reading room on the Lower East Side. The furniture looked like leftovers from a public school, and the worn red carpet had a similar surplus feel. But the walls were covered with books, and the owner (all flowing skirts and frizzy blond hair) had discreetly returned to the front room, leaving them alone.

"Okay," Dee announced in the tone of someone formally calling a meeting to order. "Now this place is pretty good, but I've also brought some resources from home." She tapped a heavy-looking military-style backpack beside her wooden chair. Then she turned to Jane expectantly, and Harris followed suit.

After a moment's uncomfortable silence, Jane slammed her unevenly glazed mug of tea on the scarred table. "You two are supposed to help *me*. If I knew where to start I wouldn't be so pathetically screwed right now."

Dee smirked. "Well, we could start by voting in a club president, but I'm afraid Jane just shot herself in the foot. It'd be down to the two of us, Harris, and I'd hate to see you get beat by a girl."

"Touché," he said with a sly grin of his own.

"Anyway . . ." Jane prompted. "What did you bring?"

Dee kicked open her backpack and turned it upside down.

"You lugged all that from Brooklyn?" Harris asked in an impressed tone. Dee smiled modestly. Neither of her friends had been thrilled about the idea of bringing the other into Jane's quest to learn magic, but it seemed they were quickly warming up to each other.

Jane rolled her eyes and rifled through the pile. There were a few dusty, cloth-covered books, an assortment of crystals in muted amber and rose, a vial of lime-green powder, a bronze pendant, and a silver knife so slim it had to be a letter-opener. "I guess we could all just take a book and start reading," she suggested.

"Don't be a wuss," Dee complained. "I've been waiting twenty years to meet an actual witch. Now that I've got one—well, one-and-a-half," she amended with an apologetic nod to Harris, "I want to play!"

Jane frowned. They had tried to access her magic for over an hour after the botched Wicca meeting earlier that week, but without success. Jane knew she needed to learn about her magic and she was willing to try, but there was such a thing as too much pressure. Dee seemed to read her look because she playfully poked Harris in the side. He jumped. "We have three people now," Dee reminded Jane pointedly. "That's a magic number, a Circle. Like the seven of us back at my place, before you sent them all running for the hills, at least. And one of us is even packing a little extra power this time."

One of them was back at your place, too, Jane thought, remembering Brooke's wide-eyed stare when she had realized that Jane's mind was touching hers. But Jane had kept that theory private, even from Dee. No one deserved to be outed as a witch if they didn't choose to be.

Jane obediently helped Dee to arrange the letter opener—"the athame," Dee corrected piously—and a couple of the crystals on the table between them. Dee scattered some of the green powder around it, giving a husky laugh when Harris sneezed.

"Is it okay that we're doing this here?" Jane asked uncertainly.

"I'm friends with the owner," Dee replied. "She doesn't care if I make a mess, as long as I come armed with baked goods."

Jane sat sharply upright. "You have cookies? *Here?*"

"They will be your reward, *if* you cooperate." Dee looked so smug she was practically purring. "Everybody hold hands," she ordered serenely. "Jane's about to knock over that blue crystal in the middle."

Jane glowered at the blackmail, but she obediently reached out her hands. Dee's was warm and calloused, Harris's cool and smooth. She ignored the little spark that skittered down her spine when he pressed his palm to hers. She closed her eyes and tried to quiet her mind. The shop smelled like green tea and patchouli, and a dog was yapping its little head off a few floors above them.

"Every inch of your body holds magic." Dee's husky voice was hypnotic. "Begin at your feet, and look for it."

Maybe when all this is over and I'm tucked away on some private island, I'll get a dog, Jane thought to the pink darkness behind her eyelids. *Maybe a boxer or one of those wiener-looking ones. A dachshund?*

"Focus. Feel the power in your feet."

A spark shot through her left ankle. Soft as cat whiskers, it twanged and purred and tickled her Achilles tendon. *Or maybe a Doberman or a rottweiler, in case Lynne ever comes looking for me. Do they make Doberweilers?*

"Focus, Jane. Keep your mind on your power."

Jane sighed, but concentrated on emptying her mind. She tried to put her thoughts on a cloud and let them float away.

"Good. Now, gather it up and let it flow to your knees and spine," Dee intoned.

Jane's spinal column shivered with electricity.

"Okay, now lift it gently and concentrate every scrap of power behind your eyes."

Suddenly the warmth spreading through her body took flight and nestled behind Jane's eyelids, which vibrated as if her skin had been hit with thousands of tiny shocks.

"Ow!" Jane's eyes flew open. "That hurt!"

Dee grinned. "Small price to pay for having 'the power.'"

Jane scooped up a book and threatened to throw it at her.

"Hold hands!" Dee reminded her insistently, and Jane was pretty sure that Harris was trying not to laugh. Another jolt ran through her stomach, but this one had nothing to do with magic. Were Dee and Harris . . . flirting?

Dee pushed a strand of dark hair behind her ear. "I want you to gather your power again and focus every prickle of magic on moving the crystal off the pile."

Jane nodded and fixed the blue stone with a ferocious stare. Her eyes narrowed and she refused to blink, even though the dusty air was making her eyes water.

Nothing happened.

She sighed and slumped forward. *Bet Lynne could do it on the first try.*

Harris squeezed her hand reassuringly. "You can do it."

"Copper Top is right. I know you have it in you." Dee centered the crystal once more.

"Thanks, Elvira," Harris answered sardonically.

Irritated, Jane stiffened her spine back upright. Focusing intently, she gathered the magic again, clenching her jaw grimly as she fought to hold on to the electricity. It instantly slipped through her fingers. She blew through her lips and stared balefully at Dee. "Okay, I suck at this."

"You don't suck at *this*," Harris supplied helpfully, stretching his long legs out to the side of his undersized chair. "You just suck at focusing."

Jane stuck her tongue out at him.

"Try again," he urged gently, and she felt herself begin to glow under his sparkling green eyes. *Stop that,* she told herself firmly, but her self didn't seem to be listening.

"You've mentioned that things around you tend to break when you're upset. Tap into that feeling, if you can," Dee suggested. "What makes you mad?"

Lynne.

Jane's fists automatically clenched and her lips curved into a frown. Crossing her legs, Jane took a deep breath and thought about everything she hated about her soon-to-be mother-in-law. *Lynne picking that stupid pouf dress. Lynne cutting those annoying egg-white rectangles. Lynne making her son seduce me. Lynne running Maeve down.*

Suddenly, all Jane could hear was the pounding of her heart, and all she could see was her targeted crystal. It was blue, but one corner was filmier than the others, so milky as to be almost white. There was a flaw running most of the way through the middle, and a few smaller ones at the poles. Electricity crackled in Jane's ears and she sent sparking mental feelers out toward the crystal to study it further, to bring it closer to her eyes.

The crystal shuddered.

Then it began to swim and waver, and it seemed as though sparks were inside the crystal and it was glowing as if it were on fire. Then dark spots filled Jane's eyes. She fell limply out of her chair, her head striking the thin industrial carpet.

When she came to, Harris and Dee were leaning over her, grinning from ear to ear.

"I fainted?" she asked, but her leaden tongue turned it into something more like "Ah fayagh?" She grimaced.

"Not before you moved the thing," Harris told her proudly, fanning her with one of Dee's paperbacks.

She glanced at Dee for confirmation. Dee, her mouth so wide it looked as though her smile would split her face, stuffed a cookie into Jane's mouth, which Jane took as a yes.

In the midst of their gloating, Jane caught sight of the book that Harris was using to fan her face. She tried to grab it out of the air, but her reflexes sucked, and instead she wound up brushing her hand lightly across Harris's smooth chest. He didn't seem to mind, and a small part of her liked that fact. *Down, girl.* She refocused her attention on the title waving back and forth in front of her face: *A True History of Witches and Magick*, by Rosalie Goddard.

"This," she whispered, tapping the book lightly with two fingers. She was happy that her mouth seemed to be a little more obedient now, but there was no need to push her luck with unnecessary words. "We start here."

Dee snapped into action as crisply as a soldier, all traces of laughter and cookie bribes vanishing instantly. She slid the book into Jane's bulky purse, leaving Harris clutching empty air in confusion. "Love that one," she chirped. "Misty—that's the owner—has Goddard's diaries in the back, so I'll take those. And Harris, you need to start talking to your family, any time you don't need to be with your sister. Jane, get me a list of Goddard's sources to cross-check as soon as you can, but in the meantime your main responsibility is to practice your little blond head off. Okay. Everybody know their jobs?"

The three of them glanced around at each other, their eyes grave and their jaws set determinedly. If this was a war, they had just become an army.

Thirty-two

Five days later, Jane rode the uptown 6 near the MoMA to Lenox Hill, clinging to the metal pole for dear life. The train was crowded with after-work commuters, and a teenager with a faux-hawk and a Ricky's NYC bag was pressed awkwardly against her.

As part of her magical training, she'd worked diligently to read the mind of a grouchy-looking elderly woman in a white fur coat, and an African-American girl who looked to be about seven and kept touching her sparkly headband anxiously. Unfortunately, while Jane could guess at what they might be thinking, she couldn't seem to focus enough to hear anything actually coming from them. But as the train hurtled out of the 68th Street station and jolted to a stop at 77th, Jane hurtled into the chest of the faux-hawk guy.

. . . hot. I wonder if she did that on purpose? Maybe she likes my hair?

Oh man, I hope that guy at Ricky's didn't see me take the extra bottle of hair gel . . .

Jane practically skipped off the train and through the turnstile, pushing outside into a light, misting rain. The one moment of mind-reading had been exhausting, and she had a fine sheen of sweat on her forehead, but at least she hadn't blacked out.

The Hot & Crusty on the corner smelled deliciously of bagels and French vanilla coffee, and Jane had to resist the urge to go inside and devour a pain au chocolat. Or three.

She crossed the street and entered the hospital. The antiseptic smell burned her nostrils and her euphoria vanished. She could only think of Maeve, lying battered on the cold pavement outside the MoMA. The longer she had gone without actually seeing her friend, the more battered her mental picture had gotten, until she was sure that she would find Maeve at death's door with broken bones jutting through her skin at crazy angles. *She won't look worse than she looked right after she was hit,* Jane told herself as firmly as she could, but her heart still sank all the way down to her toes.

She knocked on the door of room 1070, waited a beat, and then let herself in. Harris looked more haggard than he had in the bookstore, and she guessed immediately that he hadn't been sleeping. Over the course of the last week, an increasingly droopy Harris had insisted that Maeve was "doing well," and Jane kicked herself mentally for having believed him. Clearly, there had been complications, and, just as clearly, he had been bearing the stress of it all on his own.

Maeve stirred in the bed, traces of yellow puffiness still distinctly visible across her face. Her copper eyes were open, but they looked faded and muddy, missing their usual spark.

"Oh God," Jane murmured, rushing to the bed.

"I know. I look like I tried to stop a cab with my face, right?" Maeve attempted a smile, and Jane fought the urge to burst into tears.

"She's in and out," Harris said softly from behind her. "She's still on a *lot* of drugs."

"I've missed you," Jane whispered. She took Maeve's limp hand, careful not to disrupt the IV tubes, and slid onto the stool beside the bed. She gave herself exactly one minute to despair over Maeve's bruised body, then snapped into Cheery Friend mode. Adopting a conspiratorial tone, she said, "I think Archie's about to lose it. There's this gala thing the mayor puts on every year, and I guess Archie's been trying to get it at the MoMA for, like, a decade, but the Met keeps making better offers. And now he finally got a 'source'—seriously, he called it 'a source on the inside'—that was supposed to break things our way, but now the Time Warner Center suddenly decided they want in, so he's tearing out all the hair he's got left." She gave every gossipy detail she could think of, and was sure that by the time Maeve's eyes closed and her breathing settled into a sleep-filled rhythm, the corners of her mouth had lifted in a faint smile.

Jane turned her face up to Harris, who was also sleeping lightly. He shook himself awake a moment later though, and grinned at Jane. "She spends about three hours a day awake, and she's spent most of them asking about you," he commented.

"I'm sorry I couldn't come sooner," Jane told him honestly.

Harris shrugged her apology off casually. "She wouldn't have remembered until maybe yesterday. She needs a lot of rest."

He yawned, and Jane raised a Doran-esque eyebrow. "So do you."

"Hey, I'm not the one who needs energy right now, Ms. Witch Hunter," Harris pointed out.

Outside the room, a cart clattered past, carrying trays of food, and an overhead intercom paged a Dr. Davis to floor nine. Jane frowned. She had kept a close eye on Lynne for the past week, doing her best to monitor the matriarch's closed-door meetings with her cousins, her afternoon errands with Yuri, and the many hushed phone calls. It seemed the woman was more focused on the wedding than on killing anyone, but Lynne was also a master plotter capable of the deepest deceptions.

"Lynne hasn't been here, right?" Jane asked anxiously.

"She hasn't even tried," Harris said.

A tableful of flowers stood in the corner, along with several get-well balloons and teddy bears. A thought struck Jane. "Have you told your parents the truth about what happened?"

"No. No good could come of waging a war with the Dorans."

She saw his eyes momentarily flit to the ostentatious diamond on her left hand. She instinctively turned the stone so it faced her palm.

"So!" He rubbed his hands together and assumed a perky grin, signaling the end of that conversation. "Show me what you can do."

"Harris," Jane demurred, "I'm just here to see Maeve. This isn't a . . . I didn't come to practice."

He stood and placed his hands on her shoulders. Heat emanated from his fingers, massaging her stiff muscles. She felt the first spark of her power igniting—along with something else. "I don't care what you came here for. I want to see your progress."

The air seemed to crackle around them, and Jane realized just how close Harris was standing. Now that she was alone with Harris, the magic now rising in her blood felt somehow wilder, more dangerous and unpredictable, than it had when they were with Dee in Book and Bell. She felt that same pull she always felt with Malcolm, that same need to erase the few inches that stood between them.

Magic calls to magic, she reminded herself.

"Call the power to you, Jane," Harris said. "The more you practice, the more you control it, and the stronger you'll get. Right now it's radiating off you and dissipating into the air. But when you learn to focus it, you won't believe what you'll be able to do."

After a thickly charged moment, Jane took his hands in hers. She felt the energy flow between them as though a circuit had been closed. "I hope I don't crash any of Maeve's machines," she said, trying to force a light note into her voice to ease the mounting tension.

"You won't." Harris's cool voice washed over her, and suddenly she believed him. His green eyes bored into hers. "I can feel it, you know. I can feel how strong you are."

Jane felt it too. Under the steadying influence of Harris's voice, the wild shock of her magic was settling into a steady thrum. It coiled through her body, twisting and turning, even passing momentarily from her hands to Harris's. It snaked languidly down her lungs to her abdomen and then moved . . . lower. Jane felt her breath grow ragged and shallow. Harris's pupils began to dilate and their chests heaved up and down, up and down, up and down, together.

The pressure built, heat rose, and she felt as though she were on fire. Harris touched his forehead to hers. Then his breath was on her lips and . . . oh God. It was too much. She needed to release the power in her body—somewhere, somehow—*now*.

Malcolm.

Malcolm is giving up everything for me, something in the back of her mind shouted faintly over the pulse of the magic. Not that he had any right to judge . . . not that he hadn't lied to her . . . not that this would be a betrayal on anywhere near the same scale . . . not that he didn't practically have it coming . . .

The lightbulb overhead burst and sparks showered around them.

Jane jerked her hands away from Harris.

Harris just stared at her, his eyes moving from her collarbone to her lips to her eyes. "I'll let them know about the light on my way out," Jane whispered. She kissed Maeve's sleeping forehead, then hitched her purse up onto her shoulder. Harris stood frozen in place. Jane met his eyes for the briefest of moments, then stepped awkwardly around him, shutting the door to 1070 firmly behind her.

Thirty-three

JANE ARRIVED BACK AT THE DORANS' SOAKING FROM THE COLD rain that had begun as soon as she had stepped out of the hospital. Glancing at the clock as she passed through the (thankfully empty) kitchen, she grabbed a pear from the center island's fruit bowl and took a large bite. *Take that, Lynne,* she thought cheerfully, still buzzed from the magic in her system. *I'm not just snacking between meals—I'm snacking on carbs!*

A furtive movement in the shadows of the hall caught her attention, and she froze mid-swallow. "Sofia?" she asked softly, but she knew that it wasn't the timid maid. The figure that she was beginning to make out was tall, broad, and the slightest bit stooped. *Charles.*

He was watching her from the hallway, his dull, dark eyes riveted on her body. Willing him not to move, she circled slowly around the marble-covered island. He was out of her line of sight now, but here she had more access to weapons: there were about twenty copper pots and kettles within easy reach, and the massive butcher-block knife-holder was just a few steps away. She armed herself with one of each for good measure and began circling in the opposite direction toward the kitchen's other entrance, the one closest to the nondescript wooden door that led to the stairs and the street. It was cold and wet outside, but surely that was better than being cornered by a lunatic.

Her position by the door afforded a view of the hallway again. She lifted the kettle at the ready, then blinked. The corridor was empty. Charles was gone.

Before Jane could register what this might mean, a footstep sounded loud and clear . . . and right behind her. She let out a short shriek and spun around.

"Goodness, dear," Cora McCarroll tsked. "Are you *cooking* something? Did you forget where the staff call button was?" She gestured vaguely toward the electronic panel in the wall and stared hard at Jane, sucking in her lower lip speculatively.

"I . . . I thought I saw Charles," Jane admitted, and mentally kicked herself for her uncertain tone. She didn't "think" anything. "He was in the hallway just now," she declared a little more firmly.

Cora blinked her gray eyes and ran her fingers along her pink pearl necklace. "He certainly wasn't. Poor thing just can't stand being downstairs; he's happiest where he is. Now. Perhaps you would join me for a soothing cup of tea?" She nodded pointedly at the kettle in Jane's hand; Jane set it down gently on the back of the range.

"Thank you," she recited automatically, slipping the knife back into its slot, "but I think I had better get changed."

"Yes," Cora mused, her eyes raking Jane up and down. "You're positively dripping."

Jane gave a forced smile and beat a hasty retreat, tapping the code to bolt her bedroom door as soon as she was safely inside. She let out a loud sigh and kicked off her sopping suede boots. They were probably ruined—she couldn't remember if Vivienne, her shoe shopper at Barneys, had said that they were waterproofed or "needed to be" waterproofed. Either way, they looked distressingly soggy.

She was about to go to her en-suite bathroom for a towel to pat them dry when a spark of leftover magic tingled in her fingers, giving her a better idea. *"If you have a free minute, you might as well be practicing,"* Dee had been reminding her about three times a day.

Jane set her dripping left boot in the center of the dark wood floor and sat down cross-legged in front of it. She worked to still her mind the way Dee had taught her, trying to gather her thoughts like fireflies in a jar. It was difficult: the loose, unconstrained power she had felt in the room with Harris kept trying to fight its way free. And as much as she knew that she couldn't just go off like a grenade every time she got worked up, that wild magic felt . . . good.

Eventually, after many yoga fire breaths, her mind calmed. Her thoughts flowed out, and magic took their place. Electricity vibrated in her blood, unusually clear and strong. She tried to pack it all together, like a snowball, but over and over it slipped from her control.

Perhaps I should keep my distance from Harris, she considered. *I clearly can't be trusted around him, and he has enough on his plate with Maeve. Besides . . .* The magic began to settle low in her body, and she shook herself all over. *Snap out of it. Just focus.*

Sweat dampened her temples and the nape of her neck, and Jane finally managed to concentrate a small bundle of energy behind her eyes. Snapping her eyes open, she sent the magic skittering toward the boot in a warm burst.

The boot shivered noticeably in place, like a dog shaking off after a dip in the ocean. A few droplets of water scattered onto the dark floorboards.

Jane's muscles throbbed in exhaustion. *Magic: the new core-blasting workout.* That raised an interesting point: anything this tiring had to burn calories. Maybe if she practiced enough, she would lose an inch or two off her hips, and Lynne would quit harping on every little thing she ate. *Maybe I'll even be allowed to finish a complete meal sometime in the next month without something being removed, substituted, altered, or just plain snatched out from under my nose.* Newly motivated, she straightened her back once again and fixed the boot with her witchiest stare.

Ten minutes later, the boot was mostly dry and lying on its side, and Jane was prepared to call that a victory. She collapsed heavily on a particularly ugly but very cushy Oriental rug, the magic still singing in her veins. Her muscles might be tired, but the power was still there, and that was somehow comforting.

Worn out though she was, the humming drone of the magic made her mind feel awake and alert, as if every sense was heightened. Her breathing sped up, and her thoughts scattered, shifting from Malcolm to Maeve and finally landing on Harris. In the steady quiet of her new focus, she could recognize that her attraction to him stemmed directly from the magic in both their bloodstreams. She also knew that there would be no happy ending for their friendship, or whatever it was they had, so long as Lynne was watching them like a well-dressed vulture.

Jane stretched her arms above her head, the magic beginning to flow out of her. That was where all of the trouble had started, anyway: those magical impulses that had drawn her so strongly to Malcolm and then to Harris.

She thought of her first encounter with Malcolm: the spark of his touch at the auction, just from his hand brushing hers when he'd given her his card. The flame had shot through her entire body when he had lifted her, broken shoe and all, off the sidewalk and into his waiting limo. No reasonable woman could be expected to resist that kind of overwhelming assault on her defenses. She pictured the dark blond waves of his hair, the deeper color of his eyebrows, and then his deep, liquid dark eyes. When her mental eye conjured the full curve of his lips, she sighed, recalling the fiery shudders those lips had sent racing across her skin.

Just like magic.

Jane's hands moved down across her body as if they had a life of their own, following the same path that Malcolm's large, strong hands had that very first night. The magic thrummed in response, and it felt as if every nerve ending in her body was poised and ready to fire. She undid the tiny shell buttons running down the front of her sweater and let it fall open, thinking wryly that if Malcolm really were there, a few of those buttons would be gone for good. Her fingertips brushed against her bare skin, raising goose bumps on the pale flesh.

In her mind's eye, Malcolm's warm mouth moved up her thighs, bare under her fluttery layered skirt, and her fingers followed after it, stroking and caressing in the best approximation of his tongue that she could manage. The pulse of the magic in her blood more than made up the difference; it was as if Malcolm were actually in the room, his breath hot against her body.

The delicious tension built, her fingers moving faster, until she reached the most powerful climax of her life. She opened her eyes, breathing hard, and honestly expected to see Malcolm's dark gaze peering down on her. But of course the room was still empty.

A tear slipped down her cheek, salty with exhaustion, release, and longing. Then her eyes fluttered shut, and she fell asleep where she lay, half-naked on the wooden floor.

Thirty-four

LYNNE'S TRILL OF LAUGHTER ROLLED BACK OVER THE CROWD, SO
clear and brittle that Jane worried that it might crack her champagne flute. Her mother-in-law-to-be-slash-nemesis was in fine
form, statuesque in a beaded silver Valentino and surrounded by
three congressmen and a major hip-hop star.

Jane, whose main goal was to get through the entire fund-
raiser without being noticed, pressed herself against a none-too-
sturdy window and tried to gage the approximate temperature
outside. *Early February . . . in New York . . . on the water . . . and the boat's
moving,* she tallied. *Nope, outside isn't an option.* Unless, of course,
she got desperate enough to throw herself into the Hudson River,
which was impossible to completely rule out.

"Jane!" Laura Helding shouted over the din of earnest Demo-
cratic Party donors (Lynne had briskly informed her that the Re-

publican fund-raiser, held in April, was also mandatory for the entire family). Jane glanced around, but the only viable cover was behind a tuxedoed cocktail waitress, and besides, Laura had already seen her.

Peeling herself away from the cold window, Jane pushed her way reluctantly through the clusters of her animated fellow cruisers. Drinks had been circulating for over an hour, and between that and the gentle sway of the ship, crossing the room was no simple task. Jane had to be vigilant to keep her floaty silk Roberto Cavalli dress ("It'll do for the liberals, dear, but please find something in a solid color for the Republicans") from being spilled on. Her toes ached, having been stepped on twice already. *Being a Doran is not for amateurs,* she told herself grimly.

A flashbulb burst somewhere to her left, and Jane lifted her lips into what she hoped looked like a carefree smile. The action still wasn't as automatic as she wished, and she barely managed to hold the pose during the rapid burst of about a dozen more shots.

By the time she reached Laura's little clique near the buffet table, Jane's cheeks ached, but she turned the smile up another notch and greeted her heart out. Laura introduced her giddily to the wife of a senator, the wife of a technology guru, the wives of two NBA players. *The wife of, the wife of . . .* Smiling for all she was worth, Jane reflected that Laura herself was a "wife of," and apparently considered Jane to be heading into the same category. Which she was, in a way . . . except that, technically, she would be the power half of her particular power couple. Malcolm had the money, the status, the connections . . . but Jane was the piece that was truly irreplaceable.

That realization combined with the champagne to give Jane a warm glow in the pit of her stomach. She wasn't just some mousy fugitive: she was strong. She could make shoes shake, and could almost count on being able to read minds on purpose.

After a round of gossipy small talk about some mistress's horribly unflattering sequined dress, Jane politely excused herself, trying not to notice that Laura's face fell just a fraction of an inch when she did. In her own way, Blake's wife was trying for solidarity, at least, if not for real friendship. It had to be hard to be attached to a family like this one, responsible for all of their secrets but never quite allowed all the way inside.

Jane cut her way carefully to the door, suddenly desperate for a moment alone. The icy air hit her like a solid wall, but it cleared her head instantly. She was in the back of the ship—the stern, she remembered from the captain's brief safety lecture—and a trail of turbulent water disappeared behind them into the dark night. She leaned against the rail idly, watching the wake rumble and churn beneath the hull. To her right, the lights of Manhattan glittered like a million impossibly close stars that had been shrunk into a snow globe just for her. The Statue of Liberty loomed in the distance, and Jane made a mental note to come back out here when they passed it to enjoy it in private.

Or not.

She heard the distinct squeak and click of the door behind her, and felt the hairs on her arms stand on end. She turned and peered into the inky blackness. Finally, she saw an approaching figure pass under a deck light, and groaned.

Lynne.

She looked about nine feet tall in the dark, her sleek brown hair swept up into a shining twist. She didn't seem to feel the cold at all, and Jane, whose own pale mane was quickly turning into a heap of cotton candy in the whipping wind, couldn't stifle a pang of jealousy at Lynne's apparently unruffleable updo. *Maybe there's a spell . . .*

Stop. No matter how many people assured her that Lynne couldn't read her mind, it still felt unsafe to think things like that around her.

"Jane?" Lynne gasped. She seemed more alarmed than anything, and immediately slid something into her silver clutch. She balled her hand against her side, looking almost uncertain.

What the . . . ?

"Hi, Lynne," Jane chirped, enjoying the rare sight of Lynne looking so off-balance.

"I hope you haven't been out here too long, dear," Lynne managed in a reasonable approximation of her usual implacable tone. "Catching pneumonia before your wedding would be simply dreadful." She stepped to the left, arching one eyebrow significantly. It was clear that she wanted Jane to go back in, ASAP.

But if I go back inside, I'll never find out what's making you so antsy, Jane wanted to say. In this particular moment, Lynne had ceased to be a dangerous enemy and had become, however temporarily, a fascinating puzzle.

"Jane?"

Sighing a little, Jane reluctantly stepped toward the door. As she did, she nearly slipped on a small, dark patch of liquid pooling near Lynne's stiletto. She grabbed onto Lynne's shoulder to steady herself, then looked into the older woman's dark eyes, astonished. "Lynne, are you . . . bleeding?"

From Lynne's clenched left fist, another drop of red blood welled up and fell to the deck. The impossibly tall woman's peach mouth pressed into a flat line. There was no sign of pain on her face, but there was a fairly terrifying amount of annoyance. "That idiot Blake attempted a toast, and sheared my martini glass off right in my hand."

The wind pressed painfully against Jane's eardrums, stinging her eyes and chapping her lips. Lynne's tone was perfectly natural, but her hesitation confirmed that she was lying.

That and the fact all she ever does is lie, basically.

"Well, can I get you a Band-Aid or anything?" Jane asked perfunctorily, remembering her role as a doting daughter-in-law.

"Just run along, dear."

Jane slipped back through the door into the well-lit party room. Rubbing her hands on her upper arms to warm them, she scanned the crowd for Belinda and Cora. *The last time Lynne was somewhere she wasn't supposed to be, someone almost died.*

The twins were laughing merrily with a silver-haired man in the corner though, looking no more threatening than the average socialite. Nothing, in fact, seemed out of place in the room. There was no sign that someone, or something, had just cut Lynne's hand deeply enough to make it bleed, and no real danger seemed to be brewing.

Making her way to the window with a view of the stern, Jane gazed out at Lynne. The matriarch was at the rail, just as Jane had been moments ago, leaning slightly over the water. She looked for all the world as though she was just enjoying the view. But when Jane looked closer, she saw that Lynne's left hand was stretched over the metal guard. From her palm dripped a steady stream of dark red blood.

Thirty-five

AFTER TWO WEEKS OF UNIMPEACHABLY GOOD BEHAVIOR, JANE was starting to get antsy. She had trekked to Brooklyn nearly every day to meditate with Dee, practiced on her own in between sessions, and made excuse after excuse to exclude Harris from it all. It was exactly what she had told herself she should be doing . . . and it was getting dead boring.

There was no denying that the work was yielding results, though. She could burn out lightbulbs on purpose, and she could (usually) stop herself from blowing them out when she was angry. Her telekinesis was stronger, too. Just that morning, she had dragged Dee's wooden bench across the living room, though the effort had left her spent, and her mind-reading was getting easier and more reliable with every attempt.

But her progress felt slow when measured against the rapid

approach of her wedding in two weeks, and after that . . . well, she had no idea what life would be like in hiding. She didn't even know which continent Malcolm would take her to. The world as she knew it would cease to exist after March 2, and that date was bearing down on them all like a freight train.

The looming uncertainty left Jane grouchy and unfocused, which was why she groaned when Dee had announced it was time for her to practice her craft in public. It felt risky, but she had to admit that it also sounded like progress.

Dee had suggested Rockefeller Center, but Jane had cringed at the image of skaters tumbling everywhere. Instead she had chosen Barneys, with the hopes of checking out the lingerie se-lection afterward. "It's so freaking crowded," Jane whispered, the adrenaline rushing out of her as the crowd of well-dressed shop-pers pressed around to try on hats, jewelry, and handbags. Her almost unbearable cabin fever vanished abruptly into thin air, and she wanted nothing more than to be sitting on Dee's saggy couch. "It's a Thursday, for God's sake. Don't they have anywhere they need to be?"

"Well, we're here," Dee pointed out reasonably, grinning in re-sponse to Jane's glare. "Maybe they're practicing *their* magic." She all but skipped to the elevators, forcing Jane to follow close on her chunky black heels.

I'm the witch here, so why's she the one dressing the part? Jane thought irritably. Of course, the bright side of that was that if anyone noticed the magic she planned to work, they would most likely blame it on Dee. Jane knew she was being the slightest bit unfair: tons of New Yorkers dressed in black, heels were in for spring, and the bright red tartan coat Dee had thrown over her ensemble didn't look the slightest bit mystical. But knowing that she was moody because she felt nervous about trying out her magic in public, and snapping out of her funk were two entirely different things.

When they reached the cast-bronze bank of elevators, Dee spun around, her face annoyingly cheerful. "Which floor?"

"Just pick one," Jane growled. They had both agreed that the upper floors were likely to be a little calmer than the street-level one, but when it came to the actual decision between designer sportswear and shoes, Jane couldn't care less.

Dee rolled her amber eyes, but she marched into an open elevator and punched a button at random.

"Evening wear?" Jane said, picturing piles of expensive delicate silks and satins in jagged shards on the floor. As the doors glided shut, she opened her mouth to suggest a less couture floor, but someone stuck their hand in the doors just before they closed, and suddenly Jane and Dee were surrounded by chattering shoppers.

Unable to have a meaningful conversation and momentarily distracted, Jane glanced around idly at the newcomers. *Coral is back in,* she noted, *and woven-leather bags. A year and a half behind Paris, as usual.* She couldn't help but feel a little smug until a perfect blowout in the far corner of the elevator caught her eye. Its owner was wearing the head-to-toe black of a salesperson, and Jane had a nagging feeling she'd seen those glossy chestnut tresses before. Then the mystery employee raised a hand to rake her scarlet-nailed fingers through her hair, and Jane was sure.

Madison.

Luckily for Jane's composure, Malcolm's ex never turned

around. When the elevator reached the fine-china floor, Jane grabbed the red hem of Dee's coat, cautioning her to stay put. As long as there were enough people in the elevator to camouflage them, she felt a reckless desire to follow Madison. She had expected the girl to exit on the seventh floor, where the personal-shopping department was based, but Madison and three other shoppers stayed on until the very last stop. FRED'S AT BARNEYS, the lit-up button announced, and Jane realized that she was tailing Malcolm's ex on her lunch break.

Kind of stalkerish, Jane admitted, but the curious, envious part of her brain hushed the thought. And anyway, wouldn't a restaurant be as good a place as any to practice magic?

The restaurant boasted a pleasant milk-chocolate-colored wood motif, and a massive stone fireplace sat in one corner. When the hostess led her and Dee to their table, Jane plunked down in a chair with a sigh, picked up her menu, and glanced around it the way that she had seen people do in spy movies. The ploy felt awkward and the menu made it hard to see, so she gave up, dropped it on the table, and leveled with Dee. "That walking tanning-bed ad on the elevator with us used to date Malcolm," she whispered. "Do you see her anywhere?"

Dee nodded. "Two tables back, to your right, with some guy," she confirmed, barely moving her lips. *Dresses like a witch, spies like a spy,* Jane thought wryly. *She's like the Swiss Army knife of friends.* Dee leaned out into the aisle subtly before returning with her assessment. "Kind of hunky, but if Malcolm looks anything like his photos, you win. Listen to her."

"I'll never be able to hear what she's saying over this din," Jane pointed out. "I could probably muss up her blowout a little, though. That could be fun."

Dee rolled her eyes. "I meant listen to her thoughts."

"Oh, right." Jane put both hands on the table to anchor herself and took a deep breath. She then closed her eyes and focused until the voices around her diminished into white noise. She cast her mind out like a net, touching, probing, until she found a mind that felt familiar.

But it wasn't words that occupied Madison's mind right then. Instead, she had a fairly detailed, full-color fantasy going on, in which she crashed Jane's wedding with her lunch date—who, in Madison's view at least, was considerably better-looking than Dee had implied. Of course, in the fantasy, Jane's hair was so peroxided that it was falling out in clumps, so Jane decided to take the details with a grain of salt.

The vision-Madison was wearing a skintight white dress (which she currently had on hold on the seventh floor), and Malcolm turned from his overweight straw-haired bride to see his radiant, model-thin, tropically tanned ex with her handsome oil-heir date. Predictably, Malcolm shoved Jane out of the way so he could beg Madison to marry him right away, in front of all of these witnesses, because he had never stopped loving her.

Jane gagged theatrically and reported her findings to Dee. "Nice work," Dee said, her amber eyes glittering. "Now spill something on her."

Jane obediently reached her mind out again toward Madison, this time looking for something inanimate. The last couple of weeks of practice had obviously yielded results; it felt as though she were running her fingers over the table behind her.

"Concentrate," Dee whispered, and Jane almost snapped that that was harder to do with her friend talking at her, but then her mental fingers found the cold, brittle edge of a water glass, and she pressed her mouth shut and pulled. A squeal from some-where behind her confirmed her success, and a waiter ran franti-cally past their table.

Jane opened her eyes and grinned at Dee, who was flashing a wide, white grin of her own. Suddenly the idea of a "real-world" practice session seemed absolutely brilliant all over again.

Thirty-six

"AND THEN SHE STARTED SHRIEKING AT THE WAITER FOR BUMP-ing into her table, and it turns out there was a guy from *Star* there, and the whole thing turned into a huge mess," Dee gloated. Jane grinned. Her friend was so giddy that she was practically dancing in her chair to the club's thumping techno beat.

Harris cheered obediently and congratulated them both before disappearing to order another round of drinks. It was true that Jane wasn't comfortable working magic with him anymore—and, in fairness, it wasn't like he'd asked her to, either, since the awkward disaster in the hospital. But she had been so flushed with her victory over Madison at Barneys that when Dee had sug-gested calling Harris to celebrate with them, Jane hadn't objected one bit.

Her confidence had wavered just a little when he arrived. He seemed somehow taller than she remembered and he smelled like rain and mulled spices. His dancing green eyes had hit hers like a spotlight, and her head had spun in a way that it was far too early to blame on the chardonnay. *Really?* the rational part of her brain demanded sternly. *Two weeks of work and all it takes to spin your head is a pretty pair of eyes?* She focused on a couple of three-part breaths, and began to feel a little bit more grounded.

"Jane's getting really good on her own," Dee went on seamlessly when Harris returned from the bar. "It makes me wonder what she could do with us forming her Circle again, like we did in Book and Bell. Too bad you've been so busy," she concluded with a pout that could melt stone.

Jane choked a little on her wine, but passed it off as a cough. She had spent the last two weeks fabricating all kinds of iron-clad excuses for Harris's continued absence from their practices, but she hadn't thought ahead to when Dee might mention them to him. It was technically true that he did have Maeve to worry about, plus a job, a family, and presumably some other friends, too. But Jane had embellished and invented for all she was worth to convince Dee that he was booked around the clock . . . and, naturally, she hadn't troubled Harris with the details of her increasingly elaborate lies. Or even with actual invitations to their near-daily meetings, in point of fact. She shot him a sideways glance to see if he would give her away.

But he was nodding along amiably. "Sometimes things just get completely crazy. I've been wanting to get away, but it's been just impossible. I'm glad I haven't held you girls up, though. Cheers to Jane's progress!"

Jane drank gratefully at his cue. His cover-up had been flawlessly bland: convincingly sincere but without a single unneeded detail to conflict with Jane's version of events. *He's such a gentleman,* she thought with a near-swoon, and set her glass down firmly. Clearly it was never too early to pace her drinking.

"So?" Dee swiveled on her chair to face Jane squarely. "Show him what you've got."

This time it was Harris who choked on his drink. Dee patted his back solicitously before turning back to Jane. "Can you do anything about the stupid spotlight that's *right* in my eyes?"

Oh, right. Magic. Harris looked as sheepish as Jane felt, although her emotions took a slightly different turn when she noticed that Dee's hand was lingering on Harris's smoothly muscled back. A hot ball of jealousy congealed in the pit of her stomach, and she felt a familiar rushing electricity in her blood. "I think I can," she managed to say around her clenched jaw.

Calm down, she told herself frantically as the jealousy began to melt into an angry, sparking mass of magic. *Don't get sloppy over a pointless, meaningless crush, of all things. Just do what you've been practicing.* Nevertheless, the spotlight that she attempted to swivel actually fell from its perch, clattering dangerously through the rafters until it reached the end of its cord. It was still a good foot or two above the heads of the super-chic twentysomethings grinding on the club's dance floor, but Jane felt as guilty as if she actually had brained one of them.

"It's a good start," Dee told her encouragingly, but her amber eyes were troubled. In their no-boys-allowed practices, Jane had had to struggle to summon her power at all, not to control an excess of it. Dee could obviously tell the difference, but without knowing what to attribute it to, she looked more than a little anxious.

Her face compounded Jane's guilt. She had intended to tell Dee about the unstable chemistry between her and Harris any number of times, and she knew that she should have. But she hadn't wanted to admit to having both a fiancé *and* a crush who made her go weak at the knees. And she really, really hadn't wanted to hear that Dee was interested in him too.

"Let me try again," Jane offered lamely. It wasn't quite an apology—or an explanation—but it was the best she could do under the circumstances.

"There's a really cute couple back at the bar," Harris suggested. "Or they would be a couple if they had a reason to start talking."

Most of Jane wanted to stop and dissect his words for coded messages, but the smaller, saner part of her won out. She also managed to avoid glancing at Dee, sure that her friend's nerves at the idea of Jane using her magic near people right now would be written all over her tawny-skinned face. And Jane really didn't need any additional reasons to be jumpy, because she wasn't a hundred percent confident herself.

She sent her mind wandering out to the bar the way that she had in the restaurant earlier, and quickly found the two people that Harris had mentioned. The girl was short, with dirty-blond hair; the dark-haired guy probably qualified as "gangly." They were standing back-to-back, practically touching, each in conversation with their own group of friends. Skimming their minds, Jane was impressed with Harris's intuition: they had noticed each other several times, and were both hoping for a tap on the shoulder.

This would be a nice thing, Jane told herself, closing her eyes and pulling stillness over her mind like a blanket. *This is being a better person. One who doesn't lust, covet, or envy, but just takes opportunities to make the world a little better for other people. I could be a good witch.*

The pair at the bar turned simultaneously as invisible hands touched their shoulders. The girl's drink knocked into the guy's elbow and spilled. He apologized profusely and signaled the bartender; she smiled shyly. By the time Jane was fully present back at her own table, two of the pair's friends were even hitting it off.

Jane's face relaxed into what felt like her first genuine smile in ages. She felt refreshed. Even the dark club looked brighter, cleaner somehow. The experience was so potently positive that it made her want to do something else nice.

Reaching out for the dreadlocked DJ's mind, she took in the next songs in his playlist. She sensed that he was holding back something special—a request? a dedication?—in a shelf to the right of his booth. She furrowed her brow and concentrated hard, trying to get some purchase on the slick album cover. Her hands began to tremble with the strain, but she managed to pull the corner out.

She sat back in her chair, breathing hard. Harris's and Dee's concerned faces swam in her peripheral vision, but she waved them away limply. She was almost there.

Gripping the table for support, she reached for the DJ's hand. It was much, much harder than moving a glass or a record, even though it was technically smaller, because it already had a purpose behind it and a trajectory ahead of it. She had to choose her moment, and then jerk as hard as she could.

The DJ's hand bumped the protruding edge of the record she had moved, and she felt more than heard the idea skitter across his mind. Severing the connection, she slumped back in her chair.

"Jane, what the hell?" Harris demanded, a note of panic in his voice. Dee looked scared, too, but maybe also a little relieved that Jane hadn't inadvertently killed or maimed anyone with her magic.

"I got them together, I think," Jane said, "but it was really hard." She had expected to have to act a little, but her voice was weak and trembly all on its own. As if on cue, the music changed. Sultry, haunting, Auto-Tune-distorted notes filled the club, and the writhing twentysomething dancers slowed a little, their hips and arms beginning to find graceful arcs. "I need a moment. But go dance, spy, and let me know what they're doing. Take your time. Blend in."

Dee and Harris exchanged intrigued glances, and obediently turned and headed for the dance floor. Dee cast one last suspicious look over her shoulder at Jane, who could swear that her friend was mouthing "thank you" before they disappeared together into the mass of moving bodies.

So she *was* interested in Harris. Jane tried to feel good about her second romantic setup in a row, but her earlier glow was conspicuously missing. *I'm just tired,* she told herself. And she was. But she was also sad to see Harris go off with another girl, no matter how much she liked that girl, and no matter how often she reminded herself that she and Harris were just friends.

And. I. Have. A. Fiancé! Why was that so hard to remember when Harris was around? No wonder she didn't have the same altruistic high she'd had after giving the two strangers at the bar their little push. She had gotten that from acting like a good person . . . and her second try at playing Cupid was a timely reminder that she really wasn't one.

I'll just have to try harder, she resolved, sipping at her wine and swaying a little to the music. She gently turned the two rings on her left hand. One for her past, one for her future. That was all that mattered . . . it was all that could matter.

Thirty-seven

TEN DAYS BEFORE THE WEDDING, JANE FOUND HERSELF ALONE IN the Dorans' parlor. She had worked a half-day at the MoMA. She was planning a reception for a visiting professor from London's Slade School of Art. The work went quickly, but she still missed Maeve's presence in the office. She had finally been released from the hospital three days prior—an infection and a slipped stitch had slowed her recovery considerably . . . as if it hadn't been slow enough already.

Jane had wondered if Lynne or one of the twins had had a hand in Maeve's complications, but she had decided not to mention the possibility to Harris. He had to be worried enough as it was, and besides, he'd probably already thought of it.

Jane walked over to the marble wall that held Lynne's family history. She felt like she could draw most of it from memory by now, from Ambika all the way down to Annette. She had tried once to calculate in her head how long ago Ambika had begun this family's legacy, but she had lost track somewhere around the twelfth century. She found herself wondering about Ambika and her dubious legacy. Was she one of the original seven witches Rosalie had talked about in her book? What kind of a world had she lived in? And if she was one of the first seven, what exactly had caused the fight between her and her siblings that had lasted through so many generations? Was it a struggle over power . . . or something more?

Or maybe she was just a Dark Ages version of Lynne, Jane thought wryly, trying unsuccessfully to picture Lynne without a chauffeured car or five-star restaurants to call in from. But thoughts of Lynne—and Yuri—made her feel like an ice cube had been dropped down the back of her dress. It was getting harder and harder to smile pleasantly, talk about the wedding, listen to gossip, all the while holding her breath, waiting for something to give her away or for someone else to get hurt.

Jane reached out her fingers toward the wall and found Malcolm's name, tracing it gently over and over. Postcards had begun to arrive in the last week: brightly colored, information-less scraps of paper addressed to the entire family. He had sent one from Madrid, one from Barcelona, one from Marrakech. They had alluded to complications, delays, additional business in undetermined parts of the world. He hadn't bothered to spring for express air mail, so Jane was sure that they would keep coming, full of bland excuses, even after she and Malcolm were long gone on their "honeymoon." It was a smart plan: as long as the family was still getting weeks-old news from Malcolm, they would be less likely to realize that he and Jane had disappeared. They could have a month's head start before someone noticed that his postcards had stopped coming.

He would arrive home just the one day, for her, and then they would start their new life together . . . wherever that turned out to be.

In the meantime, each card ended with a sterile *"Love to J—see you soon."* It wasn't much, but it was enough to keep her going. Wherever he was now—and she was fairly sure that he hadn't ever been in Spain or Morocco at all—he was thinking of her. He was doing all of this for her. All she had to do to keep up her end was not give them away, for just another week and a half.

Her fingers slid to the right along the marble wall, exploring the grooves of Annette's name. She remembered optimistically wondering if Malcolm's little sister might have been a friend to her if she'd lived. After everything she had learned about Manhattan's magical families, and about this one in particular, that seemed extremely unlikely. Annette would have been a full-blooded witch, just like her. Lynne wouldn't have needed Jane in the first place if her own heir had survived, but if she had decided to bring Jane into the family anyway, as extra insurance, Annette almost certainly would have been raised to see her as a rival.

Seven magical sisters. Had Ambika known what the magic would do to her extended family? Just how far it would spread around the world? Just how many magical families were out there now? Hundreds or thousands, maybe, if the size of the Dorans' tree was any indication. The Montagues were part of another one that would probably have just as many branches, and even orphaned Jane

Boyle might have a couple of long-lost fifth cousins with traces of the gift in their DNA. Malcolm had mentioned something about two families dying out completely, but how many witches were left in the world? And, inherited or not, magical lines changed names in nearly every generation. When the seven original families had branched and divided and intermarried, it would be impossible to know where the power had gone unless you followed it closely. So Manhattan's witches watched each other like hawks, Harris had told her, tracking each other's power with obsessive jealousy. Not exactly a warm, loving environment.

Her eye landed on the strange smooth patch next to Annette's name. *A mistake?* she wondered again, and then she realized: that was the space for Charles. It must have been prepared when Lynne had gotten pregnant again. Maybe the baby's name had even been chiseled in, before the whole area had been erased to cover up Charles's existence. Jane felt a pang of sadness, even pity for the family that had been touched by so much tragedy. It wasn't that Lynne hadn't earned her karma in spades—she had, and more—but it was still more sorrow than Jane could comfortably wish on her worst enemy.

The thought of Charles, living his whole life in the attic, left her somewhere between pity and fear. Since the night she had spotted him in the kitchen, every creak and shadow in the halls had made her jump at the thought that Malcolm's troubled younger brother might leap out and attack her again. Although he was supposedly safely closed in the attic, she kept smelling the stale, rotten air that had filled her lungs that horrible night when he had grabbed her.

A floorboard groaned behind her, and Jane spun toward the door, a scream dying in her throat. The shape that blocked the light was much too small to be Charles. The hall light glinted off a silver-streaked bun, and Jane had the figure narrowed down to one of two.

"What are *you* doing here?" the newcomer snapped brusquely. *Belinda, definitely.*

"I had a headache," Jane improvised. "I just wanted a little peace and quiet."

Belinda Helding sniffed disapprovingly. "You'll skip dinner, then. Have something sent to your room."

Jane suppressed an unexpected smile. *She doesn't want me here any more than I want to be here,* she realized. By the Doran standards, Belinda was practically an ally. Jane was seized by an irrational urge to giggle. "That sounds good," she replied instead, trying to make her voice sound appropriately weak and faint. "Thank you for your concern."

Belinda's head tilted quizzically, as if she honestly couldn't understand why anyone would imagine that she was concerned about Jane. Jane plastered a half-grateful, half-apologetic smile onto her face and made her way to the door.

Jane got close enough to smell the dusty-violet scent of Belinda's perfume before the older woman budged at all. With a sigh that would be more appropriate to a mother dealing with an exasperating child's temper tantrum, Belinda took one reluctant, shuffling step to the side, leaving only barely enough room for Jane to pass through. *Lynne would tell me to diet,* she reflected. Then Belinda's trailing gray sleeve brushed Jane's arm. A static shock—or maybe a shock of another kind—passed between them, and Jane cringed involuntarily.

She snapped her default smile back onto her face as quickly

as she could, but she could still feel Belinda's eyes, like hard little chunks of pewter, boring into her back as she forced herself to walk, not run, back to her suite.

Ten days. Just ten more days. The wedding couldn't possibly come soon enough.

Thirty-eight

THE DAY BEFORE THE WEDDING, LYNNE DORAN HAD OFFICIALLY entered crisis mode. Sitting on her favorite perch at the kitchen table, thumbing through a pages-long to-do list, she threw up her hands in disbelief. "Then he tried to say that it wasn't in our contract, as if I give a damn what his middle-school-educated brain thinks our contract says. How he thinks he can run a business going around contradicting clients the day before their weddings is beyond me, but come Monday he won't be able to *give* his so-called creations away."

Jane wondered idly where in the printer's contract it could possibly say that the man had to hire an acceptably attractive staff to hand out programs at the church, but decided that asking would only invite trouble. It was clearly too late to save the printer's reputation; Jane could simply focus on saving her own skin. And in a backward sort of way, Lynne's tirade was comforting: she wasn't planning on ruining the printer until next week because she still needed him for the wedding tomorrow.

I'm safe so long as she needs me, too, Jane told herself over and over, like a desperate sort of mantra. *As long as she thinks she can use me. As long as she thinks I want nothing more in the world than to marry Malcolm and have his babies.* And Lynne's relentless drive to keep up appearances guaranteed that she would do almost anything to ensure that this massive, crème-de-la-crème wedding would happen as planned. She would need irrefutable proof, a one-thousand-percent certainty that her family's reputation was unsalvageable, before she would make an overt move against Jane.

It was T minus twenty-eight hours until Jane and Malcolm would leave their wedding reception hand in hand. Malcolm was probably packing his bags now, preparing to fly out of some foreign airport to find his way back to her.

Malcolm. She hoped he hadn't hit any snags in his preparations, or made some kind of mistake, or slipped in a bathtub in Prague and broken his neck. *Someone probably would have called here about that last one.*

Jane fidgeted with the enormous stack of response cards on the table, turning the "yes" card from Mr. and Mrs. Henry Sondmeyer—whoever they were—over and over in her hands. True to form, Lynne had invited five hundred of her nearest and dearest friends and family members, along with a few select individuals from the media. She had even gone so far as to express relief that Jane had no living family, as that might have forced them to consider a larger church so as not to risk choosing between the Piaggias (who were, technically, more important) and the Byrne-Chaitworths (who were known for holding a grudge). Jane had gritted her teeth, nodded along, and let her thoughts return again and again to Malcolm.

Maybe he's at the airport already? But that was probably wishful thinking. He wouldn't be able to come back until the very last minute before the wedding. He couldn't afford to be around his mother for a moment longer than necessary; there was only so long that he could studiously think about unimportant things under Lynne's intense scrutiny.

"And I'm so glad you came to your senses about those Montagues."

Jane snapped to attention at the mention of Maeve's and Harris's last name. Since the night of the collision, Jane had been careful to give the impression that Maeve was as over their friendship as Jane claimed to be. She had been sure to mention that she hadn't seen Maeve since the accident and didn't care to.

"You're too new to New York to know this," Lynne rattled on, oblivious to Jane's sudden interest, "but they're an absolutely wretched family. That mother of theirs is just horribly vulgar, and the father's no better. Always putting on airs and trading on his family name when everyone knows he's all but disinherited and no one with any sense will so much as have them over for lunch. If I had known their girl worked at the MoMA, I never would have let you accept that *job* there." Lynne sniffed rudely. She still hadn't managed to let the fact that Jane was working go entirely, and it showed clearly every time she puckered her mouth and spat out the word "job." "You are absolutely better off dropping them," she declared. "I dare say the world would have been a better place if that cab had just ..." She waved her long-fingered hand eloquently, like Maeve was no more than a pesky fly that needed swatting.

Jane gaped and tasted bile at the back of her throat.

Lynne smirked to herself obliviously, clearly enjoying what she believed to be a private joke. Jane's entire body trembled and saw red, her boiling rage overriding all of the control she had spent the last month learning. The recessed lights in the kitchen ceiling began to flicker, *on, off, on, off, on, off*. The microwave glowed to life, and a KitchenAid mixer began to whir and then rumble on the green marble countertop.

Jane clamped her hands down on the counter. *Shit! Shit! Shit!*

She closed her eyes and fought with the magic that coiled through her body and radiated off her in hot, uncontrollable waves. She breathed in and out, trying as hard as she could to force the electricity down to its resting state. The entire kitchen faded to nothing as she centered her mind, imagining the power receding like waves back into her body. After a few tense heartbeats, she felt the power begin to shift and subside, following the path that she visualized for it. Through her eyelids, she could tell that the lights were steady again, and when she heard the mixer shut down, she opened her eyes.

Lynne's dark stare was cold and appraising.

Jane's head started to buzz and her heart pounded wildly as the reality of the situation crashed down on her. What had she just done? Why hadn't she just pretended there was some kind of wiring problem in the kitchen? Lynne would still know it was her, but all that mattered was that Jane *not* know. Instead, she had controlled her magic, which was as good as announcing that she knew she had it. *And if she knows I know . . . and that I've been practicing . . .*

It would all be over. Maeve's injuries, Malcolm's absence, all of the help Dee and Harris had given Jane, Jane's own work and effort over the last month . . . none of it would mean a thing.

She tried to arrange her features in the most innocent possible expression. "Sorry," she chirped brightly, although she could hear the strain in the high pitch of her voice. "Power surges kind of freak me out. From when I was little and there were these thunderstorms. And I just remembered that I wanted to get a new manicure before tomorrow, so I'll be back tonight and if there are any problems just call, okay?" It sounded hopelessly inane, and she didn't wait for Lynne's response.

Instead, she shoved her heavy wooden chair back and bolted out of the kitchen, saying silent thanks that the door to the back stairwell was so close: it took her only moments to reach the street.

Thirty-nine

STILL BREATHING HARD FROM HER FLIGHT DOWN THE FIVE flights of stairs, Jane hailed the first cab she saw on Park and gave the driver Dee's address in Brooklyn. "No," he said firmly. "My shift is over in—"

"Your shift is over as soon as you get me to where I'm going," Jane snapped. "I've got a cell phone and a close personal friend on the Taxi and Limousine Commission."

The driver sighed but started moving without another word of protest. A month in New York—during which she had been willing to go to great lengths to avoid riding with the Dorans' creepy driver—had clearly hardened her, Jane reflected grimly.

She tried to relax against the cracked leather seat, but couldn't help glancing in the rearview mirror every few seconds, a learned habit from the few times she'd had to go somewhere with Yuri. The fourth time she checked the mirror, she saw something.

I know that car.

It was ridiculous, obviously. Manhattan was packed with black sedans, and there was nothing special about the one three cars back. But four blocks and a turn later, there it was again. Jane's hands started to shake. *There are only so many ways to get downtown,* she tried to tell herself, but the whole thing just felt wrong. Jane's phone began to vibrate, and she felt like she was about to jump out of her skin. The call was coming from the Dorans' mansion, and Jane tapped "Ignore" a little harder than necessary.

A minute and a few nervous checks of the rearview mirror later, her voice-mail alert dinged with unnerving cheerfulness.

"Jane, dear, the couturier is having an absolute fit," Lynne's voice purred, making Jane's skin crawl. *"We have an emergency fitting in fifteen minutes, so your nails will have to wait. Please come back to the house. Immediately."*

Like hell, Jane thought, her heart racing. The sedan was still behind them.

"Hey—um, excuse me?" she croaked to the sullen driver. She cleared her throat awkwardly. "I know I should have said this sooner, but can we take the FDR?"

"It's crowded this afternoon," the driver grunted.

"Oh." Jane eyed the encroaching sedan, replaying Lynne's message in her head. *What would Lynne do?* "Look, my husband hired this detective guy to follow me around because he thinks I'm cheating on him. So could you, you know, go in a big square or something, like they do in the movies? I promise you that if you help me out here, I'll be the best tipper you've ever met." She fished a hundred-dollar bill out of her wallet and waved it for emphasis. "It's my husband's money—what do I care?"

The driver raised an eyebrow. "Fine," he sighed, and cut a sharp left.

She tensed as she stared into the rearview mirror.

"Is he still there?" the cabbie asked, avoiding a bike messenger by inches.

"I don't know," Jane admitted. *Was* that the same sedan? Did the car have circular or square headlights? *I suck at this cloak-and-dagger bullshit. Why didn't I look at the license plate?* But then she saw the bald head behind the wheel just before the car disappeared behind a Hummer. "Yeah. He's still there."

Without signaling, the driver spun the wheel, cutting off a city bus and careening across three lanes of traffic before bumping over a curb to turn onto 50th Street. He made several more turns before flying onto the FDR.

She spied a black sedan—*the* black sedan?—two more times before they left Manhattan, but by the time she reached Dee's block, it seemed her driver's wild risks had paid off: it had been over fifteen minutes since Jane had seen any hint that they might still be pursued. She tossed some bills at the driver without looking at them, and ran up the concrete steps to Dee's place. She burst into the tiny apartment, gasping for breath.

Dee had a plate of cookies ready and waiting, but Jane was in no mood for comfort food. "I think I blew it," she almost sobbed.

Dee set the plate down and checked the deadbolt on her door. "Start from the beginning."

Jane opened her mouth, but instead of her voice, a loud, booming knock filled the room. Jane felt a hysterical scream rising in her throat. "It's Yuri," she whispered. "He followed me here. Lynne knows!"

Dee's hand closed around Jane's wrist with a surprisingly strong grip. Jane could barely blink before her friend was dragging her toward the open door of her bedroom. She had just enough time to register a patchwork bedspread and giant pentacle on the wall before Dee had opened the small window at the back of the room. Dee shoved her out onto a rusty fire escape that quaked and swayed beneath Jane's weight.

"Whoa," she gasped, clinging to the rail. It left orange flakes on her palms. Since Dee was only on the second floor, it was just one flight down and a short, five-foot drop to the alleyway below.

Still, the shock of the fall knocked her to the ground, and sent stabbing pain up her right shin. Rolling to her feet, she saw that Dee had made a much more graceful landing, and was beckoning her to the mouth of the alley. She followed Dee's back as fast as her aching feet could carry her.

A moment later, Dee jolted to a stop right at the sidewalk, and Jane grabbed Dee's shoulders to keep from crashing into her.

"Oh my God," she whispered. "Yuri."

He stood before Dee, blocking the entire alley. He was dressed head to toe in black, and the March sun reflected off his bald head.

"Miss Boyle," he said.

Jane tightened her grip on Dee's shoulders. She had never heard Yuri speak one single time in the entire time she had been here. His tone was courteous and pleasant and not at all like the voice of someone who had just been chasing her all over New York.

"Missus Doran sent me to find you for a dress fitting. Excuse us, please," he added, with a polite nod to Dee.

For a half-second, Jane fully intended to go with him. He sounded so reasonable that she almost doubted her own sanity.

But then his meaty hand reached for her shoulder, and her instincts kicked in fiercely, propelling her back into the alley.

"Right this way, Miss," Yuri prompted in the same pleasant tone, closing the distance between them with alarming speed.

"No!" Jane shouted, stumbling out of his reach.

"I'll drive her!" she heard Dee yell from the sidewalk. She knew it was a bluff—Dee didn't have a car—but Yuri didn't even seem to hear it.

"The car is right here," he announced, his hand finally closing hard around Jane's elbow.

At his touch, Jane's body went rigid. Her mind was flooded with image after image of terrified girls, begging, crying, running. She felt the sickening rush of Yuri's enjoyment as his mind savored his favorites. A blonde with enormous brown eyes, a deep gash running across her sternum. A teenage boy passing out as Yuri severed his hand with a machete. A woman, young and beautiful and familiar-looking, her mouth forming a terrified O as Yuri wrapped his fingers around her throat. Jane's scream rattled the windows above them.

"Get off her!" she heard Dee shout, but the pictures kept coming. A strawberry blonde bled from a cut on her cheek, clutching at her torn clothes as she staggered backward. Madison Avery's arm twisted up painfully behind her back. Sobbing and pleading filled Jane's ears.

When Yuri let go of her arm, Jane was so unprepared that she fell to her knees. Expecting an attack, she jumped up, but the space directly in front of her was empty. A few yards away, Yuri's back was to her, and he was moving, catlike, in a crouch. She could see three fresh, bloody scratches on the side of his neck, and on the ground in front of him . . .

"Yuri! Stop!"

The driver had pinned Dee to the pavement, his knees on either side of her prone body. He was lifting something made of metal— a tire iron, Jane recognized in a nauseating flash of comprehension. He swung it at Dee's head. Jane screamed, but Dee managed to twist out from under him just in time, narrowly avoiding the weapon in Yuri's meaty hand. She didn't get far, though, and Yuri pinned her down again, wrapping his free hand around her throat this time. She thrashed violently, trying to wriggle free, but she didn't seem to be able to use her right arm properly, and Jane knew that she had used up all of her luck dodging the first blow.

Jane ran forward, casting around for something to distract the giant about to kill her friend, but there was no way she could get to him in time.

Your body is too far away, her mind shouted at her. *Just your body.* Her head snapped up sharply. The tire iron was descending. There was no time for doubt.

"Stop," she hissed through her teeth, sending a surge of raw power at the driver. Her voice was a low, animalistic growl, like no sound she had ever uttered. The iron stopped in midair as if it had just struck bulletproof glass. Sweat beaded on Jane's forehead, and the effort of resisting Yuri's considerable muscles threatened to make her knees buckle.

While Dee struggled under his grip, Yuri twisted slowly to face Jane, teeth bared in a snarl. "Bitch," he snarled. There was nothing human left in his face, and Jane knew immediately that she and Dee would both die in this dank alley unless she could get the tire iron out of Yuri's hand.

Electricity crackled behind her eyes, and she twisted up hard with her mind. The iron shot toward the sky as if dangling from an invisible fishing rod. Yuri's beady eyes began to follow it, but Dee chose that moment to kick him clumsily in the groin. With a growl of rage, he turned his full attention back to her, wrapping both hands around her throat. Dee gurgled and her eyes bulged. Barely aware of making the decision, Jane swung the iron back down as hard as she possibly could. It connected with Yuri's temple with a sickening thud. The huge man collapsed to the ground like a puppet whose strings had been cut. He didn't move again.

Jane collapsed several feet away from him, chunks of gravel scratching her cheek. Her heart pounded against the unyielding pavement, and her breath came in loud rasps. *Inhale, and then exhale. Inhale . . .* When she had counted five breaths, she pushed herself to sitting, ignoring the pain that radiated throughout her entire body. She dragged herself over to the large hulk of a man. His eyes had rolled back in his head. They were milky and unseeing, and a trickle of blood leaked from the corner of his mouth. His chest was still beneath his black jacket.

Dee's amber eyes were huge. "I think he's dead," she rasped.

"I know," Jane whispered. And then she stumbled to the end of the alley and vomited.

Forty

"OH MY GOD, I KILLED HIM," JANE GASPED WHEN SHE COULD speak again, a sob rising in her throat.

"Stop that. Stop that now!" Dee hissed, rubbing her injured arm. "He was going to kill us. You had no other choice."

"I could have hurt him—just knocked him out, maybe," Jane whispered wildly, the moment when she had swung the tire iron downward playing over and over in her head. She had been afraid—terrified, actually. But was that really all, or had there been anger, too? Had she just been defending herself and her friend, or had she also wanted Yuri dead? She had been absolutely disgusted by what she had seen in his mind: his perverted cravings for fear and pain. Had she made a decision without even realizing it? Had she judged that Yuri deserved to die?

"You did the only thing you could. This is the only way to be sure," Dee remarked, startling Jane out of her thoughts. Dee was rubbing at her collarbone; angry finger-shaped welts were forming on her neck. "I was running out of time."

"He followed me from the house," Jane said numbly. "Lynne sent him after me. I knew he wasn't just a driver. I can't believe . . . God. This is all my— Are you okay?"

Dee waved away her concern. "Why was the Dorans' driver trying to kill us?"

"I don't think that was the plan." Jane shook her head miserably. "But it's not like we can ask him." She felt herself sliding into a cold, foggy daze. First Maeve, now Dee . . .

"*Focus*, Jane!" Dee begged. "Come on. I need you. You saved my life, so no wallowing!"

"It was to save you," Jane repeated slowly, the words sinking in. That was important somehow. "So we can just tell the police—"

"Okay, *I'll* do the thinking," Dee said gently, "because I don't think you're quite there yet. You don't have time to sit around some police station! Lynne sent this freak after you; you have to go now. I know you wanted to wait for Malcolm to get back, but you're going to have to run tonight."

There was something wrong with Dee's logic, and Jane fumbled through the fog that was descending on her mind to try to figure out what was wrong. "I don't think that's why he was here," she managed finally. Once it had been said out loud, she became more sure that she was on the right track. "I read him when he touched me," she mumbled, hearing an unfamiliar hoarseness in her own voice. "It was horrible. *He* was horrible. But I don't think he was planning on hurting us—"

"—until I took a couple of chunks out of the side of his neck," Dee finished grimly, holding up three bloody fingernails. She twisted a handful of her coarse black hair in her left hand. "I thought he was hurting you."

"Well, he was," Jane admitted, "but he wasn't trying to." She glanced toward the huge, still body. Just beyond it, out on the sidewalk that butted up against the alley, was a very pregnant woman pushing a stroller. She didn't turn to look toward the gory scene in the alley, but Jane watched her pass anyway. The woman had curly black hair and dusky skin stretched tautly over high, fine cheekbones. She reminded Jane of her friend Elodie. The resemblance was so strong, in fact, that Jane only barely stopped herself from calling out to the unknown woman. Then she remembered.

Oh my God. We're standing around chatting over a dead body in plain sight. The sun had moved down below the roofs of the buildings behind them, but there was still sufficient light that anyone who actually looked their way would see enough to be alarmed.

"We need to get inside," Jane blurted. "We need to get Yuri . . . I don't know, somewhere. Not here."

Dee nodded briskly and strode to a rusted blue door just below the fire escape. "Back door," she explained tersely. "For the trash." She produced a brass key, and they slipped inside. Jane felt a brief moment of disorientation seeing the familiar foyer from an unfamiliar perspective, but it resolved as they approached the creaky wooden staircase. Jane knew that walking would look less conspicuous if anyone happened to see them, but she couldn't help herself: on the third stair, she began to run, and by the time Dee's door slammed shut behind them, they were both out of breath.

Dee ducked into her narrow galley kitchen and reappeared with the plate of cookies from what felt like hours ago. "You said something about Yuri not trying to hurt us," she prompted skeptically, folding her long legs under her on a large blue cushion.

The finger marks on her neck had become so vivid they nearly glowed. Jane broke the cookie over and over into smaller pieces, until it was nothing but a pile of sugary dust on her lap. She couldn't imagine eating right now. Couldn't imagine eating ever again. She had taken someone's life.

Jane's tongue felt thick and heavy, and her limbs craved a bed to crawl into. But her mind refused to stop whirling. She had to make sense of it all.

"Jane, you have to leave tonight. You know that, right?" Dee said again.

Jane shook her head. The effort hurt and the room spun around her. "No. He tried to get me to go along willingly. He did not want us to make a scene. Which means Lynne still cares about making everything look good."

"You said Lynne was onto you," Dee reminded her stubbornly, pushing her tangled black hair out of her face. Her hands were twisting over and over each other anxiously. "He tried to kill us, Jane. The rest of it is just details. We need a plan. Do you have your passport? Any cash? Misty, my friend from Book & Bell, can—"

"Lynne told him to make everything look normal," Jane repeated stubbornly. "Dee. She can't *know* anything for sure because she's still planning on going ahead with the wedding."

A low whine began in the kitchen, and Dee jumped off her cushion. Jane froze for a panicked moment, but the whine climbed steadily until it was recognizable as the shrill of a boiling teakettle, and Jane relaxed back against the red wall. She heard the cozy, comfortable sounds of the kettle being removed from the burner and water pouring into mugs, and she sighed: how could her world have gotten so dangerous in such a short period of time?

Dee's dark blue jeans scissored back across Jane's field of vision, and a steaming mug found its way into her hands. The surface of the liquid rippled; Jane realized that she must be trembling. "You mean . . . you are going to go back?" Dee said quietly, her husky voice so low it was almost inaudible.

"I have to," Jane whispered. The heat of the mug emanated up her arms and made her feel more present in her body. The horror of the afternoon was still there, but the emptiness had been replaced with a plan—and a sense of certainty about how the next twenty-four hours of her life would play out. "If she had been sure that I knew about her, Yuri would have just attacked. Instead he was nice—or he tried to be—because Lynne still thinks she can get away with her plan. She wasn't ready to blow her cover; she just wanted me to come back to the house where she could keep an eye on me. And if I don't go back, she *will* know."

And I'll be nothing more than an ill-prepared moving target. She would have to run with the clothes on her back, just like she had meant to do the night of the disastrous cocktail party at the MoMA. True, she had her credit cards this time, but the end result would be the same: she'd be caught before she made it out of the state. Malcolm would come home and find . . . what? A forged note saying that Jane had gotten cold feet and flown back to France? A call from the coroner, saying Jane had passed away in a freak car accident that was no one's fault? He wouldn't believe either story, but he wouldn't be able to save her then. And if Lynne caught wind of what *he* had been up to over the past month . . . "I have to go back," Jane repeated more firmly, "and you need to run."

Dee shook her head dismissively. "I'll be fi—"

"You won't," Jane cut her off impatiently. The police might believe that Yuri had attacked Dee at random and that she had killed him in self-defense—the police had probably heard a thing or two about Yuri before. But Lynne would figure it out immediately. She didn't know Jane and Dee were friends, but when she discovered that Yuri's body was found in an alley next to the home of someone connected to Jane—even as remotely as an assistant wedding-cake baker was—Dee's days would be numbered.

Jane cleared her throat. "You can't be involved in this. We got lucky today, but I need to know you'll be safe when I'm gone. You need an alibi so good no one will even think to talk to you, and you need to stay out of sight until the whole thing blows over."

Dee looked as though she was going to argue, but Jane stared her down. Finally, Dee sighed and nodded. "It won't be as hard as you think. This is Misty's place. It's an illegal sublet, and my name's not on anything. She wanted to be closer to the store, and I had just moved to New York and didn't know anybody . . ." She trailed off, apparently momentarily distracted by the memory. "Misty will help," she concluded confidently. "Strays and runaways are like her second job. She can handle this, no problem. And you'll know how to reach me when—if—" Dee frowned.

"I know," Jane told her gently. "I'll miss you. Just stay safe."

Dee's wide mouth curved up into a smile that held faint traces of her usual cockiness. "I'll land on my feet, Jane. And you better do the same."

forty-one

JANE HAD THE TAXI DRIVER LET HER OUT AT THE CORNER. SHE stayed close to the tall limestone buildings lining Park Avenue, wanting to avoid the sight of the gaping black windows at the top of the Dorans' mansion. In the months she had lived there, she had never been able to shake the feeling that someone was watching her from those windows. Of course, now that she thought about it, it was probably Charles.

I can't believe I'm coming back here willingly. Again.

Jane shivered and tapped her code into the panel beside the carved wooden door. Gunther was awake enough to approximate a wave, but she was reasonably sure she heard him snoring by the time she reached the narrow back staircase. At least there would be a record of her using her code to come home, even if he didn't remember. She had been sorely tempted to use the service entrance instead of the ostentatious front door, but had changed her mind after imagining Lynne in a black fury, demolishing half of Brooklyn because she didn't realize that Jane was back.

When she slid open the door into the kitchen, her heart zoomed down to the tips of her toes. Lynne was exactly where she had been when Jane had run out earlier: sitting at the kitchen table, sipping tea from a delicate porcelain cup. Jane opened her mouth to speak, but found herself frozen indecisively, her mouth wide, and still holding the door handle.

"Nice try," Lynne purred. Every instinct of Jane's screamed at her to run, but whether it was fear or some kind of spell, she felt completely unable to move. "But you'll still have to go through with the fitting," Lynne went on, standing to her considerable full height. "The couturier was simply beside himself, of course, but he's a professional, and I did eventually feel compelled to remind him of that fact. So he'll just have to come a bit early tomorrow if he really can't manage with the measurements that he has already." She glided majestically across the tiled floor and tipped the remains of her tea into the sink. "Do let me see your nails, dear."

Jane felt a faint prickling in her fingers and toes, as if they had been numb and now the feeling was returning. The wooden door clicked shut behind Jane and she realized that she must have let it go. She held her hands in front of her uncertainly. Her nails didn't have blood under them like Dee's had, but the shell-pink polish didn't look new, either. "Jin Soon had a wait," she heard herself saying, "but the hairdresser said she could change out the polish tomorrow as long as it's something simple. Which is fine."

Lynne nodded slowly, her odd, dark eyes riveted on Jane's. "Dorans go to the front of the line, Jane," she said finally. "Especially on such a special occasion."

Jane forced herself to breathe; it would be harder to sound natural if her face was turning blue. She had been convinced that Lynne knew about Yuri somehow—honestly, she had believed it on some level since she had left Dee's apartment. But if Lynne *did* know that something was wrong, she was playing it impossibly cool. *So I just have to keep up the act until tomorrow,* Jane reminded herself desperately. "Of course," she said out loud. "I'm just a little emotional, I guess. About the big day. So I've been kind of out of it. I've never been married before. It's kind of a new experience for me." Jane let out an inane giggle.

Lynne's eyes narrowed, but her peach lips pursed together thoughtfully. After a long moment, she seemed to accept that excuse, and stepped away from the sink. "Perhaps you should lie down, dear," she suggested, and Jane gratefully hurried forward, toward the hall that led to her room. "Do let me know if you plan to go out again tonight," Lynne added from somewhere behind her, in a voice that could have frozen fire. A fierce chill ran down Jane's spine and, not trusting herself to speak, she nodded once before she fled down the hallway.

It wasn't until she shut the door of her bedroom that she began to sob. Her chest heaved as her anguish poured out in salty waves, and she wondered for what felt like the millionth time exactly how she'd gotten here. When she'd met Malcolm, she felt like she'd been rescued from years of heartbreaking loneliness. But their relationship had plunged her straight into hell, and she'd gone from French Orphan Swept Off Her Feet to Kill-or-Be-Killed Girl.

She kicked off her shoes and padded into her spacious closet. The discreetly hidden lighting glowed to life, making each sleeve, skirt, strap, and heel look like a work of art. She stretched onto her tiptoes to reach the Louis Vuitton hatbox that sat on the back of a high shelf ("Every New York woman who's *anyone* needs a hatbox!" Lena from Barneys had sworn) and pulled it down, narrowly missing her own head.

She brusquely tossed the lovely Lanvin hat inside out of the way. It settled on the closet floor, glossy black feathers quivering. Four layers of tissue paper followed it quickly, and finally Jane felt the dusty-soft paper of the manuscript that Dee had given her to read—discreetly—at home. The curious and eventually institutionalized Rosalie Goddard had not been especially inclined to share the source material for her controversial book. But in her diaries, she had mentioned the names of a couple of books and their authors. Misty Travers had located one of them in her extensive back room. *Hope she has enough room back there to hide Dee,* Jane thought, and then she shut those thoughts out. There was nothing she could do now, and fretting wouldn't help.

Instead, she carried the manuscript gently back to the carved and canopied bed, pulled the silk duvet over her aching body, and began to read. Because she was tired and tense, the words mostly ran together, but after a few minutes she began to get the sense of what she was reading, and another minute after that, a familiar name jumped out.

> The first woman to discover this amazing reserve of natural magic and bend it to her will was a queen in her own land. Before Ambika died, she divided her massive wealth among her seven sons, and bequeathed her magic among her seven daughters.
>
> The sons have disappeared from history, but for centuries the descendants of those seven daughters passed their magic through the female line, just as

Ambika did, and seven distinct families emerged. Gradually, perceived inequalities between the families' powers caused jealousy and strife. In the Middle Ages, plain fighting broke out when witches realized that a fallen witch's powers could be stolen at the moment of her death. These battles eventually attracted attention even from the non-magical community, inciting fear and hysteria.

In the resulting hysteria and suspicion, most of the accused and executed "witches" were innocent. When the occasional real witch was caught and killed, however, the power was transferred to her survivors, and so, most active witches were willing to overlook the civilian casualties of their wars. By the late seventeenth century, however, two of the seven families had been wiped out completely, and this danger was considered less acceptable to the witches. A truce was called amongst the remaining five, and once again magic went underground.

The world grew steadily smaller, though, and the signatories of the truce grew further and further from their descendants' collective memories. Once the danger in Salem had passed, large numbers of witches immigrated to the New World to establish control over unclaimed swaths of the Americas, and the vast new territory reignited old conflicts.

A floorboard creaked, and magical pulses arced between Jane's fingertips. The power that began to pulse in her veins felt so strong that she was almost surprised she couldn't see it moving under the skin of her arms. *If someone comes in here, I could kill them,* she realized. A dead body at her bedroom door would be a lot harder to walk away from than Yuri's had been, not to mention the fact that there was a decent chance that, in her panic, she might blow up someone relatively harmless, like Sofia. It was kind of no-win, and she wished for an old-fashioned key-and-tumbler lock on her door.

After a moment, it occurred to her that she could put her extra magic to use to make the next best thing.

Focusing her attention on the heavy mahogany bookcase beside the door, she tried to pull enough magic together to move it. Her attention was scattered, though, and the magic responded accordingly. An antique clock covered in gold plate crashed from the fourth shelf to the ground with a loud *bang*. Its glass face shattered into thousands of tiny glittering pieces on the carpet. She guessed it had probably cost a small fortune, but even more important, it had made an impressive amount of noise for its size. She wondered if someone would come to check on her.

Or just burst in and attack her.

Jane redoubled her assault on the bookcase, willing it to move just a little, but it only rattled in its place, sending a couple of dusty, leather-bound books onto their sides. She could almost hear Dee chiding her for focusing on the wrong thing, and she closed her eyes. The bookcase wasn't the point; it was just an object for her power to act on. Before she could make it act, she needed to concentrate on the power itself, and make it obey her will. She spun Gran's silver ring on her finger and turned her focus inward, exploring her magic.

After a stubborn moment, it began to respond, like millions of tiny pinpricks in her veins. She drew it together slowly, patiently, so deep in her own mind that she could no longer feel her own body. With her magic at the ready, it was almost easy: the massive piece of mahogany slid in front of the door as if it were gliding across ice, and, for once, Jane didn't feel entirely spent.

In spite of its bulk, the bookcase looked somehow fragile against the door—thin and almost insubstantial. It certainly wouldn't stop Lynne if she wanted to enter; it might not stop Charles, either. Maybe even slight, bulge-eyed Sofia could still get in. With a sigh, Jane pulled herself upright again and turned her attention toward an antique armoire in the corner, narrower than the bookcase but definitely more solid-looking.

By the time she felt safe, she couldn't have opened her eyes if her life had depended on it, and she sank into a dreamless sleep.

Forty-two

THE MORNING OF THE WEDDING DAWNED OVERCAST AND HUMID, but the scene inside of Jane's suite was so hectic that the weather was at the absolute bottom of her list of worries. Lynne was on the warpath because something was wrong with the flowers ("I quite clearly stated, 'Nothing whatsoever involving hibiscus,' so I simply do *not* understand why you're standing there like the village idiot holding that awful bouquet full of them when you *could* be taking this opportunity to redo the centerpieces"), the brass octet were stuck in heavy traffic on the George Washington Bridge, and the couturier just would not stop fussing.

Jane could only assume that no one had yet wondered where the Dorans' personal driver was. All of this frivolity on the heels of a violent death felt obscene and ghoulish to her, but no one else seemed bothered in the slightest that Yuri had never shown up for work. While two women and a very skinny man clumped around Jane, curling bits of her hair, pinning others, and spraying makeup onto her face before carefully sponging most of it off again, it was all Jane could do to not explode out of her seat and flee from the chaos. Why had she ever agreed to any of this? Twisting her silver ring around her finger, she reminded herself that it would all be over in a matter of hours. Those hours couldn't pass soon enough.

"Well, I have no idea why anyone would have told you that, but now *I'm* telling you to turn yourself back around and get those over to the Met where they belong," Cora McCarroll screeched, sounding nearly unpleasant enough to be mistaken for her twin. "Alicia's there with the seating chart." There was a brief pause before she added, "Is there any reason you're still blocking our doorway?" and then a door slammed shut and Jane could only conclude that the place-card debacle was on its way to being resolved.

The couturier stabbed Jane in the ribs with a pin and she jumped, causing one of her hairstylists to burn her own wrist with a curling iron. "Sorry," Jane mumbled, but noticed the couturier didn't seem the least bit contrite, even though it was all his fault. Instead, he was muttering something about Mrs. Doran having promised that Jane would cut out carbs entirely between the last fitting and now, and who could blame him for believing it, when any sane person would *want* to look good in a one-of-a-kind haute couture masterpiece like this one?

"I'm sorry, but all of the press invitations went out last—" Sofia's voice wafted down the hall with barely enough force to make it to Jane's ears, but she sounded desperate. "I understand that," she went on miserably, "but I have the list right here, and it says . . . No, that's what I'm trying to tell you: Mr. Lavandeira simply isn't on the list . . . I know . . . I know . . . I'm sure that if it were an oversight someone would have caught . . . No, I know . . ." She drifted out of range, and Jane sighed. She felt horrible that otherwise normal people had to be sucked into the massive tornado that was The Wedding.

And speaking of tornadoes . . . she thought confusedly as the four people working on her swirled into some new and mysterious configuration. They formed a human shield in front of her, her stylist actually brandishing her curling iron. *What now?*

"No! You're not allowed to see her yet!" the makeup artist squealed. "It's bad luck."

"Well, now." A molten-gold voice rumbled through the air between them. "We certainly don't need any of that."

"Malcolm," Jane exclaimed, the breath rushing out of her in relief. Her entourage was crowded around her, blocking her view, but he was there. He had come back, and they would get away from all of this insanity, and everything would be all right again.

"I want to talk to him," she announced in a loud, firm tone. "Figure something out." She realized that she sounded alarmingly like Lynne or Cora, but she didn't care: they got results and she wanted some now.

It worked. Seconds later, she was shielded by a carved-rosewood screen, and the room was empty except for her and Malcolm. She could feel the heat of his body radiating through the wood, and she seriously considered shoving the stupid thing out of the way, but he was right: today, of all days, they needed luck on their side. "I missed you," she said instead, and tried to put all of her longing into the words.

"I missed you, too," his hoarse whisper came back. "I've been worried sick about what was happening to you. Are you okay?"

"I'm—" Jane hesitated. She'd been about to say "fine," but Yuri's final snarl, Charles's constant lurking, and Lynne's terrifying scheming all flashed in her mind at once. "Well, I'm still in one piece. But so much has happened . . ." She trailed off helplessly, unwilling to risk sharing the details, with so many of his mind-reading relatives around.

"I know," he murmured. "It's just a few more hours. Can you make it?"

"Of course," she assured him softly, but a grim part of her wondered how he'd react to knowing *everything* she'd done in the month since he'd been gone. The prank on Madison, the pyro-technics in front of Lynne, the killing . . . she shuddered and the scrambled eggs she'd eaten that morning flipped in her stomach. She closed her eyes. *"You saved my life,"* Dee's voice rang out in her head and she forced down the wave of nausea. As horrible as it was, she had done what she had to do.

"I love you," he said.

"I love you, too," she whispered. The screen moved a bit and she knew he was resting a hand against it. She raised her own, guessing where his might be so they would almost be touching through the thin layer of rosewood.

"I have to go," he told her after a silent minute. "The guy from Valentino is freaking out and my dad looked like he'd cry if we didn't have a scotch-and-cigar moment, so . . ."

"Get through the day," she reminded him. "Everything else can wait."

"Right," he said, but then paused. "Oh! I almost forgot: there was this girl outside who said she knew you. She didn't want to come in, but she gave me this." His golden-skinned hand appeared over the screen, holding a small packet of waxed paper. "I wasn't sure if I should check it first, but I figured you'd know if it was something . . . um, dangerous."

Jane sliced through the tape with a Goa Sand fingernail, not caring that the fresh polish chipped in protest. She doubted she would recognize a magical booby trap any more readily than Malcolm would. But considering that all of their enemies were currently inside the house, it didn't seem efficient to worry about an attack from some random person on the street. When the packet unfolded, she began to giggle in relief. "The girl outside—dark hair, kind of tall, with a hoarse voice?"

"Sounds about right."

Jane broke one of the chocolate-chip cookies in half and passed it back over the screen. She wished Dee hadn't risked coming up here, but at least she knew her friend was okay.

"This is our unofficial wedding cake. I made a friend while you were gone."

"Yeah?"

"Yeah."

She felt a genuine smile come to her lips as they chewed silently on opposite sides of the screen.

For the first time in a month, Jane knew deep down in her bones that everything really was going to be all right.

forty-three

THE BEGINNING OF THE WEDDING MARCH BOOMED THROUGH
the cathedral, and Jane hummed along in her head. When the
familiar *dum, dum, dum-dum* began, the ushers swung the doors
open theatrically. Approximately five hundred of the Dorans'
closest friends and family (plus selected press) rose to their feet
simultaneously, and Jane paused for a moment to allow them all
to get a good look at her dress. It was absolutely perfect—a simple
sheath with a satin ribbon right below the bustline. Considering
the very many "helpful" suggestions and sarcastic asides she'd en-
dured from Lynne about her "ridiculously casual" gown, *someone*
had better appreciate the damned thing.

As she started down the aisle, she thought for one moment
about the family that, in another world, would be here for her,
escorting her through the church to her new husband. Gran, no
doubt, would have shaken her head at the ostentatious event. Jane

had no idea what her mom or dad would have done, but she liked to think that her mother would love the clean lines of her cream-colored dress and satin shoes.

She twisted her grandmother's ring around her finger for luck, and then found Malcolm's dark eyes at the front of the church. He was staring at her in what looked like awe. His eyes shone, swimming with what she suspected were unshed tears. *Guess he's one of the "someones" who like it,* she smiled to herself. She knew the clinging column accented her curves while the delicate cap sleeves added an air of innocence and vulnerability. She figured both probably appealed to Malcolm in equal degrees. And then she forgot the dress, the guests, the obnoxious trailing sweet peas of her bouquet, Lynne, and everything else, because Malcolm was waiting for her at the end of the aisle, and all she wanted in the world was to get to him.

The music set her pace, but it was Malcolm's eyes that carried her over the rose petals strewn in the aisle. *We made it,* she thought with exhilaration as he held his hand out to guide her for the last couple of steps. He had kept his promise, and she had held on long enough to see that he was on her side. She couldn't concentrate on the sermon and didn't try; she just rested her hand in his and breathed in his spiced-champagne scent. She knew some of this need to be with him was magic, but she didn't care. *Magic is natural,* she reminded herself, knowing that that was what Dee would tell her. *And so is love.* There are certain things in life you simply can't fight.

She dimly heard Malcolm repeating after the minister, and then it was her turn. "I, Jane Boyle, do promise . . ." It was easy; it was natural. Looking deep into Malcolm's eyes, she knew that together they would be unstoppable. He had a lifetime of experience with the power she now had in spades: there was nothing they wouldn't be able to face. *Let her come,* she thought fiercely. *Let that bitch try to track us down.* She jammed Malcolm's platinum wedding band on his finger with such passion that he winced a bit, and she twitched her mouth apologetically.

He leaned forward, wrapped an arm around her waist to pull her as close as he could, and kissed her forcefully on the lips. Bells began to toll joyfully above them, and they turned to walk hand-in-hand down the aisle through the parted sea of smiling faces.

"We made it," she whispered triumphantly to him.

"I love you," he replied, his eyes shining.

Near the exit, Jane found herself searching for one face in particular, even though she knew that she wouldn't see it. Even if Harris had had some burning desire to see her off, he wouldn't have put them all in danger by crashing a wedding full of killer mind-readers. He had had the good sense to stay away, and Jane reminded herself that that was a good thing. *Good-bye,* she thought at the memory of his face, *now you and Maeve will both be safe.*

Or would they? The thought ricocheted around her mind as they approached the outer doors of the cathedral. What would Lynne do when she and Malcolm didn't return from their supposed honeymoon? Jane had assumed that Lynne's focus would be on finding her, but would the thwarted witch really leave the Montagues in peace if she thought they might know where she was?

Jane and Malcolm stepped out into the feeble sunlight. Malcolm smiled at her, but she was too wrapped up in her fears to smile back. *I can't go without knowing that they're safe, but it's not like I can ask him in the middle of our stupid receiving line.*

It occurred to her as the breeze ruffled the waves of his hair that she wouldn't really have to ask. She hadn't been able to read Malcolm's mind before he had left, but she had come really far since then thanks to Dee ... and Harris. She fought down a twinge of discomfort at the idea; it felt intrusive. But she needed this information—now. And besides, he had given her permission, sort of, the night that he had left New York. *I'll tell him later,* she decided. *He will have to understand how important this is.* She took a deep breath and concentrated. She found the thread of his thoughts easily. *I really am getting good.*

Malcolm flinched when she touched his mind, and she realized belatedly that he had had enough experience with witches to know when magic was directed his way. She stared meaningfully into his eyes and squeezed his hand, trying to convey silently that it was all right; it was just her. She didn't understand why his eyes widened in fear, or why he suddenly took a step away from her— did he not understand?

All around them, people cheered, clapped, and cried. She was vaguely aware that someone had stepped on the short train of her dress, but Jane kept her focus on Malcolm, and on his thoughts. And then, the world narrowed around her, and she was seeing what he was seeing, and she understood why he had shrunk away from her. But it was too late to pull back now.

Malcolm crept through the dark farmhouse, careful not to make any noise with his body or his mind. There was no movement, and no probing thoughts brushed his own, but he knew he had to stay vigilant: danger could come from anywhere. Weak yellow light spilled from the living room—was she still awake at this hour? He waited a few breaths in total silence before peering around the corner, keeping his head low to the ground. She was facing him, and for a moment he thought he'd been caught, but his breath steadied when he realized her eyes were closed, and a book lay open on the table beside her.

He hesitated: it would be too risky to creep slowly across the room. She could wake up while he was stuck halfway. He would be completely helpless, and, old or no, she was lethal. But youth and speed were on his side, and he sprang from his crouch and crossed the room in three large bounds. Her eyes flew open when he jammed the syringe into her thigh and depressed the plunger, but it was too late by then: the poison was already speeding her heart past the point where she would be able to fight him.

It was over in seconds. When he felt the shuddering of her body begin to slow, he pulled a small silver knife from his pocket and held it in front of her mouth, waiting for her final breath. It came and went, though, and he felt no change in the athame; no electric hum to tell him he had succeeded.

How was this possible? He had magic in his blood. He should have been able to receive her magic. Unless . . . she had already taken her last breath as a witch, and given it away. But the only person she might have given it to was the girl, and *she* hadn't been here in years. He straightened with a shrug: it would have been a useful bonus, but his main task had been accomplished.

Celine Boyle was dead, and so was the protection spell she had set around her only heir.

Now, finally, he could get to Jane.

Suddenly, Jane was catapulted out of the old, familiar farmhouse and was back in her body, back in New York, with the full knowledge of what had happened. The sun felt too bright, her shoes pinched her toes, and her dress chafed her entire body. The din of the voices around her sounded louder than a concert at full blast. It was all just too much. Jane put her hands to her face, and then felt herself retching on the cathedral's steps. Screams of alarm fluttered into her mind as though through mounds of cotton. But all she could see was Malcolm killing her grandmother over and over again, on an endless loop. And then everything went blissfully, mercifully dark.

forty-four

WHEN JANE WOKE UP, SHE HAD NO IDEA WHERE SHE WAS. THE
ceiling above her was supported by wood rafters that sloped at a
steep angle. Light filtered in through two dusty windows, and the
walls were bare save for a small, gold-framed photo near the door.

She tried to sit up and get a better look around. The satin of
her dress rustled, but her limbs wouldn't move. *I was getting married,* she thought foggily. *I'm almost sure of it.* But that wasn't right,
not exactly. *I did* get married. *And now I'm in a bed . . . in an attic?* She
tried harder to move, and this time the source of the resistance
was clearer. *I'm tied to a bed in an attic.* Had the honeymoon started
already? *You'd think I'd remember that . . .*

But that wasn't right, either. Hot tears began to spill from
her eyes as her mind recalled the image of her husband leaning
over her dying grandmother. *No wonder the dog barked at him,* she
thought, but that reminded her that the dog hadn't been the only

one to recognize him. The old man in the flower shop—what had he said? *"Normal people come one time. They do not again."* His dark tangle of anger at the funeral suddenly made a lot more sense: he knew that Malcolm had been in Saint-Croix once already. He must have seen something that had made him suspicious, especially once Celine had turned up dead. *Why the hell didn't he say something?* she fumed impotently, but it was hard to really blame the stranger. Either he had been afraid to get involved or he had thought that Jane was a party to the murder; either one was more forgivable than Jane's marrying the man who had killed her grandmother.

And the more Jane thought about it the more she realized the full magnitude of her mistake. She had been so foolish. All the clues pointing the way to the truth had been laid out in front of her, like dainty little breadcrumbs, but she'd been so blinded by love, by her need for Malcolm, that she had put the picture together all wrong. She'd questioned the timing of Malcolm's arrival in her life, sure, but she'd overlooked the most obvious problem with the "coincidence." Malcolm was a son of a witch with bad intentions: he could never have gotten anywhere near her so long as the ever-paranoid Celine Boyle was alive. *And apparently the Dorans weren't willing to sit around waiting.*

Bile rose in her throat. Malcolm was a liar and a murderer, and she had put all of her trust in him. She had *married* him, for God's sake. There was no light at the end of the tunnel anymore. She had no one to love, no one to trust. But she did have someone to blame.

"Lynne Doran!" she shouted at the top of her lungs. "Lynne, you lunatic psycho-bitch, get your bony ass in here!"

There was a brief silence, and then the aging wood door swung open. "Really, dear. Do you *have* to be so crude?" Lynne sniffed. The twin cousins filed into the room behind her like bodyguards. "At least you won't be around to pass on your appalling lack of manners to my granddaughter. I shudder to think how she'd turn out under your tutelage."

Rage boiled through Jane, followed by the familiar prick of magic, but it was weak and faint, impossible to grasp, as if all her weeks of practice had been undone—or had never occurred at all.

Lynne laughed unpleasantly. "That's a useful little spell we hit you with, Jane. I'd offer to teach you sometime, but I doubt it'd be worth my trouble."

"Don't worry, it'll wear off . . . eventually," Cora tittered.

"I'll kill all three of you," Jane sputtered, although behind the hollow threat her mind was racing. So the cousins had done something to dampen her magic. But they hadn't taken it away. She just had to figure out how to access it.

Belinda smirked. "It's three against one, Jane, and let's be honest: you're not really much of a witch even when you *haven't* just been knocked out."

Jane swallowed hard. Maybe she wasn't much of a witch, but that was because these women had killed her grandmother before she'd had time to teach her anything.

"Killing your thug wasn't all that hard," she spat at Lynne, whose eyes narrowed in response.

"Yes," Lynne mused. "I suppose I'll have to punish you for that. Will taking your baby and slitting your throat do it?"

Jane rolled her eyes. "Your golden boy never did manage to knock me up, so you might as well get to the throat-slitting and spare me having to listen to your obnoxious voice for another moment." Anger rattled through her, igniting tiny sparks of her magic. She focused hard on them. If she could summon just enough, perhaps she could get the photo frame beside the door to fly off the wall and lodge in Lynne's brain.

"As tempting as that is, dear, your throat will remain intact for another nine months. I do need you to have that baby for me one way or another. Although, unfortunately, Malcolm is *unavailable* at the moment." A shadow flickered across her face and was gone before Jane could interpret it. "How very lucky that I have two sons."

Charles. Jane swallowed a gasp. This woman was truly sick.

"From what I heard, 'luck' had nothing to do with little Charlie's birth," Jane retorted, trying to mask her terror. Lynne flinched. "Malcolm sold you out," Jane went on softly, forcing Lynne to step a little closer to the bed to hear her. She gave the framed photo a hopeful try; it rattled so faintly that it could have passed for a loud exhale. *Come closer. Get distracted. Give me something to work with, here.* "He made up some nonsense about 'experimental drugs,' made it sound like a mistake of a desperately hopeful woman. But you and I know better, don't we? You weren't hopeful. You didn't wait to see how the pregnancy would go, and you sure as hell didn't bother with anything the FDA will ever see. The moment you knew you were pregnant, you locked it down. You just kept forcing and forcing more of your witchcraft on his fragile little brain until you broke it." Jane chuckled grimly. "Shame you couldn't figure out how to move chromosomes around. It would've all been worth it to have a broken *daughter*, right?"

Lynne's eyes blazed with rage and she took a menacing step forward.

"Lynne," Cora cautioned.

After a violently still moment, Lynne straightened up and

smoothed the peach gown she'd worn to the wedding. It matched her lipstick perfectly. "Well," she snapped very precisely. "I guess you'll find out soon enough." Then she strode out of the room, her cousins on her heel.

No, Jane thought desperately. *I need more time.* She thrashed against her ropes, but there wasn't the slightest bit of give in the complicated knots. And then she saw the hulking figure lurking in the hallway. *Charles.* Her stomach turned and for a moment she thought she might pass out again.

"This is seriously your sickest idea yet," she called to Lynne, hearing a note of desperation creep into her voice.

"Be a good boy, Charles." Lynne appeared in the doorway. She kissed her younger son on the cheek and smiled aloofly at Jane. A moment later, she slammed the door shut behind her. Charles padded toward Jane, a horrifying gleam in his eye. A key turned in the lock, and then they were alone.

Forty-five

MAGIC CALLS TO MAGIC, JANE THOUGHT WILDLY AS CHARLES MOVED closer to the bed. "Wait a minute," she pleaded urgently. "Charles, wait. Is it 'Charles'? 'Charlie'?" He stared at her, momentarily confused. *Whichever.* "Just wait a second."

He shook his head and grabbed her ankle; she instinctively shot her focus out toward the painting again. This time, free from the other witches' stifling presence, it flew off the wall, but it drooped low before it reached Charles's meaty shoulder, and ended up bouncing harmlessly off of his leg. In spite of herself, she caught herself admiring the older witches' skill. *How the hell long before their knockout wears off?*

Charles wrinkled his nose, then touched her other ankle and squeezed. Hard.

"Stop!" she demanded, cringing from the feel of his meaty fingers on her skin. *What now? What now?* A wave of panic threatened to overcome her. How could she stop him—and how could she do so quietly enough that Lynne and her drones wouldn't hear the slam of his body against the wall? If they rushed back into the attic, she'd never get another chance to get away.

And even if she did manage to hit him hard enough to do real damage, she'd still be tied to the bed, with her power coming back in slow dribbles.

Charles's clammy hand grabbed her big toe and wiggled it back and forth, almost as though he was playing "This Little Piggy." Jane thrashed her legs, trying to sit up and free herself from the bed. Charles's smile drooped and he shook his head. He wrapped his fleshy hand around her throat and pinned her back to the bed.

She shuddered violently, and a flash of confused images invaded her mind—a tattered doll with the smiling face half wrenched off, a shattered mirror, a threadbare blanket. *Charles's thoughts.*

But his thoughts didn't feel lustful, as Lynne clearly wanted them to be. They just felt . . . lonely. Jane set her jaw, struggling to take a breath. *I'll have to work with him,* she decided. *There has to be something in there.*

Summoning all her energy, she dove into Charles's mind. Like Malcolm's, it offered just a thin skin of passing resistance—but unlike Malcolm's, it was a jumbled mess.

Charles howled and increased the pressure around Jane's neck. *No, no, no!* Jane thought frantically, gasping for air. With her mind's eye, she grabbed onto one of the memories spinning in Charles's brain. Miraculously, the movement stopped and a scene blossomed in her mind.

"You'll be getting a new friend in the house," Lynne told Charles lovingly, in a distant memory. But before Jane could see more, colors

blurred and suddenly a slightly younger Charles was in the attic, pounding on the door and ripping apart the bed as footsteps retreated down the hallway, leaving him all by himself. In the memory, Charles took a tarnished silver object out of his pocket and clutched it in his palm.

Jane fought desperately to take a breath. Still locked inside of Charles's disordered and confused mind, she pushed as hard as she could.

The thought moved.

"You'll be getting a new friend in the house," Lynne repeated, more clearly this time. *"Do you understand what I mean by 'friend'?"*

Charles's eyes widened. For a moment, he loosened his grip on Jane's neck and stared at her. Jane took a greedy gulp of air.

Charles tried to brush the memory away, but Jane held on for dear life. After a few moments, Charles returned obediently to the memory she held in front of him.

"I'm your brother," a bored-looking eighteen-year-old Malcolm told Charles, who was still in diapers in spite of looking too old for them. Charles gaped at him, and Malcolm rolled his eyes in annoyance. "Whatever—it's like having a friend. Except you're never going to have one of those, so . . . Mom, do I have to? The kid's a turnip." Lynne's response was too soft for Charles to hear, but Malcolm was apparently chastened because he turned back to his little brother. "Look, we're friends, okay? It means I'll always be nice to you, and that I'll look out for you, and that you do the same when you can. I'm leaving tomorrow for school, so it's not like—" Malcolm glanced to the side where Lynne was presumably standing before going on. "So I'll be away for a while, but I'll visit. I'll be back at Thanks—" Another glance. "Christmas." He began to turn toward the door, and sadness welled up in Charles.

Abruptly, Malcolm turned back, holding out something in his hand. "You could hold on to this for me, until I get back."

Charles held out his hands eagerly, and Malcolm dropped a silver Yale key chain into them. Charles stared up at him with adoration before leaning forward and sinking his teeth into Malcolm's leg.

"Ow! Damn it! Mom, would you—" He shook Charles off violently, and the child collapsed on the ground, sobbing. "Oh, for the love of . . . Never mind. I got it." He bent down to look Charles in the eye, holding him firmly by the shoulders just in case. "We're friends, remember? That means you never, ever hurt me, and I don't hurt you, either."

"You're hurting me, Charles," Jane told him firmly, forcing her voice not to tremble. "This hurts."

Charles backed away, confused, and Jane dug through his mind for what she needed, to drive the point home.

"*You'll be getting a new friend in the house,*" Lynne said, showing Charles a snapshot of Jane that Malcolm had taken on one of the narrow back streets of the Marais. She was laughing happily, pale blond hair whipping around in the wind like a flag. They had gone to a museum and then sat for hours in her favorite café with the orange walls, sipping hot chocolate.

"*We're friends, remember?*" Malcolm said. "*That means you never, ever hurt me, and I don't hurt you, either.*" The key chain spun between them, the silver gleaming.

Charles inhaled deeply, and Jane almost cried with relief when Charles reached into his pocket and pulled out a tarnished Yale key chain. He turned it over and over in his hands.

"We're friends, Charles, so you won't hurt me, and that's good! Because I need you to help me right now. And then we'll go to my room and you can pick out anything you want, like that key chain, to remember that we're friends, just like you and Malcolm. Okay?"

He stared at her balefully, and then turned and shuffled toward the door.

"Wait—Charles! Wait!" she squeaked. Charles flinched at the sound of her voice, but he didn't open the door. "I can't go anywhere right now; that's why I need your help. Can you untie these ropes? Otherwise I can't . . . help you find your present." She almost said, "Otherwise I can't leave," but realized just in time that Charles might not consider that to be as much of a problem as she did. She showed him Malcolm's key chain again, pushing the memory discreetly away before he bit Malcolm.

Fortunately, Charles seemed to like the present idea because he returned purposefully to the bed. The knots were complicated and extremely tight, but she merged her thoughts with his. Her mind helped direct his, and within minutes, she was rubbing her sore wrists and legs.

"Good," she breathed, casting her mind toward the locked door. The tumblers felt simple and blissfully loose to her tired magic, turning almost of their own accord, and then she was free. For now, at least.

forty-six

Jane pressed her ear to the door, searching for any signs of life. Silence greeted her, and Jane said silent thanks that Lynne hadn't stayed around to listen to the show. She opened the door as carefully as she could, wincing at the tiny creak. In the quiet, and in her fear, the click sounded almost like a scream. But there was no hint of voices or footsteps, so she had to assume that most of the noise was just a product of her frayed nerves.

Jane made Charles walk ahead of her to give her as much room as possible to escape if they ran into someone. Fortunately, they made it to her room without incident. Once the door clicked shut behind them, she went straight for the closet, feeling more and more urgent every second. Her luck couldn't hold out forever, and her room only had one exit; she had to hurry or she could get cornered. She whipped her navy Burberry trench over her tired-looking wedding dress and scooped up the compact little flight bag she had packed for her "honeymoon." She glanced at Charles, who was standing fixedly in front of her bathroom mirror, apparently entranced by her moisturizer.

She thought about just sneaking out of the room, but her conscience got the best of her. "Charles," she whispered, and his head swiveled around. "You remember what I said, about picking something as a present? You can take anything you want, and then go back to your room, okay? Because your mom might be angry if she sees you here." She dug quickly through his mind for illustrative examples, showing him Lynne in a variety of unflattering snits.

He ambled over and, with a hopeful expression, held up a little stuffed dog a MoMA vendor had sent her. Jane nodded, her heart panging as he hugged it to his chest.

"Okay, fine. Now I'm going out and then you count to ten— do you understand? You count to ten and then come out and go back to your room." She caught a glimpse of his mind's interpretation of her instructions, which involved her tied to his bed again in just a thong. She began to rifle through his thoughts for something a little closer to her plan, but her focus was abruptly interrupted when he slapped her across the face. She reeled back. He stared at her with a reasonably pleasant expression on his slack face, all things considered, and she reminded herself that he wasn't just misunderstood—he was also nuts. "Ten," she reminded him firmly, rubbing her stinging cheek, and slid silently from the room.

The hallways remained mercifully deserted, but it felt like it took her a month to reach the staircase. She chose the service entrance rather than the main door, in case Gunther was awake at his post for once, but didn't really breathe until she was on the street.

It was surreal: bright, peaceful, normal, and completely separate from the lunatic world just a few stories above it. The trees in the median, leaves just beginning to bud, waved gently in the breeze. *I'm free,* she thought, trying to make the news sink into her still-terrified brain. Her hands were shaking and she clenched them, trying to steady her heart. *I can go anywhere I want now, and they'll never—*

"Jane," a molten-gold voice murmured behind her, and she let out a tiny scream.

Malcolm.

She spun around, but the sidewalk was empty.

"Jane," Malcolm's unmistakable voice said again, and she whipped her head back and forth, trying to find him.

Just get in a cab and get the hell away! her brain shouted, but something was wrong. His voice sounded wrong. Her body hovered halfway between the stairs and the curb, between danger and freedom, waiting for her mind to click to a decision.

"I have to get to Jane," Malcolm whispered, and she finally understood: she wasn't hearing his voice. She was hearing his mind.

It doesn't matter. Just get in a damn cab! But she hesitated again, glancing at the main door a few yards away. No one was coming yet, and she'd see them first if they did, wouldn't she?

It'd be useful to know as much as I can before I go, she told the skeptical part of her brain, but the truth was that Malcolm's "voice" sounded choked and desperate, and she just wanted to . . . check. *On your grandmother's murderer,* the skeptical part reminded her, but she shushed it. As true as that statement was, so was the desperation and love she felt in his thoughts. She stood frozen, indecisive, then flattened herself against the gray stone of the mansion, pushing very quietly into Malcolm's mind.

He was somewhere dark with stone walls—a basement? It was hard to get a clear picture of his surroundings through his eyes, though, because he had surrounded himself with mental images of Jane. Everywhere she looked, there she was, laughing, blushing, brushing on lip gloss, eating, showering, working. They were meeting, flirting, arguing, making love, and getting married, but fear infiltrated every image. She followed the thread of fear, and there she was again: bloodied, broken, tortured, and dead in hundreds of painful-looking ways. In most of the images, Lynne was there, gloating, and something nagged at Malcolm's memory wherever his mother appeared. Jane couldn't quite catch it the first few times that it flickered by, but the repetition felt significant.

She tapped her foot impatiently while, in the newest vision, Lynne snapped her neck and she fell to the ground. She waited for the flicker to pass by again, and this time she saw it coming. *I chose wrong,* he was thinking and, carefully so as not to alert him to her presence, she drifted toward that thought.

"No other member of this family requires so much handling, Malcolm. Can't you try a little harder to remember your loyalties?"

"I don't see why we can't just—"

"Malcolm," Lynne snapped, twirling a gleaming black pen between her long fingers. "You're simply not qualified to make this sort of decision."

"It's murder," he said, but his voice wavered, lacking conviction.

"It is," she snarled softly, dropping the pen. "But do you remember what happened the last time you had the slightest bit of responsibility for our family's welfare?" Malcolm flinched, and his mother leaned toward him, dark eyes glowing cruelly. "Don't you realize that you are the reason why it has come to this at all? We only need this girl because you have never wanted to be responsible. So I'm making it easy for you: no hard choices, no moral dilemmas. All you have to do is exactly what you're told. Enough of that and maybe you'll come close to making up for what you did to my darling girl."

Malcolm recoiled as if he'd been slapped, but Lynne's hands had risen to cover her face, and her shoulders shuddered with what looked like sobs. He crossed the distance between them in two long steps and knelt by her feet, tears standing in his own eyes.

Then memories of Annette crashed in on him and Jane both: a little girl with a round face and a light-brown bob, in a pink bathing suit, shoveling sand into a bucket while the grown-ups hid from the sun's glare in their shady house. Malcolm, thin at twelve but already growing tall, had wandered off down the beach, drawn by the sight of older boys playing soccer. Then there were frantic calls behind him that quickly became desperate wails, and he saw that the bucket and shovel were still on the sand, purposeless and ownerless.

"You're right," Malcolm whispered against Lynne's trembling knees. "I'm sorry, Mom. Of course I will. I'll do whatever I have to. Just don't cry. I'll get the girl here. I'll make this right."

Jane threw herself violently away from the memory, revulsion making her clumsy. Everything spun around her as Malcolm became aware of the intruder in his thoughts.

Jane! his mind shouted. *Jane, get the hell away from this place!*

Then, with a snap, he expelled her from his mind. She gasped and fell into her own body again. The everyday New York sounds of cars revving, pedestrians laughing, and cell phones ringing swooped in on her at full volume. Jane kicked the stone wall in frustration, leaving a gray smudge on the point of her ivory shoe. She could never forgive Malcolm for what he'd done, but now she had to admit that she couldn't hate him, either. His family had twisted him until he broke. It was Lynne who had made him what he was . . . but that could also make him an asset to Jane. No one knew Lynne better—strengths, weaknesses, everything—than the son who had disappointed her so thoroughly.

Jane tapped in the code to the service door, feeling a reckless rage boil up slowly but steadily. It was time to storm the freaking castle.

forty-seven

THE STAIRWAY WAS JUST AS STILL AS IT HAD BEEN ON HER WAY out, but there was a charge in the air that made the hairs on the back of Jane's neck stand up. She tried to tell herself it was just her nerves, but her nerves were telling her quite firmly that the hunt for her was on. She wasn't sure how far along it was, but there was no doubt she'd been missed.

The door at the bottom of the last flight of stairs looked like it had been built to withstand a nuclear blast. It was reinforced steel with three dead bolts on the outside—not one of them locked. She flew through it, the maze of pipes indicating that she was in the basement. Although with its array of hooks, chains, and what she was fairly certain were a variety of medieval torture devices, "dungeon" would have been a more appropriate term.

Is that a freaking rack?

Chained to the far wall and naked to the waist was Malcolm.

He raised his golden head in terrified disbelief. His right eye was swollen almost shut, and a trickle of blood ran from a nasty cut on his nose. But the worst damage she could see was the absolute despair in his eyes. "Jane, what the hell are you doing?" he rasped. "You need to get out of here."

"Malcolm, honey," she choked, her voice barely more than a whisper. "Did *you* know your mother was this kinky?"

"Jane, seriously," he wheezed.

She crossed the dungeon at a run, her stupid wedding shoes clacking obnoxiously over the concrete floor. "I'll go as soon as you do," she promised him, reaching for his chained wrist. "Just tell me where those bitches hide their keys."

He shook his head and winced. "No keys. She conjured the chains out of thin air."

The rage was boiling faster and redder now in Jane's body, co-alescing behind her eyes. A familiar electric tingle came with it, and she knew her magic had fully shaken off the dampening ef-fects of whatever Lynne and the twins had done to her. She took a step away from Malcolm.

"Thank God," he mumbled, clearly taking her step back as a retreat.

Footsteps sounded overhead, along with shouts. Time was running out. Inhaling a deep lungful of stale air, Jane called to-gether all of the power in her body. *Conjuring? They're not the only ones who can do tricks.* She let out a dry laugh as the magic formed a hard, angry ball in her chest.

Malcolm's head lolled up, uncomprehending. "Jane . . ." he began, but he met her eyes and clamped his mouth shut.

She moved the ball of fire outward, toward her fingertips, and clenched the chains around his wrists. She felt a detonation somewhere inside her, and at the same time the chains exploded into rusted sand that rained down on their feet. Without the chains to support his battered body, Malcolm slumped to the damp cement ground.

"Jane," he whispered, dark eyes wide.

"Shush," she told him. "Talk later. Right now we're in the middle of a daring escape." They headed for the service door, Malcolm limping miserably on an injured leg while Jane tried to contain her impatience. *You're the moron who insisted on rescuing him,* her mind informed her huffily, and she smiled in spite of herself.

The smile lasted through their slow progress up the stairs, but disappeared abruptly when the service door refused to open. "Shit."

She entered her code again, and then Malcolm's, and, finally, what she was pretty sure was Laura Helding's, but the little LED flashed red and the door didn't budge. "Shit shit shit shit." The footsteps sounded louder now, more frenzied. She channeled a few exploratory tendrils of magic into the keypad, but they bounced back painfully into her hands. *Magic-proof—I'd want that, too, if I spent my time going around killing other witches' families.*

"Let me try," Malcolm offered, stumbling toward the door. He winced, and she wondered if he'd cracked a rib or two.

"No point," she disagreed. "They've locked the place down."

Malcolm looked stricken. "Then it's over. They've won."

Jane fought the urge to shake his broken-looking shoulders. "What is wrong with you?" she demanded. "Why are you so in awe of your family? They're just witches, not gods. Are you really going to just give up? Stand here and wait for them to come and make up a new set of chains for you?"

Something changed in Malcolm as he processed her words.

He seemed to stand up straighter, and his eyes blazed beneath his puffy, blackened lids. "We have to get to Gunther's desk," he said resolutely. "Which means—"

"That we have to go through the main house."

He nodded slowly, and without waiting for more discussion, she dragged him grimly toward the main hall: if this was the end, they'd go down swinging.

A shout echoed through the high-ceilinged entryway when they burst into it, and Jane spun toward the sound. Belinda Helding was raising a bony finger to point at them, but Jane—who didn't bother with the dramatic gesture—was faster, and the woman smashed against the wall before slumping to the floor in an unconscious heap.

Jane had never felt so powerful, so angry—but also so in control. She ran toward Gunther's desk, shoving Belinda's limp body out of the way with her shoe. "Malcolm, tell me what all this is," she urged. The control panel was an incomprehensible mass of buttons and lights.

He shook his head helplessly. "Can't you just . . . ?" he wiggled his fingers as a demonstration.

She consulted the magic sparking through her veins for a moment, finding power but no intelligence, and shook her head. "I'm pretty sure I'd blow the whole thing up, which probably wouldn't open the doors."

He turned back toward the console. "What if we—"

Ding. It was the softest noise, but they both turned toward the sound as if it were machine-gun fire. It had to be Lynne. Heart pounding, Jane funneled all the electricity in her body to her hands, where it crackled almost visibly.

The elevator doors slid open painfully slowly. Jane started to launch her magic at it, but managed to pull it to the side just in time as Malcolm's father stepped out, scotch glass in hand, looking beyond dazed.

"What are you kids doing setting fireworks in the hall?" he slurred, crashing into the door frame as he staggered toward them. He didn't appear to notice the charred hole in the marble wall beside his head, the remnant of Jane's aborted attack. He did stop when he reached Belinda's prone form on the floor, but only for a brief moment before he stepped over her body. "Huh. Never liked her." He turned to his son. "Malcolm, Blake's got a poker game on two"—he frowned suddenly—"but this isn't two."

"Dad," Malcolm said carefully, "do you know how the security system works?" Jane stared at him incredulously: the man couldn't even work the elevator. But Malcolm nodded reassuringly as his father tottered toward them.

"I always did think these gizmos were neat," he announced happily, setting the scotch down so hard on the desk that some sloshed out. "Malcolm, have you talked to your mother? I think she's mad at you. You know how she gets. I got worried so I locked her in our room upstairs, but I think she'll find a way out. She always does."

Malcolm put a hand on his shoulder. "Dad, we're leaving," he said softly.

The older man turned his bleary eyes up to his son's face, taking in the damage there for what appeared to be the first time. "That sounds right," he agreed, turning back to the control panel with a shrug. "Wish I had . . . well, water under the bridge. You remind me of her," he added suddenly. Jane, who'd been watching the stairway for more intruders, frowned in confusion when she realized that he'd been talking to her. She was like *Lynne*?

"She was sweet when we met," he explained, his words alternately hesitating and running together. "Smart young thing, and pretty, too. More like you, less on her shoulders. You two should go now," he added sadly, and a soft beeping noise was followed by an audible click. He frowned at Malcolm's naked torso, quite possibly noticing it for the first time. He unbuttoned his own pink shirt and handed it to his son before settling into Gunther's padded chair in just his undershirt. "Even taxis still have standards. Some things do stay the same." He sounded sleepy.

"Malcolm, come on," Jane urged, pulling him toward the door, but he resisted, wincing at the pressure on his ribs. "It's only a matter of time before your mom gets free."

"No!" Malcolm cried. "We have to—*you* have to do something about my dad. When she finds out he helped—"

"Don't worry 'bout a thing," his father slurred in a relaxed singsong, swiveling the chair back and forth. "Never did figure out how you managed to hide things from her, kid. Bet it's good— you always were a smart one. But my way works, too." He winked and raised his scotch glass pointedly and drank a lengthy farewell toast as Malcolm finally let Jane pull him through the carved wooden door for what she fervently hoped would be the last time.

forty-eight

THE STREETLIGHTS HAD COME ON ALONG PARK AVENUE, AND Jane strained to see the familiar glow of a free taxi. She pushed Malcolm, bloodied and limping, down the avenue. The light changed and a fleet of taxis rushed toward them. One screeched to a halt several feet in front of them, the red taillights flashing. Jane slid across the seat and Malcolm slammed the door behind them.

"Grand Central," he announced.

The driver put the car in gear and pulled away from the curb. Jane breathed a sigh of relief, relaxing into the seat as the car lurched forward. But just two blocks later, the wheels locked with a sharp thud and the cab jolted to a stop in the middle of the road. "What the—" the driver muttered darkly. A black BMW zoomed past, and a minivan taxi leaned on its horn, coming within inches of their stalled cab.

"What are you doing?" Jane cried to the driver. Malcolm breathed heavily through his mouth; his nose had begun to bleed again.

"I'm not doing anything! It's the damn car." The driver threw the car in and out of gear a few times to no avail, and even shut off the engine before restarting it. The car hummed to life, making all of the right noises, but wouldn't budge so much as an inch along the pavement.

"Forget it," Malcolm ordered, grimacing as he reached for the door. "Let's just take a different cab."

Jane clutched Malcolm's wrist urgently, every hair on her arm standing on end. The air had changed. It was thicker somehow, foggy almost, and the world outside looked as if it were unfolding in slow motion. Each drop of moisture in the air sparkled like crystal.

"Malcolm," she whispered, her gaze transfixed on the rear window. "Don't get out of this car."

"What?" he asked, baffled, but she turned in her seat and he swiveled to follow her gaze. "Oh shit."

A wind had picked up, blowing brown leaves across the wide, tree-lined avenue, and the trees in the median and along the sidewalk bent in the sudden gust. But all Jane could see was Lynne, her peach wedding jacket billowing around her as she strode purposefully toward their beached taxi. Her hands were at her sides, and her eyes looked as dark as the night sky. She was walking in the middle of the street, but cars swerved harmlessly past, as if the entire world had bent itself around her. From what Jane could tell, it more or less had.

"She's doing it," Jane whispered.

"I know," Malcolm said. In the front seat, the driver swore and tried the ignition again. "Can you do anything?" Malcolm whispered to Jane.

As if I hadn't thought of that, Jane thought darkly, probing for any hole in Lynne's defenses. "She's too powerful." Jane turned her attention toward the taxi, but the wall of energy holding them in place was even more intense than the protective cocoon around Lynne. Jane felt like a child who had picked a fight with a grownup, and she spun the rings on her left hand in frustration. Celine Boyle's silver band sparked, sending a bolt of electricity down her finger.

Jane's heart pounded and her eyes narrowed. *That bitch killed my grandmother.*

Lynne was less than a block away now. Jane knelt on the bench seat, calling her magic and feeling it spark to life in her veins. *She stalked me, murdered Gran, attacked my friends, destroyed Malcolm, and tried to have me raped.* The power in her grew with every offense Jane recounted, and she suddenly felt very sure that her eyes were as black as her raging mother-in-law's. The magic thrummed in her veins almost painfully, but she held on, knowing she couldn't afford to release it carelessly.

An SUV swerved blindly around Lynne's tall form, and Jane sent out feelers to the protective bubble around her mother-in-law. It was solid and seamless, but it was taking a lot of energy, too: between maintaining her shield and holding the taxi in place, Lynne had nothing left over. *We just need one good distraction,* Jane thought urgently. *One thing to make her forget about us, even just for a second.* The trees in the median continued to thrash wildly in the wind that was coming down the avenue along with Lynne. A plan formed in Jane's head, and she could only hope it would be enough.

She focused hard on the large maple just behind the car. Reaching out with her mind, she felt the rough edges of the dark, splintering bark, and probed the frozen ground that was packed in around the thick roots. She wrapped her mental fingers around those roots, and then yanked back as hard as she could. The blood drained from her face, but she kept pulling, knuckles white on the back of the seat. A tearing noise reached them over the whipping of the wind. Jane's muscles burned and screamed in agony, each one clenched and focused on the massive trunk.

With a final creak, the tree crashed down lengthwise across the road between Lynne and her prey. Surprise flickered across Lynne's face for just a moment before it was hidden by the dense branches, and then came the squealing of brakes and the crumpling of metal on metal. Lynne let out a howl of rage as she found herself in the center of a five-car accident that would, Jane hoped, take every ounce of her magic to avoid being crushed under. *Or she could just be crushed. That works too.*

Jane spun around to face the front of the car. "Drive!" she shouted to the cabbie. *"Now!"*

Using the last strains of her magic, she shoved the surprised driver's foot down on the pedal for good measure, and the taxi jolted forward, speeding recklessly down the avenue until the fallen tree was out of sight. To his credit, the cabbie kept the car steady. "Grand Central?" he asked in an almost normal voice, although he was glaring suspiciously at the couple in his rearview mirror.

Malcolm just nodded at him in the mirror, and Jane sank down into the seat, feeling her eyelids force themselves closed.

Twenty blocks of napping, she promised herself, *and then back to the daring escape.*

forty-nine

Five minutes later, they were dashing through the bustle of Grand Central Station.

"White Plains," Malcolm told her, pointing to the electronic screen over the ticket window; there was a train in nine minutes. "They've got an airport, and I've got cash. Mom will have people looking for us at LaGuardia and JFK, but there's a good chance she won't think to—what?"

Jane was shaking her head. "You've been around your mom all day. She has to know what you have planned."

"She doesn't!" Malcolm said forcefully. "I promise. I would have known if she'd seen it. And we can still change our plans—get on a different plane, go to a different airport." His voice was verging on hysterical, and Jane put her hand on his arm to calm him.

A man with a Prada roller-duffle ducked around her, clipping her toe with one of the wheels. Jane barely registered the pain.

Malcolm was looking at her, pleading with his amazing, hypnotic eyes.

"Too risky," she explained gently. "Airports have rules and security; you could get cornered. You need to stick to trains: pay in cash and get off early, change to a different one, backtrack. Keep moving, and keep her guessing."

"*We,*" he corrected cautiously, and then rushed on before she could say more. "Hundreds of trains pass through here. We'll go wherever you want, however you like. We just have to go, now!"

He tried to pull her toward the gates, but she resisted. "We're getting on different trains, Malcolm." His face fell, but he didn't seem nearly as surprised by her news as she had feared. "I'll never be able to look at you without seeing her," she added in a whisper, and bit her lip fiercely. Now that she knew how Lynne had manipulated Malcolm, using his guilt over Annette, she couldn't hate him for what he had done to her life. He was just a tool of his family, not some evil arch-villain. But he also was not the person she had once imagined that she'd loved. She couldn't in good conscience leave him to be tortured in some dungeon, and she might be able to use his help someday, if they could both survive Lynne's current rampage. But that was as much as she owed him, and it was all she could feel for him anymore.

He nodded, his dark eyes closing in pain. "I'm so sorry," he whispered roughly.

"I know," she said, touching his temple lightly. "I saw."

"You will need money," he said, pulling out his wallet and tucking a thick wad of cash into her purse. After a moment's hesitation, he added three blue passports and one dark red one to the money. "Can you at least tell me where you're going?"

"It's safer if you don't know," she told him gently. "But I'll need to be able to reach you. Set up an e-mail account. I'll find you."

He gripped her arm suddenly.

"It won't help," he warned desperately. "It doesn't matter how far you go: you'll only buy time, not safety. They'll never stop looking, and they *will* find you. I need to be there to protect you. I have to do *something* to make up for what I've done."

"You're right," she said carefully, ignoring his fleeting hopeful look. "They'll keep on coming until they reach me, but that'll happen no matter where you go. And I'm not going to let you die playing bodyguard just so you can feel better about what you did." He flinched, and she felt a stab of guilt, but she couldn't really regret telling him the truth.

After a moment, he nodded slowly, and she exhaled a breath that she hadn't even realized she'd been holding. "But I mean it," he went on fiercely, eyes blazing with a new, darker kind of determination. "Jane, if there's ever *anything* . . ." He waved his hand, dismissing the rest of the sentence. She knew that he meant it: there were no limits or qualifications on his offer to help her hide from his family. "Whenever you need me, Jane, I'm on your side."

"You better be," she told him seriously, and then winked. "After all, I am your wife now."

The corners of his lips quirked up in his familiar smile, and she felt a twinge of regret when she realized that this might be the last time she saw it. She stood on her tiptoes to kiss his cheek, and then turned before she could change her mind, plunging into the shifting crowd. A cluster of giggling teenage girls in way-too-short miniskirts filled the space where she had been almost as soon as she left it, and by the time they cleared, Malcolm was gone. *It's for the best,* she told herself firmly. *I need to learn more. I need to move forward, not just crouch down and wait for them to get me. And I can't afford to be protected anymore. I have to figure out how to do it myself.*

She glanced up at the sign that pointed toward the trains, but as she did, something else caught her eye.

SUBWAY, an adjacent archway read, complete with a helpful arrow pointing in the opposite direction. 4, 5, 6, 7, S.

Jane stopped in the middle of the giant marble-vaulted hall, the beginning of an idea swimming idly around her mind.

"It doesn't matter how far you go," Malcolm had said.

So why go far?

The orange constellations painted into the blue ceiling twinkled, and the crowd flowed around her as though she was simply part of the scenery—no more conspicuous than a tree or potted plant. She'd run to Paris when she was eighteen, and then to New York when she met Malcolm, but she'd never been able to shake off her fate.

Now Lynne and her cousins would be stalking her the same way her own magic always had, and she realized that she had absolutely no desire to run again. She had put down roots, had made a family. There was Dee, with her useful knowledge and boundless curiosity. There were Maeve and Harris—though Jane hesitated to ask any more of them. Plus, New York was the last place anyone would think to look for her: no sane person would stick around in the same town where they'd just crashed a bunch of cars around Lynne Doran.

She gave the arches one last look: Metro-North trains to the left, the subway to the right. *Guess I'm not all that sane,* she thought with a grin, smoothing her jacket over her torn wedding dress.

Heart pounding, she turned to the right and headed for the maze of tunnels and trains that would hide her in plain sight . . . right below the Dorans' feet.

Gabriella Pierce

GABRIELLA PIERCE is an American living in Paris with her two dogs. This is her first novel.